Fatal Game

I didn't have any facts about the case, or how the killer operated, but then again, it wasn't my job to solve the case. I was there for moral support, along with a prod every now and then if I thought my husband's investigation was going off-course. No one knew about my input but Zach, and for my protection, he didn't tell anyone that I was his unpaid and extremely unofficial consultant.

And I liked that just fine myself. I had no desire for the limelight or any credit for solving one of my husband's cases any more than I wanted his name on one of my puzzles, even if he did spot mistakes from time to time. Most of them went straight to my publisher, but every now and then I had Zach solve one to make sure I was playing fair. We were a team, both in our professions and in our marriage, and I wouldn't have it any other way.

And now we were going to try to find a killer before he had the chance to strike again.

□ □ □ □ □ □ □ □ □ □ □ □ □ □ □

A DEADLY ROW

Casey Mayes

□ □ □ □ □ □ □ □ □ □ □ □ □ □ □

BERKLEY PRIME CRIME, NEW YORK

THE BERKLEY PUBLISHING GROUP
Published by the Penguin Group
Penguin Group (USA) Inc.
375 Hudson Street, New York, New York 10014, USA

Penguin Group (Canada), 90 Eglinton Avenue East, Suite 700, Toronto, Ontario M4P 2Y3, Canada
(a division of Pearson Penguin Canada Inc.)
Penguin Books Ltd., 80 Strand, London WC2R 0RL, England
Penguin Group Ireland, 25 St. Stephen's Green, Dublin 2, Ireland (a division of Penguin Books Ltd.)
Penguin Group (Australia), 250 Camberwell Road, Camberwell, Victoria 3124, Australia
(a division of Pearson Australia Group Pty. Ltd.)
Penguin Books India Pvt. Ltd., 11 Community Centre, Panchsheel Park, New Delhi—110 017, India
Penguin Group (NZ), 67 Apollo Drive, Rosedale, North Shore 0632, New Zealand
(a division of Pearson New Zealand Ltd.)
Penguin Books (South Africa) (Pty.) Ltd., 24 Sturdee Avenue, Rosebank, Johannesburg 2196,
South Africa

Penguin Books Ltd., Registered Offices: 80 Strand, London WC2R 0RL, England

This is a work of fiction. Names, characters, places, and incidents either are the product of the author's
imagination or are used fictitiously, and any resemblance to actual persons, living or dead, business
establishments, events, or locales is entirely coincidental. The publisher does not have any control over
and does not assume any responsibility for author or third-party websites or their content.

A DEADLY ROW

A Berkley Prime Crime Book / published by arrangement with the author

PRINTING HISTORY
Berkley Prime Crime mass-market edition / September 2010

Copyright © 2010 by Tim Myers.
Cover illustration by Bas Waijers.
Cover design by Rita Frangie.
Interior text design by Kristin del Rosario.

ISBN: 978-0-425-23641-3

BERKLEY® PRIME CRIME
Berkley Prime Crime Books are published by The Berkley Publishing Group,
a division of Penguin Group (USA) Inc.,
375 Hudson Street, New York, New York 10014.
BERKLEY® PRIME CRIME and the PRIME CRIME logo are trademarks of Penguin Group (USA)
Inc.

PRINTED IN THE UNITED STATES OF AMERICA

10 9 8 7 6 5 4 3 2 1

For my inspirations,
Patty and Emily;

and Michelle Vega,
for all of her hard
work on this project!

AUTHOR'S NOTE

Charlotte, North Carolina—the Queen City—is obviously a real locale, and in many respects, the city is a key character in this book. Some of the places mentioned here exist, including Luigi's—the best pizza in the city, in the author's humble opinion. Several of the places mentioned are actual neighborhoods and businesses, and at the time of this writing, were all thriving in real life. Other information—such as the location of police headquarters and its distance from the mayor's office—has been fictionalized in order to aid in telling a good story. Trust me when I say that the architecture in Charlotte is beautiful, and the people as a rule are genuine, but there are killers in many locales, big cities and small towns alike, and Charlotte is no exception.

It's important to remember that when all things are considered, Charlotte is a city with many sides and facets, worthy of exploration.

Puzzles are like songs—A good puzzle can give you all the pleasure of being duped that a mystery story can. It has surface innocence, surprise, the revelation of a concealed meaning, and the catharsis of solution.

—STEPHEN SONDHEIM

Prologue

. . .

*T*HE MURDERER STARED AT THE MAP, CAREFULLY CALCU-
lating the next strike. The complication of the scheme
was delightful, adding another layer to the fabric of the
plan. Crime was too easy when it was random. There was
grace and beauty—dare the killer be bold enough to admit
elegance?—to the transgressions committed, and if the
world was too blind to see the pattern of the actions, it
would all be revealed in the end.

No one could stop the plan once it was in place, certainly not the police.

No one would even realize what was happening—the
completion of the grand scheme—until it was too late.

By then, the ultimate prize would be achieved.

The life of the last target would rest in a single out-
stretched hand, and then it would be squeezed until there
was nothing left.

Chapter 1

...

"**A**RE YOU STILL FIDDLING WITH THAT PUZZLE, SAVANNAH? I need some help in the bedroom with that blasted shelf I'm putting up. You're the one who wanted it in the first place, remember?"

"Hang on a second. I've almost got it." My dear husband loomed over me as I worked on the couch with paper and pencil, toiling over my latest creation. My name's Savannah Stone, and it's my job to create a variety of the math and logic puzzles you find in your newspaper every morning, just as long as you subscribe to one of the forty-two papers my syndicate sells my puzzles to every day. While I might not be in *The New York Times*, I am in the *New Bern Register,* along with the *Covington Chronicle* and the *Grandfather Mountain Gazette*. I taught high school math in Charlotte until puzzles came into my life, and though the money I make now is somewhat less than I made before, the freedom my current career provides is well worth the cut in pay.

I wasn't sweating literally like my husband was, but the math on this new puzzle was taxing me just the same. Working a puzzle and creating it were two very different things.

I looked up and saw beads of sweat traipsing down Zach's nose and threatening to despoil the puzzle I'd been toiling so hard over for the past two hours. As I pulled my work safely out of the way, I noticed that the silver touches of frost around his temples were matted with sweat as well. Why was it that my husband's graying hair looked so distinguished? On me, it looked like I was nearing my expiration date—though I wasn't even up to my fortieth birthday, while he was two years past his.

He looked at me, the exasperation clear on his face. "Seriously? You can't put that down for one minute to help me? It won't take that long, Savannah, I promise."

"Zach, I've almost got it. That shelf is going to have to wait until I'm finished. You're supposed to be retired anyway, remember? So why don't you be a dear and go retire somewhere else until I wrap this up?"

My husband had been the police chief in Charlotte, North Carolina, when a bullet had hit him in the chest and ended his career. The irony had been that he'd been stopping a robbery when he was off duty and heading home to me. My husband was a hero, no matter how much he downplayed what had happened. Zach had managed to save three people with his intervention. Just thinking about that night sent me into shivers. It still felt like yes-

terday when I'd gotten the call, the one every police officer's wife dreads. As I'd raced to the hospital, I frantically
worried if I'd be a widow by the time I got there. Fortunately the gunshot wound hadn't been nearly as bad as it
might have been, but I didn't think I could ever go through
that again. At least no one would be shooting at him anymore. Or so I hoped.

Unfortunately, the wound had left him technically dis-
abled with an injury too close to his heart, though you'd
never know it by the way he acted. Zach had taken early
retirement—though not willingly—but he'd soon been
bored with his idle lifestyle. Instead of puttering around
the garden on our mini-farm on the outskirts of Parson's
Valley in the foothills of the Blue Ridge Mountains or
tinkering in his woodworking shop, Zach began working
as a consultant to various police forces in North Carolina, and occasionally even the rest of the country. He was
good at what he did, and the freedom of my job allowed
me to travel with him whenever he was on a case.

"You know how hard it is for me to slow down and take
it easy," he said as he mopped his brow with a colorful
bandana he always kept in his back pocket, even when he
was wearing his nicest navy blue suit. "I get bored if I sit
still too long. Why isn't anything happening? Surely
there's some case somewhere that needs me." Almost as an
afterthought, he glanced down and pointed at my formula.

My eraser struck and removed one of the offending
digits. "That's why I said I wasn't finished yet. Honestly,
you need something else to keep you busy. Isn't there anything besides police work that interests you? I thought you
loved it here near the mountains as much as I do."

"This place is nice." He gestured around our cottage, tucked away in the western North Carolina Mountains. We had four acres, half of it wooded, and enough open land left to have a magnificent lawn and garden. It had always been our dream to own something like it some day, and I enjoyed it even more than I ever could have imagined. It would have been fine with me if we never left our serene enclave again, but my husband was a different story altogether.

"But . . ." I said, waiting for him to fill in the rest.

"It's not the big city. Savannah, I can't help it. I'm used to being in the middle of the action."

I had a tough time understanding the pull that tugged at him constantly. "Zach, that's why we came here, remember? I know your police consultant business isn't getting you as much work as you'd hoped, and goodness knows our life here isn't as stimulating as your old job used to be, but we've had our fill of that kind of excitement in our lives, haven't we?"

He frowned at me, and it was all I could do not to laugh. My husband could be an imposing man—six foot three and two hundred ten pounds of lean muscle—but to me, there were times he looked like a little lost puppy. Sometimes it was all I could do not to rub him behind the ears.

"Don't be so glum," I said. "I'll be finished with this puzzle in a jiff, and then I'll help you with your shelf."

He shrugged as he stared at my layout grid. "I don't get it, Savannah. They're just numbers. Why do they take so long to make?"

"I'm not solving the puzzle, Zach, I'm creating it.

You know that takes a great deal more time and concentration."

"You should give it up," he said. "We don't really need the money. We're both supposed to be taking it easy now, not just me."

I laughed. "Now why on earth would I do that? I'm in my puzzle-making prime." I was good at what I did, just as good as he had been at his job, and I wasn't about to stop.

Zach clearly didn't know how to respond to that. After a look I'd seen a thousand times in our marriage that said he'd clearly lost interest in our topic of conversation, he said with a sigh, "Come up when you're finished, then." Zach tromped back to our cozy bedroom suite upstairs, which happened to be the hottest part of our cottage at the worst time of day. While I loved the warm sun that nurtured the rows of beans, corn, and tomatoes in our vegetable garden, I avoided the attic space devoutly in the summer afternoons; my husband's internal thermostat was much more tolerant than mine. The mountain breezes we counted on to keep us cool had stalled somewhere else at the moment, and we were enduring a particularly miserable summer.

Before he left, I suggested, "Why don't we get cleaned up and go into Asheville after I finish this? We can eat out, and maybe even catch a movie. What do you say?"

He grumbled something and continued up the stairs, and I knew enough not to pursue it. It was clear that the man was bored, but I wouldn't have traded our new life for the old one in Charlotte for all of the money in the world. I'd help my husband with his shelf project just as

I'd promised, but there was no way I was going to rush what I was doing. Stewing upstairs would give him time to cool off a little, as odd as that sounded in the heat of the day. I glanced at the puzzle with a sense of pride. I reveled in creating them too much to rush the process. I stared at the proposed puzzle formula, enjoying the elegant beauty of it. I knew that some of my peers created their puzzles by computer, but I liked to do them with a pencil in one hand and an eraser in the other. Building the logical progression into my creations was just part of the experience for me. I liked the test of balancing the results of the puzzles to challenge my readers. As I worked, I created my puzzles for one particular challenger, though she existed only in my imagination. As I finished each one, I could see her worry her way through the numbers, and I could almost hear her shout of joy as she finished.

I transferred the completed puzzle to a pristine sheet of paper, then studied the finished puzzle one last time before I faxed it to Derrick—my syndicate editor—a man I was not particularly fond of, despite the checks he sent me for every completed puzzle.

After glancing at my computer email and stalling a half dozen other ways, I realized I couldn't delay my trek upstairs any longer.

I was going to have to help with that blasted shelf after all. I knew it was going to be miserably hot up there, but there was no way to avoid it. I'd promised for better or for worse on our wedding day, and enduring scalding temperatures helping install a shelf I didn't really need was just one more check in the worse column, though that side was happily sparse.

My foot was on the bottom step when the telephone rang, and in my ignorance, I nearly skipped as I raced to answer it. If I'd known who was calling—and more importantly why—I would have pulled the blasted thing out of the wall and chucked the telephone out the window instead of picking the receiver up.

"Hello," I said, not suspecting a thing was amiss.

"Er, hello, Savannah. I need to speak with Zach."

Before I could protest, he hastily added, "I wouldn't ask if it wasn't important."

I didn't need caller ID to tell me who was on the other end of the line. At least he'd had the decency to sound embarrassed by his request.

"Sorry, Davis. You can't. He's busy right now." Zach would have killed me if he'd overheard my end of the conversation, but I was tired of him being bothered by his former employees. It wasn't just because they were reluctant to pay for his services, though they felt free to tap into his knowledge any time it suited them. I didn't care about the money—we were doing just fine on his retirement and my income—but I didn't like anyone taking advantage of him.

I started to hang up when I heard a whining protest. "Savannah, please. This is something he needs to hear."

I took a deep breath, and then said, "Davis Rawles, my husband is retired. He doesn't work with you anymore. He's a consultant now. If you'd like his fee schedule, I'd be glad to fax it over to you."

"Send it. You know the number. There shouldn't be any problem covering it this time."

That caught me off guard. I'd never dreamed I'd hear

him say he was actually willing to pay for Zach's services. He must be in real trouble. "What's going on, Davis?"

"Savannah, Zach is my very last option. We've got a killer case on our hands, and there's no one but your husband who can solve it."

Davis Rawles had been my husband's immediate subordinate on the police force, and upon Zach's retirement, Davis had stepped into his shoes. At least he'd tried to. But no one could get inside a criminal's mind like my husband, and Davis had grown to rely on him too much in the past few months since my husband's retirement.

I'd never heard that level of desperation in Davis's voice before, and there was something about it that chilled my blood. This sounded too dangerous to me, and it wasn't my husband's battle anymore. "You know what? I'm sorry, but the answer's still no. You'll just have to muddle through this time by yourself," I said, and then on an impulse, I hung up the phone.

Please, oh please, don't let Zach have heard that ring.

To my dismay, his size 12 shoes clomped down the steps two at a time a second later. "Who was that on the phone?"

"Wrong number," I mumbled, hoping he'd take me at my word.

There must have been something in my voice that told him I was lying, no matter how hard I'd tried to disguise it.

"Savannah," he said softly. There was a steel edge as he said my name that made me bite my lower lip.

"It was Davis," I admitted. *Never lie to your husband*, I told myself yet again, especially when he's a retired police detective.

"What did he want?" Zach asked keenly. I could see his yearning for another murder or jewel theft. He was like a racehorse waiting for the gate to open, eager and chomping at the bit.

"He was asking about the weather here," I said lamely. Even I wouldn't believe that one. Without waiting for my husband to comment, I added, "He also wanted your opinion, but I told him you couldn't help him this time, even when he agreed to pay your fee. You're retired, remember?"

"I'm trying to get my consulting business going," he said as he dialed the number by heart. "I can't be too picky about the jobs I take on at this point."

"He sounded scared, Zach. I don't want you to get involved."

My husband's voice softened as he explained, "If it was easy, they wouldn't need me."

I tried one last thing. "The money's not worth it, even if they really do pay you, which I still doubt."

Zach's finger hovered over the last digit before he pressed it. "They will this time, or I won't do a thing to help them. Savannah, I know you feel like they've been taking advantage of me, but we could use the extra money, and you know it."

Great, I'd brought up a point I didn't really believe in without meaning to, and my sweet but literal husband had taken it at face value. It was time to switch positions, an art I'd mastered over the years. "Nonsense. We're doing fine. We have everything we need."

"True, but we don't have everything we want, do we?" he asked with a grin. "It won't hurt to hear what the man has to say," Zach said as he pushed the last number.

During the one-sided conversation, I had no idea what they were talking about, but my husband's face turned darker and darker in the silence. After a few minutes of mostly brief comments, Zach hung up the telephone.

"Pack your bags, Savannah. We're going back to Charlotte."

I couldn't believe my ears. In all our years of marriage, my husband had never given me a direct order before. "Are you kidding me? Don't I even get a say in this? Business is business, but at least you've run it past me before you've taken a job."

Zach nodded contritely. "I'm sorry, you're right. I should have asked you first. But we have to go. This is important. Grady Winslow has been getting some pretty nasty threats that Davis is sure are tied to someone who's already committed two murders, and there's a dark tone to them that's too serious to ignore." Grady was the mayor of our former fair city, a powerful man and a dear friend who had introduced us to each other a long time ago. My husband knew there was no way I could turn down that particular summons.

After a moment's hesitation, he offered me a slight grin. "You're welcome to stay here and enjoy the summer heat, but they're putting me up at the Belmont, and they've agreed to pay me a nice fee to go along with it, though to be honest with you, this is one time I'd do it for free. Think of it, Savannah. There will be full maid service, shopping in Dilworth, eating out at Morton's Steakhouse. And don't forget. We'd have air conditioning."

"I've got things to do here," I said stubbornly.

He wouldn't let me pout though. The big bear wrapped me up in his arms and said, "You can work on your puz-

zles just as easily there as you can here. They have pencils
and erasers in Charlotte, too, you know. Come on. It'll be
like a second honeymoon, only this time it will be on
someone else's dime."

"Some honeymoon. You'll be at police headquarters all
day and half the night, if I know you."

"They need me, Savannah," he said somberly. "More
importantly, Grady could be in some real trouble. This
guy isn't messing around."

I studied him a moment before I trusted myself to
speak. "And don't forget the other highlight here; you get
to be a cop again, don't you?"

"Nobody's going to shoot at me. Don't forget, I'm just
a consultant," he said. "I won't be anywhere near the line
of fire." He touched his chest lightly as he said it, gently
rubbing the scar where the bullet had entered.

I knew there was no point in arguing with him. I looked
wistfully around the cottage and realized that he was right.
There was no way he could refuse to help our best friend.
Besides, a getaway might be nice. It was just too bad that
my husband, despite his protests to the contrary, would
probably be putting his life on the line, and that was something I never thought I'd have to deal with again.

There was no use worrying about it now, though.

I smiled as brightly as I could manage and said, "Let
me pack a few things, then I'll be ready to go."

He looked at me skeptically. "It's really going to be that
easy? I don't have to twist your arm to get you to go?"

I reached my arms up around his neck and kissed him.
"If you're going, I'm going."

He smiled down at me. "That's why I love you so
much."

"One of the many, many reasons, I'm sure," I said, matching his smile with one of my own.

"**A**RE YOU REALLY GOING TO HATE THIS, SAVANNAH? I CAN turn around and we can go back to the cottage, if you're that dead-set against it. You're more important to me than anyone else in the world, even Grady. You know that, don't you?"

We'd been driving nearly two hours and we were fast approaching Charlotte. Normally the trip felt like it took forever, but it seemed like ten minutes to me this time. I was dreading every mile of it as the markers sped past, and my husband knew it.

"It will be fine, Zach. Grady Winslow is our friend. I just hate to see you putting yourself back in danger."

"Come on, you know me. If I hear even a car backfire, I'll run the other way."

"We both know better," I said. I patted his shoulder holster and touched his gun. "Don't ever try to tell me that. You couldn't wait to get back into that harness."

"You weren't supposed to notice that," he said.

"Zachary Stone, just because you were the police officer in the family doesn't mean that I don't notice things, too. My puzzles make me aware of anything that changes or doesn't fit into a situation. Life is one big math problem waiting to be solved, if you look at it the right way."

He shook his head and laughed gently.

"What, you don't believe me?" I asked, trying to keep the slight hurt out of my voice.

"No, ma'am, I would never say that, even under gunpoint. It's just that I never have understood your fascination with numbers. You see them in entirely different ways than I do."

I tried to snuggle close to him, despite the seatbelt holding me steadfastly in place. "That's all right; it wouldn't be any fun if we were exactly the same. I like to think we complement each other."

He smiled. "You do look pretty fantastic today."

"Complement with an 'e', not an 'i', you goof," I said.

"I knew what you meant," he answered with a grin, "but I stand by my earlier statement."

"If I could lose fifteen pounds, I might just agree with you," I said.

"Don't you dare lose an ounce. I love you just the way you are."

I grinned at him. "That's probably a good thing, because I'm not about to go on a diet in Charlotte. I can't wait to hit some of our favorite restaurants."

"Does that mean you're warming up to the idea?"

I thought about it, considered the possibility that despite his protests to the contrary, my husband might land himself in danger again, but then I realized that this was what he'd been made to do.

Before I could form a reply, he said, "Strike that last question. I'm not sure I want to know the answer."

"No, it's fine. I realize that you need to do this, and I want to be with you."

As he got off the interstate at an exit much earlier than the one for the police station, I asked, "Where are you going?"

"I figured you'd want to go to the hotel and get settled in before I report."

"Not on your life," I said. "We're going straight to the police station, together."

"Are you sure?"

"I'm positive."

He smiled as he gunned the engine and merged back onto the interstate. "I'm not about to argue with you. Let's go see what's going on."

W E WALKED INTO THE STATION TOGETHER, BUT I MIGHT as well have gone directly to the hotel after all. I've never seen so many people that happy to see my husband, and only a few of them even glanced my way as we walked in.

The exception, to my surprise, was Davis Rawles. Davis had been a little heavy during the years he'd worked under Zach, but he must have gone on an eating binge since my husband had left him with his responsibilities. Even at six feet tall, the weight on Davis made me doubt he could pass any police physical in the world. His hair, once thinning, had left him completely, and the lack of it made him look even rounder.

He extended a meaty hand to me, and as I took it, Davis said, "I'm sorry about this, Savannah. If there'd been any other way . . ."

"It's fine, Davis," I said as I kissed his cheek. "He wanted to come, and I wasn't about to stop him, even if I could."

I looked around the squad room expecting to see Grady Winslow. I knew the mayor had to be busy doing his job, but I was still a little disappointed that he hadn't shown up.

"Where's Grady?" I asked Davis.

He looked troubled by my question, and I didn't think he was going to answer it, but after a few moments of silence, he finally said, "That's the problem. Nobody's seen him since last night, and he's not answering his cell phone this morning."

I knew things were more desperate than we'd been told on the phone. Grady was attached to that cell phone more than he had been to any woman he'd ever dated, and he never went anywhere without it.

If he wasn't answering his calls, something serious was wrong indeed.

Chapter 2

■ ■ ■

"TELL ZACH," I SAID. "HE NEEDS TO KNOW WHAT'S going on."

"I wanted to give him a minute to say hello to everyone first," Davis said.

I studied his frown for a second, and then I asked, "Is that the truth, or are you just stalling?"

"How can I tell him that I lost his best friend?" Davis asked, the pleading clear in his eyes.

"Trust me; the quicker you do it, the better."

Davis nodded, and then made his way over to my husband. The smile on Zach's face vanished as he learned the news, and he hurried over to me.

"Did you hear?"

"Davis just told me," I said. "What are you going to do?"

"What do you think? I'm going to find him," my husband said.

Zach started conferring with Davis about tracking down Grady when I had a thought. "Have you tried checking the location of his phone?"

"They've been calling him all morning, Savannah."

"That's not what I mean, Zach. You told me you could use some kind of tracing technology to find a cell phone wherever it is, whether it's turned on or not. Why don't you ping his phone? I can't imagine him going anywhere without it."

"That's not a bad idea," Davis said.

"You haven't tried it yet?" Zach asked him.

"Cut me some slack. I just figured out that the man was missing two minutes ago."

"Being missing and not answering his telephone are two different things," I said. "There could be a perfectly reasonable explanation about where he is, and why he's not answering his phone."

"I'd rather overreact than assume everything's all right, given the threats he's been getting lately," Zach said.

"I wasn't suggesting otherwise," I answered. "Let's just make sure something's really wrong before we get the whole city in an uproar." I looked at Davis. "Did anyone go by his house to check on him?"

"I dispatched a car there right before I told you," Davis admitted.

My husband answered, "I'm not waiting around to hear what happens. Ping his phone."

Davis nodded, then stepped away from us to give the order.

While he was gone, my husband said, "I know he's probably fine, but we can't take any chances."

"I'm as worried about Grady as you are." I shivered slightly as I said it.

"He's at home," Davis said when he rejoined us. "At least his phone is."

"Well, that's good news, isn't it?"

Zach answered for him. "Maybe, maybe not. One thing's for sure; I'm not going to stand around here waiting to hear one way or the other. I'm going to Grady's. Are you coming, Savannah?"

"Just try to leave me behind," I said. There was no use arguing with me, and he knew it.

"We can take my car," Davis said.

"Who invited you?" Zach asked, an edge in his voice. It was clear that he held Davis responsible for Grady's disappearance, whether it made any sense or not.

"I've got a siren, flashing lights, and a badge. What have you got?" Davis wasn't holding back, either. He obviously wasn't in the mood to be anybody's whipping boy, not even for his former boss.

I asked, "What are we standing around here for, then?"

I wasn't sure Davis was all that thrilled about me coming along, but it was a good bet that he wasn't about to make an issue of it, not after butting heads with my husband. We raced out of the precinct parking lot, and I knew if we hadn't been with the chief of police, we would have surely gotten a ticket for speeding.

Davis's car radio went off as we neared Grady's house. "His truck's here, but he's not answering the door. Should I break in?" It was clear in the patrolman's voice even over the radio that he was reluctant to bust in on the mayor of Charlotte, and a man who was—several rungs up the ladder—his boss.

Davis snapped, "Don't do anything. I'll be there in two minutes."

There was no more conversation as we raced to Grady's house. The last time I'd been there had been during our going-away party that he'd hosted for us. Long ago, Zach and I had become friends with Grady separately, and without his introduction, it's quite possible I never would have met my husband, the man who quickly became the love of my life. When Zach had been a local attorney just starting out, Grady had taken him under his wing, helping him find his way around Charlotte, both within the legal system, and outside of it. I'd tried to return the favor by fixing him up with some of my younger friends, but Grady hadn't been in the mood to settle down then any more than he was now. If anything had happened to him, I didn't know how I was going to deal with it.

When we pulled up in front of his place in Myers Park, it didn't look like a house that might belong to the mayor. There were McMansions on his street, homes overbuilt for the lots they sat on, but Grady had chosen a rather modest Cape for his home, painted moss green with beige shutters and trim. It was neatly kept, but I knew Grady used a lawn service for that. He considered himself no better than his lowliest constituent, but he had never had any interest in lawn care, let alone gardening, no matter how much I tried to convince him otherwise.

Davis, Zach, and I got out of the car and met the patrol officer at the front door.

"No signs of life, sir," he said.

I wasn't sure if he was directing his comment to Zach or Davis, and it was all I could do not to laugh when the two men answered, "Okay," at the same time.

"Let's break it down," Davis said.

"Hang on a second," I said before they could muscle the door down. "Grady has a spare key hidden, if it's still there."

"I doubt the mayor has a hide-a-key," Davis said.

"That's where you're wrong." Grady had told me about the key years ago when I'd come by to drop off one of my homemade apple-crisp pies. I'd teased him about it at the time, but I was glad I knew about it now.

There was a rock garden near the trees by the porch, and I knew Grady had hidden one of those fake rocks there, but the problem was that they all looked a little too artificial to me. After all, it wasn't all that common to find a streambed in Myers Park, but there the stones were.

"We don't have much time," Zach said.

"Hang on a second." I studied the rocks, searching for one that didn't fit the pattern, much like what I did when I was designing one of my puzzles. I couldn't see it when I looked directly at the stones, but when I turned my head, the fake one made itself obvious by the way the light reflected off it.

I picked it up with more confidence than I felt, and was relieved to find that the weight of the stone was less than it should have been.

As I handed the key to Zach, Davis said, "We still don't know the alarm code."

"It's 0607," I said.

"Why would he choose that?"

"It's his birthday," I said.

Davis shook his head as we approached the front door. The key slid in quickly, and I moved to the alarm pad. Zach raised an eyebrow as I did this.

"Hey, I'm the one who found the key," I said.

"Go ahead before it goes off," he said.

I punched in the numbers, and was relieved to see that Grady hadn't changed the code since he'd told it to me years before.

The house was neat and tidy, thanks more to the mayor's housekeeper than his personal habits. Grady liked things neat, but he wasn't all that consistent in keeping the things around him that way. If I had to bet, I'd say that his bedroom was a mess.

"You need to wait outside now," Davis said to me.

"I'm the one who got you in, remember?" I said.

"He's right," Zach said in a voice that didn't allow argument. I had one of those myself, but neither one of us used it unless the situation was dire.

I walked outside, and saw the look of incredulity on Davis's face as I accepted the situation. Little did he know that I wasn't finished snooping, though it might appear that I was.

The patrol officer was gone, so I walked over to Grady's vehicle, a nice-looking pickup that to my knowledge had never been used for its intended purpose. Grady liked to say that he had the common touch, and driving the truck was just one way he showed it. I tried the driver's side door, but it was locked. As I peeked in through the windows, I noticed that the rear pass-through window was unlatched.

There was only one thing I could do. I hopped up into

the truck bed, not with a great deal of finesse, I'll grant you, but I managed it. After I slid the window open, I tried to imagine how I was going to get in far enough to open the door. There was no way I was going to fit, and seeing me stuck there was not an image I ever wanted in my husband's mind.

I might not be able to fit in all of the way, but I could still reach inside. The truck interior was as neat as Grady's living room had been, but there might be something under the seats, not that I could reach them from where I was squatting.

I was trying to extend my reach when I heard my husband's distinctive cough behind me.

"Have you taken up breaking and entering, Savannah?"

"No breaking, and not much entering," I said. "I noticed that the back sliding window was unlatched, so I thought I'd check it out. Did you have any luck inside?"

"We found this," he said as he held up a bagged cell phone. "There are about forty messages on it, but no sign of Grady."

"That's a relief," I said. "It must have slipped out of his pocket."

"And he didn't notice instantly that it was missing? I'm not happy about this," he said.

As Zach helped me out of the back of Grady's truck, I noticed a man on foot approaching us. He had on a cap with the Carolina Panthers logo on it, and he wore running shoes, shorts, and a knit shirt. I didn't even recognize him until he was twenty paces away from us.

"You're a hard man to track down," I said.

"That's funny, I've known where I was all along," the mayor replied.

* * *

"**S**INCE WHEN DID YOU TAKE UP RUNNING?" ZACH ASKED Grady as we joined him inside. Davis had left us the second he knew the mayor was safe, and Grady had promised us a ride back to the station when we were ready to go.

"It's something new," Grady admitted. Though he was five years younger than me, the weight of his office had aged him somewhat over the years. His face had too many added lines, and not enough caused by laughter.

Grady patted his stomach. "If you want to know the truth, I've put on a few pounds since you two left."

"At least a few," Zach said, and both men laughed. If either one of them had made that comment about me, there would have been bloodshed, and none of it would have been mine, but they seemed to find it acceptable enough between the two of them.

"So, you were never in any danger at all," I said.

Grady's smile faded. "I wish that were true, but I have been getting some threats lately."

"More than the usual ones?" Zach asked him. Though he was trying to keep his tone light, I could tell that there was an undercurrent of concern for his friend there.

"Yeah, I seem to have acquired a couple of real kooks."

"Shouldn't a police officer be guarding you, then?" I asked.

"I'm not the president, or even the governor," Grady said. "I don't exactly have the budget for police protection."

"Then find the money," I snapped.

"Are you sure you want to use that tone of voice with the mayor?" Grady asked.

"When he's being pigheaded, I am," I said.

Grady laughed. "I miss you both."

"You should at least have an officer run with you," I said.

"Does she ever let up?" Grady asked my husband.

"You know her better than to ask that," he said. "But she's not wrong."

Grady shook his head. "I'm not about to have somebody looking over my shoulder all of the time. It would feel like I was in jail."

"Better there than the hospital; or worse, the morgue," I said.

"I'll think about it."

Zach handed him the telephone he'd found, still safely ensconced in its evidence bag. "Then you should take this with you wherever you go, and I mean it. If you can't call out on it, we can still use it to track you."

"Yeah, I admit leaving it wasn't the smartest thing I've ever done. I just wanted to get away for a while, you know?"

"Is the pressure getting to you?" I asked softly.

"It's been pretty bad lately, but I can handle it." It was clear that he wasn't happy with the serious tone of our conversation. "Let me grab a quick shower, then I can take you back to the police station so you can get your car. You don't mind waiting, do you?"

"If the alternative is to have you drive us like that," Zach said, "I think we can spare the time."

"Hey, a runner sweats, you know?"

"Then you must have run a marathon," Zach answered.

"When you two boys are finished with your routine, I'd

like to check in to the hotel," I said. "It was a real strain
thinking that something might have happened to you."

"Don't worry about me. I'm too tough to get hurt,"
Grady said.

Zach answered softly, "That's what I used to think,
too."

That sobered Grady instantly. "Okay, I'll look into it.
I'll be back in a few minutes."

While he was showering and getting dressed, Zach
paced around the living room. "I don't like his attitude."

"It sounds the same to me as it always has," I said.

"That's the problem, isn't it? He's not taking this threat
seriously enough for my taste."

"Then you'll convince him that he needs to," I answered.
"He'll listen to you, Zach. You've been friends forever."

"I think you've got a better chance of persuading him
than I do," he said.

"Why do you say that?"

"I don't know, it's just something I sense about him.
Will you take a shot at it? I honestly am worried about
him."

"I'll try, but I can't imagine how I can do any better
than you could," I said.

"Just do what you can," he said. "I've got to make
some calls, and I'm going to step outside to make them."

"Who are you calling that you need privacy from me?
Are you letting your girlfriend know that you're back in
town?"

"No, she doesn't live here anymore."

He was smiling, but there wasn't much humor in it.

"Really? Where exactly did she move to?"

"She's living with me in Parson's Valley, you nit."

"Just checking," I said.

"How about your boyfriends?"

"Maybe it was a little premature, but I gave them all up when we got married."

"I feel their pain," he said with a smile.

"All kidding aside, why are you going outside to make your calls?"

"Savannah, sometimes you drive me crazy. How are you going to get some time to talk to Grady if I'm always with you? There's a lot better chance that he'll listen to you if I'm not around."

We heard the door start to open from the bedroom area, and Zach ducked outside, but not before he stopped to wink at me. I didn't like the pressure of trying to convince our old friend to do something he clearly didn't want to, but I really had no choice.

"I thought I heard voices out here," he said as he rubbed a towel through his hair. He'd changed into blue jeans and a crisp T-shirt, his casual mayor look. He glanced at his bare wrist. "You haven't seen my watch anywhere, have you? I lost it, and it's driving me nuts."

I looked around the room. "I don't see it."

He shrugged. "Have you been talking to yourself since you moved to the hills? It hasn't made you crazy, has it?"

"No more than usual," I said with a smile. "Zach had some phone calls to make."

He sat across from me. "And he couldn't make them in here?"

"He said he wanted some privacy."

Grady shook his head. "For us or for him? Come on, I've known you too long for you to lie to me."

"I'm not lying," I said. "That's exactly what Zach told me."

"No ulterior motives?" Grady asked.

"I wouldn't say that. We're both worried about you."

"I'm fine," he said, trying to brush off my concern.

"That's not the way Davis tells it. I have a feeling that he'd like to bring in the state police on this."

"Trust me, you aren't telling me anything I don't know. I told him he could handle it, or he was the wrong man for the job. It took some arm-twisting, but we finally agreed to call Zach as a compromise."

"Which one of you didn't want him?" I asked.

"Take it easy, Savannah. It's not like that."

I stood. "If Davis doesn't want us here, we're leaving. Zach can't help unless he gets the chief's full cooperation. Stay safe, Grady."

I headed for the door, but he stopped me with one small phrase. "It was me."

"You? Have you lost confidence in Zach's ability? That bullet tore into his body, but his mind's as sharp as ever."

"Would you sit back down and hear me out? Please?"

I thought about it, and then reluctantly did as he asked.

After I was settled back down, Grady said, "I fought Davis on bringing anyone into this, but he has more confidence in your husband than he does the state police. For now, I've gotten permission from Raleigh for us to handle this ourselves, but if there's one more body, they're going to take over."

"Then Zach had better get started. But there's one condition, or we're going straight home."

"This used to be your home," Grady said.

"That was before."

"It wasn't that long ago."

"Trust me, it feels like a lifetime, and I don't have any interest in ever coming back."

He sat there and mulled it over, and then finally asked, "What's the condition?"

"You have to take this seriously."

"Okay."

I looked closely at him. "What's going on? We both know you don't give up that easily."

Grady shrugged. "Not unless it's a battle I don't want to win. I'll ask Davis for protection, but it's not going to be around the clock."

"Then I'm sorry we couldn't help."

As I got up, he did, too. "Are you serious, Savannah? You'd just walk out on an old friend when he needs you the most?"

"I don't have much choice. If you aren't going to take steps to protect yourself, it puts even more pressure on Zach to figure out who your killer is, and it's going to be hard enough for him to do without worrying about you."

"Okay, I didn't think of it that way."

"Brighten up," I said. "That's why I'm here. Now, let's go find my husband so we can tell him the good news."

"I didn't have a chance, did I?" Grady asked me as we went to the front door.

"That's not true at all. You nearly lost us, but you managed to redeem yourself at the last second."

"What can I say, I'm a clutch player." He tossed his towel onto the kitchen counter and ran a comb through his hair as I opened the door. Zach was on the porch, in deep conversation with someone.

He held a finger up to us, and then said, "We'll be right there."

Before he even looked at Grady, he glanced at me and asked, "Did he agree?"

"Around the clock police protection until you find the killer," I answered.

"Good enough. Let's go."

"Are you ready to go to the hotel?" Grady asked.

"No, there's been another note from the killer. He put a picture in this one, too."

If we'd had any chance of a pleasant conversation on the way to the police station, that information ruined it. I didn't have any facts about the case, or how the killer operated, but then again, it wasn't my job to solve the case. I was there for moral support, along with a prod every now and then if I thought my husband's investigation was going off course. I considered myself Zach's unpaid and extremely unofficial consultant.

And I liked that just fine myself. I had no desire for the limelight, or any credit for solving one of my husband's cases, any more than I wanted his name on one of my puzzles, even if he did spot mistakes from time to time. Zach liked to solve puzzles, claiming they helped distract him from the cases he worked on, and he was my tester when I wasn't sure about a puzzle I was ready to submit. Most of them went straight to my publisher, but every now and then I had Zach solve one to make sure I was playing fair. We were a team, both in our professions and in our marriage, and I wouldn't have it any other way.

And now we were going to try to find a killer before he had the chance to strike again.

Chapter 3

∎∎∎

"**Y**OU NEED TO SEE THIS," DAVIS TOLD ZACH WHEN WE walked into the police station. "It just showed up four minutes ago."

"What is it?" I asked. Grady had waited around just long enough to be assigned a police officer as a body-guard, and then he'd taken off for his office. We couldn't convince him to lay low until Zach caught the killer, but he had to be safer at city hall than in his house, or worse yet, jogging alone on the streets of Charlotte.

"This is official police business," Davis said.

"Zach's not a cop anymore, either."

"It's different. He's on the payroll."

I looked at my husband, who was clearly getting impa-tient with this particular conversation. Zach just shrugged as he reached into his wallet and handed me a five dollar bill.

"What's that for? Lunch? You're not buying me off with a five, you know that, don't you?"

"Don't be thick, Savannah. That's your fee as my assistant. You are now officially on the payroll."

"Is this all I'm worth to you?" I couldn't believe he'd handed me just a five. I was worth at least twice that.

"It's just to cover our bases in case someone asks," Zach explained.

"The five's fine, then," I said as I folded it and tucked it into my jeans. "Would you like a receipt for your tax records?"

"You can mail it to me," he said as he turned to Davis. "Are you satisfied now?"

"She shouldn't be involved in this, Zach. It's too dangerous."

I was about to reply when I saw my husband bite his lower lip. He was about to handle things just fine without any interference from me. "We're a matched set, and you don't break those up. I'll protect her."

"Hey, I can protect myself," I protested.

No one even acknowledged that I had spoken.

"Maybe you'll think twice about it after you see this," Davis said.

He pulled a Polaroid snapshot out of his jacket pocket and showed it to Zach. It was safely tucked into a plastic evidence bag, and I steeled myself for whatever grizzly scene it portrayed. I could handle most things, but I still wasn't thrilled with seeing graphic acts of violence captured on film.

Zach studied it for a long time, and then handed it back to Davis.

"Hey, I want to see that," I said.

Zach thought about it, and then shrugged. "Show her."

"I want to go on the record right now. This is not a good idea."

"She has a right to know," my husband said. At that point, I wasn't sure I wanted to see what was in the picture anymore.

"Suit yourself," Davis said as he handed it to me.

In an instant, I realized why Davis hadn't wanted me to see the photograph, and my husband had.

It showed me crouching in the back of Grady's truck, my arm extended through the open sliding window and vanishing behind the seat.

Whoever had taken it had been close enough to reach out and touch me.

WITHOUT REALIZING I'D DONE IT, I DROPPED THE PHOtograph, and it fluttered to the floor.

"Are you okay, Savannah?" Zach said as he wrapped one arm around me. "I should have warned you."

"I'm fine," I said, though I clearly wasn't. I couldn't shake the belief that I should have seen whoever had taken that snapshot. Why hadn't I turned to see someone taking it? Could I have identified the killer, if I'd only had the foresight to look?

"Are you sure?"

"Zach, it's okay. He just wanted to prove that he saw us looking for Grady. It's not like he's threatening me. Is it?" Another thought jumped into my head unbidden. Was it possible that whoever had taken that photo knew how close my husband and I were to the mayor? Could it be that he was planning to use our relationship to come after Grady, or was it just a coincidence that he'd captured me on film? Either way, I wasn't too happy about it.

"How do we know this is from the killer?" I asked Davis.

He flipped the photo, and I saw that someone had carefully lettered "3A" in red magic marker. "What is that supposed to mean?"

"We were hoping your husband would be able to figure it out."

Zach took the offered photograph again, studied the sequence, and then shook his head. "I don't have a clue."

"Why does that not comfort me?" I asked.

"Give me time, Savannah. You're welcome to go back home until I figure this out. As a matter of fact, it might not be a bad idea. You'd be safer there."

"Are you kidding me? I like to think I'm pretty self-sufficient, but I'm also pragmatic about it. If someone's got me in his sights, I'd just as soon have you around, instead of being two hours away."

He nodded. "To tell you the truth, I wouldn't be able to get anything done here; I'd be worrying about you the entire time." He turned to Davis. "Let's see the rest of those photographs. Maybe something I see will make some sense of this mess."

"It's all upstairs," he said. "We were just getting ready to form a task force, so I had my men take everything up there."

"Who all is on this task force of yours?" Zach asked.

Davis grinned slightly. "Well, so far, there's you."

"Don't forget my assistant," he said.

"I'm not sure I'm all that thrilled with that title," I said.

"But you'll take it, right?"

"You bet. I don't care what you call me, as long as you let me in on what's going on."

Davis led us upstairs, and we came to a large, empty conference room with five white boxes perched on a long, folding table. The walls were blank, and there wasn't a window in the place. Against one wall were six folding chairs and a few more tables, but there wasn't another thing in the room.

"We can do better than this," Davis said.

"It's fine," Zach said. "I can use the wall space to pin everything up, or you can bring in some foil-backed foam insulation board if you don't want to ruin your walls." The construction foam board was a favorite of my husband's. It came in four by eight foot sheets, and it took pushpins beautifully.

"I'll have them here within an hour, and I'll also have a copier moved in," Davis said. "Do you need anything else at the moment?"

"No, we're good," Zach said, barely even acknowledging the man's presence. I knew my husband too well. He was already deep in thought about how to catch this killer, and I was going to do everything in my power to help him.

"It might help if you gave me a little information about what's been happening," I said.

Zach looked at me, clearly distracted by my question, but if I was going to be of any assistance, I had to have some information.

"So far, there have been two murders that are con-

nected o the threat on Grady. A high-society businessman with a lot of different companies, Hank Tristan, was
discovered in his bed stabbed in the heart after a charity ball. The second victim, Cindy Glass, was a little less
prominent, a personal assistant to a very important man in
Charlotte, but the notes sent afterward along with the sou-
venirs were from the same person, so we know they're
linked somehow."

I knew what the distraction was costing my husband,
and though I wanted more details, I understood I had to be
satisfied with the information I had. We set up the other
tables and chairs, and Zach started digging through the
boxes.

"Is there anything in particular you're looking for?" I
asked. "Maybe I can help you."

"This looks like everything was just dumped into a box
without any rhyme or reason. I need to make sense of it,
but before I can do that, I have to get it organized."

"That's something I can help with. My whole job as a
puzzle maker is to find order in chaos."

He whistled under his breath, a sure sign that he wanted
to say something to me that he didn't think I was going to
like.

"Zach, don't think of me as your wife right now. Treat
me like an assistant and tell me what you'd like me to do."

"Some of these photos are kind of graphic," he said.
"I'm not crazy about having you look at them."

"I can handle it," I said, though if I were being honest
about it, the prospect of looking at dead bodies was pretty
mortifying to me.

"Tell you what. You handle the official police documents, and I'll deal with the rest."

I started to protest when he added, "It's the way I want it done, and I expect my assistant to do as she's asked."

"Just as long as you don't expect your wife to follow orders," I said.

"Do I look that crazy to you?"

"Where do you want me to start?"

"Find the case files for the two murders," Zach said. "If you see any pictures or letters, anything that doesn't look like an official police document, put it in a pile over by the door. Stack your files on the table. Let's get started."

As I searched through the boxes, I did my best to ignore the content of the photographs I found and tried to focus on their shapes and sizes instead. Once I forced myself to look at them as geometric objects and not photographs that would give me nightmares, things started going much faster. Sorting things was like a puzzle, and that was one thing I loved, and happened to be very good at as well.

We'd just finished doing a preliminary sort when the door opened and two police officers came in, each carrying a sheet of foam insulation board.

"Hey, Chief," one of the cops said.

My husband brightened. "Sanders, how are you?"

They shook hands, and Zach introduced us. "Savannah, you remember Steve Sanders. He was my number one go-to guy around here before I left."

"Deserted is more like it," Sanders said with a grin. He was tall and lanky, with a shock of thick black hair and a clean-shaven face. I knew that he'd been in the running to take over for my husband as chief when he left, but if Steve minded them promoting Davis over him, he didn't show it.

Zach smiled gently. "Hey, they forced me out, remember?"

"I know, I'm just kidding." He looked around at the mess on the floor. "This place looks like a bomb just went off. Do you need a hand?"

"Thanks, but I've already got an assistant," he said, pointing at me.

"Three could be better than two," Steve said.

"Let me sort this out, and then I'll let you know."

"I'd do anything for you, Chief, and you know it." He glanced at his watch. "I'm getting ready to get off, but I'd be happy to hang around."

"You could put in for overtime, if you don't mind helping," Zach said.

"Excellent. It will be just like old times. What's the first order of business?"

"Find Davis and remind him that I need that copier as soon as possible. We've got some work to do."

After he was gone, I looked at Zach. "Does this mean I'm fired already? Wow, that's quick."

"Of course not," he said. "Steve can help me make copies and hang this stuff up, but then you're back on the payroll. In the meantime, why don't you get us checked in and settled at the hotel? You know how much I hate unpacking."

"Are you sure you're not just trying to get rid of me?"

He wrapped me up in his arms. "Savannah, I'd never do that, even if I could."

"Which you can't," I answered with a grin and a quick peck. "I know you're just trying to protect me, and I appreciate it, but I'm tougher than you think."

"Trust me, I know how tough you are."

"Okay, as long as that's settled, I'll take off." As I started for the door, I paused and said, "But don't think you're getting rid of me for good."

"Come back when you're finished. You can help me lay things out. There are times when I can use that organizing point of view you've got."

"See you soon."

I bumped into Steve in the hallway, and found him deep in conversation with someone on his cell phone. It was pretty clear that he wasn't happy with whoever was on the other end, but when he spotted me, the frown changed into a smile.

"Hang on one second," he said as he buried his phone into his chest. "My landlord's trying to go up on my rent," he explained to me, "and I'm trying to convince him how handy it is having a cop live there."

"Are you having any luck?"

"Not yet, but I think I'm wearing him down. If you don't mind my saying so, that husband of yours is the best cop I've ever seen."

"He used to be," I said evenly.

"I know he's retired, but I can't imagine it ever gets out of your blood, you know?"

"I'm doing my best, though, to help see that it does."

Steve grinned at me. "You keep fighting your battle, and maybe one of us will win."

"Good luck with yours," I said.

He smiled, and then returned to his phone call. "It's not going to happen," he said as he shot me with his finger.

As I made my way out of the station to our car, I wondered if what he'd said was true. Was Zach always going to be a cop, until it ended up killing him? With his pension and my income from the puzzles, we were comfortable, but it was the excitement that Zach missed, and I knew it. The only problem was that the more he worked, the greater chance there was that he'd put himself in danger. I'd come close to losing him once, and that was something I never wanted to face again.

THE BELMONT WAS EVEN NICER THAN I REMEMBERED, one of Charlotte's finest hotels. A nicely dressed man in a suit was waiting at the front entrance with a mobile rack, and he unloaded my car snappily. As he wheeled it to the front desk, I started digging into my purse for a tip, but he held his palm up.

"Everything is being covered," he said.

"Even tips?"

"Absolutely, Mrs. Stone."

"How in the world did you know my name?" I'd heard of good service before, but this was a little over the top.

"The hotel owner himself told our staff to be on the lookout for you, and we've been waiting for your arrival ever since."

I started for the front desk when he held out a paper sleeve containing room keys to me. "You're already checked in, so we can go straight to your suite."

"Suite? A room would be fine." The last time Zach and I had stayed in a suite had been our honeymoon.

"I suppose I could move you, but it would cause us all a great deal of headaches, what with the paperwork and everything we'd have to change." He smiled as he said it, so I decided to go with the flow. "Also, the owner would be unhappy with us if we allowed it, and none of us want to cause that. We would consider it a great favor if you'd accept this offer."

I laughed. "I'm too tired to fight you on it," I said.

He hit the top button on the elevator, and it was all I could do not to say anything. When the door opened, I stepped out and saw in the long hallway, there were only four rooms on the top level.

As he started to open the door to Suite Three, I said, "You're not really a bellman at all, are you?"

"My name is Garrett, and it's my pleasure to serve as the manager of the Belmont," he said. "If you need anything, all you have to do is ask."

He started inside, but then he stopped when he realized that I wasn't following him in.

"Is there something wrong?" he asked me. "I thought we'd already settled your situation."

"This is more than we need, and I want an explanation before I move another step."

He looked distressed as I stood in the hallway, but I was firm in my insistence that I wasn't moving. I knew that Charlotte couldn't afford this kind of luxury, and I doubted that Grady could either, unless he was grandstanding. I had no problem with my husband getting paid handsomely for his work. He was good at it, and he deserved whatever the market would bear. But I didn't want to take advantage of anyone in the process.

"I'm waiting," I said.

The manager appeared to go through a handful of options when he finally shrugged and reached for his cell phone. After dialing, he surprised me by handing it to me.

"Hello?" I said tentatively.

"Is this Savannah Stone?"

"It is," I admitted.

"I understand there's a problem with your accommodations."

What on earth was going on here? "No, sir, no problem. It's just nicer than my husband and I need. May I ask your name?"

"Of course. Sorry about that. Garrett is literal when it comes to instructions, and I've trained him well not to reveal anything about me that he doesn't have to. My name is Barton Lane, and I own the Belmont, among other things here and there around the world. I would appreciate it if you would be my guests while you're here in Charlotte."

"Mr. Lane, it's most generous of you, but it's not necessary."

"Young lady," he said, his voice booming so loudly over the phone that I could swear I saw Garrett flinch, "I'm unaccustomed to having my wishes ignored."

"Wow, it must be really nice living your life. It happens to me all of the time."

I wasn't sure what reaction I expected, and from the look on the hotel manager's face, I must have just committed an unforgivable act of treason. The thing was, I'd never sworn an oath to Barton Lane.

What I got was laughter, a sound so foreign in the man's voice that I was certain he rarely used it. "I like you, Savannah. May I call you Savannah?"

"Absolutely, and I'll call you Barton."

If I kept this up, Garrett was going to need a team of paramedics to revive him. As it was, he looked like his head was about to explode.

"Savannah, it would please me for you to use this suite, and anything else my hotel has to offer."

"Is there any reason in particular you're being so nice to me?"

"The second victim, Cindy Glass, was my personal secretary," he said plainly, all joy gone from his voice. "I want her death avenged, and from everything I've heard, your husband is the only man capable of catching the killer."

"Thank you," I said. "He'll do his best, and please know that we appreciate your generosity. It's very sweet of you, Barton."

"Think nothing of it. If you need anything, or would like to get in contact with me, Garrett will take care of it. I hope someday we'll have the pleasure of meeting face to face under better circumstances."

"That would be nice."

"Now, if you will, give me back to Garrett."

The hotel manager took the phone, and as he kept repeating, "Yes, sir. Of course. I understand," I looked around the suite. My gaze was drawn outside before I even looked at the furnishings. The skyline of Charlotte, in all its glory, was laid out before me, and I couldn't wait for Zach to see it. We loved the mountains, but Charlotte had a lure for us as well, and here in the clouds, we could see the Queen City's beautiful architecture from a perspective few people had ever enjoyed.

I was still standing there taking it all in when I realized that Garrett was off the phone.

"Is there anything else I can get you?" he asked.

"No thank you. I've got to get us settled in, and then I'm going to rejoin my husband at police headquarters." I looked around the room and took in a sitting area with furniture nicer than anything I'd ever owned in my life.

The style was Queen Anne throughout, with shades of burgundy and black everywhere.

"I'll take care of settling you in then, if you wouldn't mind," he said.

"Who exactly is Barton Lane?" I asked. "Forgive me, but I've never heard of him before."

"He'd be delighted to hear that, since he prides himself on his privacy. I've spoken to him half a dozen times since I became manager, and that was fourteen years ago. Mr. Lane has a policy that as long as the job is being done efficiently, there's no need for direct supervision, or even contact, for that matter."

"I'm sure you're very good at what you do," I said.

I wondered what Zach and Steve were doing at that moment, and though I knew it was too soon for my husband to investigate anything outside the command center, I was still uneasy not knowing if he was safe. I was going to have to get over that impulse when Zach was working on a case, but I hadn't managed to do it so far.

Garrett handed me the keys, and as we left the suite, I took a second to gaze once again at that skyline view. My husband was going to be thrilled, if he wasn't already in the muck and mire of a killer's mind.

Chapter 4

■ ■ ■

"**S**AVANNAH? WHAT ARE YOU DOING IN TOWN? DID YOU and Zach move back to Charlotte?"

I was in the lobby heading for my car when I turned to see who was talking to me. "Lorna, how are you?" I hugged my old friend, and then I explained, "We didn't move back. Zach and I are just visiting." I wasn't about to tell her why we were really here.

"How have you been? We really miss you around here." Lorna Gaither had gone out with Grady for nearly a year before he'd broken the relationship off shortly before we left town.

"Thanks for asking. I'm good. How are you?" Lorna and I had become friends when she and Grady had been dating, and after the breakup, we'd stayed in touch. Right after things had ended with Grady, I'd had the distinct impression that Lorna blamed me for her relationship woes, though I hadn't had anything to do with it. If she still held it against me though, I couldn't tell by her demeanor.

"I'm doing fine," she said, and I could see in her eyes that it was true. "I owe you more thanks than I can say. Breaking me up with Grady was the best thing that ever happened to me."

"I thought you knew that I didn't have anything to do with it," I said. "I was as surprised as you were when he broke it off with you."

"Then I take my thanks back," she said with a hint of laughter in her voice. "However it happened, it worked out for the best. After Grady dumped me, I took a long, hard look at myself, and I didn't like what I saw. I started going to the gym, working with a shrink, and I finally realized that I'd been sabotaging things all along."

"Good for you," I said, not really knowing what else I could say. I glanced at my watch, and then I added, "I'm truly sorry, but I've got to meet up with Zach, and I'm late as it is."

"I have a wonderful idea. Let's have dinner tonight, just the two of us."

"I wish I could, Lorna, but I can't."

"Lunch tomorrow, then. Come on, it will be fun."

"I'm honestly not sure what our schedule will be like while we're here," I said.

"Then we can make it breakfast. You have to eat sometime, don't you?"

"Breakfast sounds good," I agreed.

"I'll see you here tomorrow in the hotel restaurant. Eight o'clock on the dot."

"Eight it is," I said. I wasn't sure why Lorna was so insistent about sharing a meal with me, but I'd deal with that tomorrow. At the moment, I just wanted to get back and see what Zach had been up to.

I FOUND MY HUSBAND DEEP IN THOUGHT WHEN I GOT BACK to the task force headquarters at the police station. There had been a note on his door that said, "Quiet. Genius at Work," and I pulled it off to show him.

"Please tell me you didn't write this yourself," I said as I showed him the notice.

"What? No, it's just probably somebody's idea of a joke."

The rigid sheets of insulation—once empty silver— were now filled with copies from the files. A nice-sized copier sat in one corner of the room, and the original documents were on tables in different sections of the space, making it feel like some kind of weird maze. No doubt there was some kind of order there, but I knew no one else would be able to see it but Zach.

I avoided the area where the photographs were displayed, then studied the montage of the backs of the communiqués from the killer. Numbers and letters were interposed in the oddest arrangements, but if they made any sense, I couldn't see it, and I prided myself on my orderly mind.

I'd been focusing so intensely, I hadn't realized that Zach was standing right behind me.

"It's odd, isn't it?" he asked.

"I'm sure it means something, but who knows what the

killer's mind is like? This could be a recipe for cereal, for all we know."

"It's significant, I know that much," Zach said as he shook his head.

"How can you be so sure?"

"I can't explain it. It's something in my gut," he told me, and that was good enough for me. My husband's years as a police officer had given him instincts based on experience that I would stack up against anyone's intuition. Added to that was his uncanny ability to cut through the fog to see what was really happening, and it was no wonder that his consulting business was starting to pick up. The problem with that was that the cases he got were only the very hardest, and that put a strain on him that I didn't like.

"Where's your minion?" I asked as I looked around the room.

"Steve had to take care of a problem with his landlord," Zach said. "I'm having him reassigned to me, so at least there's that. He's going to be my gopher so I don't have to run all over Charlotte tracking things down."

"I like the sound of that," I said as I hugged him.

"What was that for?"

"You looked like you could use a hug."

"Thanks, but we should probably keep that to a minimum around here. We don't want people talking."

I laughed at him. "Zach, it's okay. We're married."

"You know what I mean. This is serious business, and I don't want anyone to think I'm treating it otherwise."

I broke free. "Message received."

"You're not mad, are you?"

"Why should I be mad? My husband doesn't want to hug me, but other than that, I'm just dandy." I smiled at him to show that I was teasing.

"Thanks. Did you get us set up in a room?"

"You might say that."

"Savannah, what's with that smile?"

"We're in a suite on the top floor," I explained.

He shook his head. "And you let them put us there? We're on the taxpayer's dime here. We don't need a suite."

He reached for his phone and I put a hand over his to stop him. "It's compliments of the hotel's owner, so it isn't costing the people of Charlotte a dime."

"Why on earth would the owner of the Belmont put us up for free?"

"I asked him that exact same question, and he told me that he had a personal stake in this."

Zach nodded. "Barton Lane."

"How did you know that? It's supposed to be some kind of huge secret. I'm fairly certain that he's not going to be happy that you figured it out so quickly."

Zach tapped a copied photograph, and though I didn't want to look at it, after a second I drove back my queasiness and examined it. At least it wasn't a crime scene photo, or one from the killer. The photograph appeared to be from an employee ID badge, and even though the conditions weren't ideal, it was a decent picture of a pretty young woman with a nice figure and coppery hair.

"She's really pretty," I said. "Was, I mean."

"Grady thought so, too."

I stared openly at my husband. "How could you possibly know that?"

"They were dating when she was murdered," Zach said.

"Is that why we're here?" I asked my husband. "Did someone kill her because she was close to Grady? It sounds like a pretty big coincidence, otherwise."

"You know I don't believe in coincidences," he said. "At first, Davis thought that it might have something to do with Barton Lane, but with the threats against Grady, they have to be tied together."

"What about the first victim?"

Zach shrugged. "If he has any connection to Grady, nobody's been able to find it so far."

"So, you're not the only one who noticed the original connection."

"That's why Davis hired me. He knows that if something happens to the mayor on his watch, he's through."

That angered me. "It's a matter of self-preservation, then. And here I thought he called you because he was worried about Grady."

"Why can't it be both?" Zach asked. "I had to watch out for political ramifications all of the time when I had his job. It isn't easy being chief, and nobody knows that better than I do. He'd done everything he can to catch this guy. I can't think of a thing I would have done differently if I was in his shoes."

"You wouldn't have had to bring in outside help," I said.

"Don't count on it. There's such a thing as being too close to a situation. I've got enough distance to look at it a little clearer, with none of the pressure Davis has."

"No, you just have to find a killer before one of your best friends is the next victim. That's no pressure at all."

"I'm surprised to see you back here so soon," Zach said. "How long were you gone?"

"Are you trying to get rid of me already?"

"No, of course not. I just thought you had another puzzle due today. You're not skipping any deadlines for this, are you?"

"I have a few in the bank. I'll call Derrick and have him run one of those if he needs to."

"Savannah, I know how much you hate doing that."

"It's no big deal. I'll do one tomorrow, okay? Right after my breakfast appointment."

"You've got plans already? Who's your date?"

"Lorna Gaither. I ran into her in the hotel lobby, and she wanted to get together. I think she misses having me around. Would you like to join us?"

Zach had never been one of Lorna's fans, and it wouldn't have surprised me if he'd been the one to break her up with Grady, though he'd never said anything to me about it, and there weren't any secrets between us.

At least I didn't think there were.

My stomach grumbled. "Zach, were you planning to eat dinner any time soon?"

"It's nowhere near time to eat."

"Look at your watch."

He glanced at it, then he said, "Sorry, I didn't realize how late it was getting. I thought I'd just send out for a sandwich."

"Wow, could we make it two, or do we have to split yours?"

"Savannah, you know how I get when I'm trying to get my hooks into a case. If you'd like to go out to Morton's yourself, you have my blessing."

"I'd rather split a sandwich with you than have a steak

by myself," I said. "Let me grab a phone book and I'll make the call."

"Fine," he said absently, but I could tell that I'd already lost him. There was something about one of the photographs on the wall that he was fixated on, and I knew I could stand on the table in front of him and spout the Gettysburg Address and he wouldn't even notice. I found a sandwich shop that delivered, placed our order, and then started looking through some of the paperwork spread out on tables. The first murder victim had been a man in his thirties named Hank Tristan. He'd been discovered in his bed with a single stab wound to the heart, and the police had determined that he'd been at the Black-Tie Ball the night before. The ball had been a fundraiser for Charity At Home, a group that raised money to help underprivileged children in the most rural areas of North Carolina. It had been hosted by Jerry Drake, one of the minority partners of the Charlotte Bobcats basketball team, a man who wasn't afraid to use the clout of his connections to solicit donations for his favorite causes. Hank's date had left the party early with a migraine headache, and he had stayed behind to dance with as many women as he could convince to join him on the floor. Nobody saw him leave, or even if he was alone at the time, and when he didn't show up at his investment firm the next morning, his executive assistant, Julian King, had gone by the house to collect him.

Evidently Hank enjoyed his partying, and had made it a duty of his aide to wake him if it was needed, help him into a cold shower, and get him ready for work. I didn't know how much Julian made, but I couldn't imagine that it was worth what he had to do. When the photo showed up, wrapped in Hank's black bow tie, things elevated to an entirely different level. It was clear that whoever had committed the murder was now taunting the police with their crime. The interview list of everyone the police had talked to read like a Who's Who of Charlotte society, and I wasn't surprised to see the names of several of my friends there, including my breakfast date for the next day, Lorna Gaither. I wondered if it was possible that she'd seen something. As I flipped through the interviews, I found the one with Lorna, and after a few seconds, I realized that it wasn't likely. She'd been attending the ball with Peter Colt, a man rich enough to own his very own mountain. Not just the peak, the entire thing. Lorna had danced once with Hank, and then she and Peter had left early when he had complained of being bored; neither of them had seen anything of note. I glanced through more interviews and found Grady's name. His interview was a little more interesting. It appeared that he and Hank Tristan had had a disagreement, and there had been the threat of a physical confrontation when calmer heads stepped in and stopped them.

"Did you see this?" I asked Zach as I held out the report.

"I haven't gotten to that stack yet. What is it?"

He took the interview sheets from me and quickly scanned them. "Funny, Grady's usually pretty good about controlling his temper."

"Unless there's sangria around," I said. "Remember the time at the Jackson barbeque he had two drinks and was ready to take on the world?"

"There's a reason some people shouldn't drink. I wonder if he had a cocktail that night."

"It doesn't say." I saw my husband watching me. "Don't look so surprised. You're not the only one in our family who notices things. That's the first thing that came into my mind, too."

"This is bad."

As Zach reached for his telephone, I asked, "Who are you calling?"

"I want to see what Grady has to say about this."

"Hang on a second. You're not actually thinking that our friend had anything to do with this, do you?"

Zach gave me a noncommittal shrug. "I'm just gathering information right now."

"Don't try to brush me off; you should know better than that by now. Do you honestly think Grady is capable of killing anyone?"

He lowered the telephone. "Savannah, if he weren't our friend and the mayor of Charlotte, wouldn't he be at the top of our suspect list? I had no idea until just now that he had a fight with the first victim the night he died. I already knew that the woman he was dating was the second victim. I'm worried, and I'm not afraid to say it. We need to consider the possibility that Grady could be faking the latest threats himself."

"He wouldn't kill anybody. He's too nice a person to do that."

"Remember when I first became a cop? I had to arrest a grandmother of seven for killing her best friend because she beat her in a gardening show. Just because she baked cookies for blood drives didn't mean she wasn't a murderer. Until I'm sure that Grady wasn't involved with either murder, I'm treating him as my prime suspect."

I knew better than to try to talk my husband out of anything. What was worse, I could see the logic of what he was saying. Was that why Davis had brought Zach in? Arresting the mayor, or even thinking that he could be guilty of multiple murders, could end his career if he was wrong. Hiring my husband was a good way to diffuse the blame if he was mistaken. Davis would bear watching. He might just be sneakier than I'd ever given him credit for.

Zach made his call, and I listened in on his end of the conversation. He'd been curt and formal with Grady, and the mayor had agreed to come by the police station in half an hour.

When our sandwiches arrived, I paid for them, though neither one of us felt much like eating. Zach was right; Grady belonged at the top of his suspect list, but I didn't have to like it.

As I nibbled at my sandwich, my husband said, "You need to make yourself scarce when Grady gets here."

"Why? I thought I was your assistant."

"Savannah, things might get a little dicey, and it would be better if you weren't here."

"Man talk, is that what you're saying?"

Zach looked uncomfortable admitting it, but he finally said, "That's part of it, certainly. Grady might open up more to me if you're not in the room."

"I can watch his expressions while you interview him," I said. "There's a chance I might pick up on something that you wouldn't see." Another thought occurred to me. "What if I think of something to ask him that you miss?

Can we afford to take that chance? Stop trying to protect me, Zach."

"It's not that. If anything, my rationale puts you in more danger, not less. Forget what I said; you can stay."

I wasn't about to give up that easily, even if it meant a win in my column. "What did you have in mind?"

"It's not a great idea."

"Why don't you let me hear it, and I'll be the judge of that. Come on, give."

My husband reluctantly explained, "If you're not here during the interrogation, it might help keep you on good terms with Grady. We may need that. I plan to explore some pretty explosive lines of questioning, and there's an excellent chance I'm going to thoroughly tick him off. If you can stay on his good side, there's a chance we won't lose total access to the man, but it puts you in a precarious situation. If Grady really is guilty, you could be in danger."

"He wouldn't hurt me," I said.

"Don't you think Cindy Glass thought the exact same thing?"

"I don't care," I said. "But you're right, I'm leaving the second he gets here."

"Savannah, I'm still not sure this is a good idea. We need to talk about it more before I'm willing to let you take such an active role in the investigation."

Things still hadn't been decided ten minutes later when Grady arrived alone.

The mayor tried to be playful as he said, "Before you chew me out, my bodyguard is downstairs catching up with his pals. I figured I'm safe enough in here with you two."

There must have been something in our expressions, because Grady added, "You two look like you've just lost your best friend. What's going on?"

"We need to talk," Zach said. That was my cue to leave, if I decided to go. My husband had ultimately left it up to me, and now was the time to figure out which option held the most promise for us. If I stayed, I might pick up on something that my husband missed, which wasn't all that likely, I was the first to admit. But if I left, I'd still have an in with the mayor, a chance that would die if I stayed.

I decided to try to have it both ways. "If you two will excuse me, I've got a puzzle to create."

"I've got to admit, I'm hooked on them myself. How often do you make them?" Grady asked me.

"Every day." As I walked out of the room, I looked back at my husband. It was pretty clear that he wasn't happy with the decision I'd made to take chances with my safety, but it was ultimately my choice.

That didn't mean that I actually had to go back to the hotel and work on a puzzle, though. I kept the door purposely ajar so I could listen to their conversation without them knowing I was there. It wasn't ideal, but it was certainly a lot better than just hiding in a hole until the storm blew over.

Once he was sure I was gone, Zach said, "We need to have a serious conversation, Grady. That means no lies, no misdirection, no holding back on me. Is that understood?"

Grady's easy tone vanished. "What's with the attitude, Zach? Was it a mistake bringing you back to Charlotte?"

"Not as far as I'm concerned. The city's hired me to do a job, and I aim to do it."

"You know I'll cooperate all I can, but I never did like

being bossed around. That's why I'm the mayor. In a way, you could say that I *am* the city."

"Funny, I thought the citizens were."

Grady must have realized how pompous he was starting to sound. The edge was gone from his voice the next time he spoke. I would have given anything to study his face as he made that transition, but I couldn't see more than a sliver of floor and shadow through the opening. "Is there any reason to have an attitude with me? We're friends; at least I thought we were."

Zach slapped his hand on the table, something that startled me from where I was lurking. I couldn't imagine the impact the sound must have had on Grady. "I'm trying to get to the truth, and if you're innocent, you should be trying to help me, not stonewalling like this was some kind of press conference."

"Sorry. What do you want to talk about?"

There was a pause, and then I heard my husband say, "Let's talk about Cindy Glass."

"Let's not," Grady said.

"I'm not fooling around here."

"Move on, Zach."

After another pause, Zach said, "Okay, fine. We'll come back to her later. I understand you had a pretty public argument with Hank Tristan the night he was murdered. Would you like to tell me about it?"

"Been spying on me, have you?" the mayor asked.

"It's in the police report. Everybody knows about it, but I thought you might like to tell me your side of it."

"Do you honestly think that I could have killed him? You do, don't you?"

"Grady, I want to believe you, but there's too much cop

in me to turn my back on the fact that a guy you had a public brawl with was murdered not long after, and then a girl you were dating was next. How do you think that looks on you?"

"I'm being threatened, too, remember?" Grady said. His voice was high and shrill, and it sounded to me like he was close to snapping.

"If you didn't do it, you're my best resource. Somebody is hovering around the edges of your life and doing some pretty terrible things. You want me to find them, don't you?"

"Of course I do. You shouldn't even have to ask."

"Then help me eliminate you as a suspect so I can go find the real killer."

The request hung in the air between them, and for a second, I didn't think Grady was going to answer. After a few more seconds, though, he said, "I'll tell you whatever I can."

"What were you and Hank fighting about the night of the ball?"

"He made a crack about my date, if you have to know. He thought it was amusing that I was there with someone's secretary, and he asked me what it was like slumming with Cindy."

"So you lost your temper with him?"

I could hear an edge of anger in Grady's voice as he said, "He was acting like an idiot. I didn't really know the girl. It was a fix up, a last-minute blind date for the ball when my original date had to cancel. I didn't know her, but I wasn't about to stand there and let some drunken fool take shots at her."

"You'd been drinking too, hadn't you?"

"Yes," he admitted. "I'm sure that's in the police report, too. But I didn't kill him. Two minutes after the argument ended, I'd forgotten all about him."

"Where were you later that night after the ball?" The
question was simple and easy, but I knew that my husband
was really asking the mayor of Charlotte for his alibi.

Grady sighed, and then said, "I was with Cindy, okay?
My alibi was murdered the night after Hank was killed,
before the police had a chance to interview her. I know they
thought they were doing me a favor by going easy on me,
but if they'd talked to Cindy before she died, I would have
had an alibi for the murder." He took a deep breath, and
then added, "I'm not proud of having a one-night stand, but
I was drunk, and one thing led to another. She was a sweet
girl. Who knows? If we'd had more than one date, something special might have developed between us."

"No one saw you then, besides her?"

"No one," Grady said.

"Let's move on," Zach said. "Cindy Glass was stabbed
in her apartment with the same type of knife someone
used on Hank Tristan. Where were you the night she was
killed?"

"You don't think I killed her, do you? Zach, I liked
her."

"I've got to ask, and we both know it."

Grady sighed, and then he said, "I was in Atlanta at a
symposium for southern mayors. You can check with the
Thorgood; that's where we stayed."

I knew my husband would verify the mayor's alibi, but
I wasn't sure how good it was. After all, Charlotte was just
four hours away from Atlanta, so it was possible he made
the round-trip to kill Cindy while everyone else was sleep-

ing. It wouldn't leave him a lot of time to get back to his conference, but it still left a window of opportunity for him to be the murderer, and I knew my husband was as aware of that fact as I was.

"Any chance you took a city-owned car?"

"No, I like to hit the open highway in my truck when I get the chance. Why?"

"Grady, it's my job to check everything."

"Davis didn't ask me any of these questions," the mayor said a little petulantly.

"I'm not about to comment on someone else's investigation techniques. This is just how I do it. Is there anything else you want to tell me? Anything that might help me solve this case?"

"If you're hoping I'll confess, I'm sorry to say that you're going to be disappointed."

"Then how do you explain two murders, both claimed by some nutcase, that touch your life?"

"Maybe it's just a coincidence," Grady said.

"Sorry, I don't believe in them."

"I don't know. What can I tell you? The only other thing I can think of is that somebody's out to get me."

"Ordinarily I'd say you're being a little paranoid," Zach said.

"Hey, even the paranoid are right sometimes." His voice softened as he added, "Zach, I know you're just doing your job, but if anybody else finds out that I'm your main suspect, you're going to destroy my political career."

"That's why you should be helping me instead of stonewalling."

"I said I'd do anything I could. What else do you need?"

"A list of your enemies might help," Zach said. "If you didn't do it, I'm willing to guess that someone you know did."

I heard him stand, and I knew I had to get out of there before they caught me listening in. I ducked down the hallway hoping to find an open door, but I made it all the way to the stairs, and every room was locked. I had no choice. I ran into the stairwell and climbed up to the next landing. I was going to wait five minutes, and then emerge to compare notes with my husband.

As I silently counted down the minutes in my mind, the stairwell door opened. I'd taken two steps down, so I hurried back to my landing.

Below me, I heard Grady say, "Call the second you have something."

When there was no reply, the mayor added, "You're not going to tell me anything, are you?"

"A lot of that depends on what I find out," Zach said.

Grady turned his back without another word and hurried down the stairs. I waited until I heard the door below shut, and then I made my way to the door to our floor.

It was locked from the inside.

I pounded on it for a few minutes, but no one answered. I had no choice but to follow Grady downstairs and make my way back up the elevator.

The only problem was that the mayor was still near the stairwell door when I walked out, and I nearly ran him down.

Chapter 5

∎∎∎

"**S**AVANNAH? WHAT WERE YOU DOING IN THE STAIRWELL? Were you eavesdropping?"

"I was up on the roof," I said suddenly, hoping that he would believe me.

"Why in the world would you go up there?"

"Sometimes I need to be above everything when I create. Who knows why? Every puzzle is different, and I don't know what circumstances I'll need until I realize what I'm doing isn't working."

"I figured you did them all on computers," he said.

"No, I'm an old-fashioned kind of gal. I like the feel of pencil lead on paper, and the way an eraser glides across the page."

He nodded absently, and I could tell that his thoughts were somewhere else. It was time to nudge him a little.

"Did you and Zach have a productive conversation?"

Grady looked skeptical, and then he said, "Your husband acts tough sometimes, doesn't he?"

"What makes you think he's acting?"

That clearly wasn't what he was expecting to hear. "Savannah, do you think I killed those people, too?"

"I never said that, Grady, and I'm willing to bet that my husband didn't, either."

"How could you possibly know that? You were listening in to our conversation, weren't you?"

"I don't have to hear my husband's words to know what he would or wouldn't say. Besides, I was on the roof, remember?"

"So you said," Grady answered. He was about to say something else when his cell phone rang. He glanced at the number, and then said, "I've got to take this. Excuse me."

"Certainly," I said.

He moved away, and I saw his bodyguard trailing after him. A sudden dark thought occurred to me. Had he protested having someone shadow him because it might limit his movements? If he was a killer, having a police chaperone would be the last thing he wanted. It was a possibility that I'd have to discuss with my husband.

Steve Sanders approached, and it was clear that he'd seen me watching the mayor. "He's some piece of work, isn't he?"

"What do you mean?"

The officer just shrugged. "I don't know. Forget I said that. I'm just a little beat."

"Then why don't you go home? I'm sure Zach can manage without you."

"What, and miss out on all of the fun? I don't think so. There will be plenty of time to sleep when I'm dead." He must have realized how that sounded. "I didn't mean anything by that."

"Don't be so sensitive," I said. "I wasn't offended."

"You're all right by me," Steve said. "Are you going out?"

"Actually, I'm heading upstairs to talk to my husband. Give us five minutes before you come up, okay?"

He saluted me, and I didn't care what he thought we were going to do with our time. I didn't like the way Steve had looked at Grady, and I didn't want him privy to the conversation I needed to have with my husband.

"I thought you went back to the hotel," Zach said when I walked into the task force room.

"I never left," I admitted. "What do you think about the way Grady acted when you questioned him? He sounded pretty defensive to me."

"You heard us? Were you eavesdropping, Savannah?"

"I kept the door ajar when I left, and I listened from the hallway."

Storm clouds crossed Zach's face. "We had a deal. You were supposed to leave the interrogation to me."

"I didn't say a word. You didn't even know I was out there, so don't try to say that I interfered."

He frowned for a few seconds. "He could have caught you."

I bit back the urge to say that he almost did. That wouldn't do either of us any good. "But he didn't. It was better than nothing listening in, but I couldn't see his face. Was he telling you the truth during your interview?"

My husband was a trained investigator, and I knew there wasn't much he missed, though I was happy to help from time to time. He stretched back in his chair, and for a second, I wasn't sure it could take the strain. "There were things he wasn't telling me, but I honestly can't say yet whether I believe the things he did say. On the face of it, it's all pretty convenient, isn't it? His alibi for the first homicide was murdered herself before the police could question her."

"Atlanta's close enough to drive back here and kill her, but it didn't leave him much time if he did it. There are a thousand things that could have gone wrong during that drive. Is Grady that big a risk taker?"

"You know him as well as I do," Zach said. "He can be foolhardy if it suits him. What I don't understand is why he's trying to hide something from me if he's innocent. All I want to do is help him, but he treated me like I was the enemy during that interview."

"So, you can't cross him off your list."

"Not by a long shot. I have to do a lot more digging before I'm willing to do that."

"I thought of something else you might want to consider," I said.

"You know I'm always willing to hear what you have to say."

"Willing maybe, but not eager."

"Come on, Savannah, spill it."

"I ran into Grady downstairs after he left you."

"Savannah, this is serious. You can't play games with him."

I frowned. "I didn't mean to run into him, but the stupid door to this floor is locked from the stairwell, so I had to use the ground floor exit. I nearly knocked him over when I opened the door."

"You told us both you had a puzzle to create. How did you explain being in a stairwell the entire time he was talking to me? Come on, tell me. I really want to know."

"I told him that I was working on the roof for inspiration," I said.

Zach smiled. "The fact that you're afraid of heights doesn't enter into the equation, does it?"

"I doubt Grady knows that."

"Maybe we should get a room in the hotel closer to the ground."

"I'm fine as long as there's steel and glass around me. It's being out in the open that freaks me out." My husband, as far as I knew, wasn't afraid of anything. He'd run into a burning building or gunfire if it meant saving someone, when anyone with any kind of self-preservation instinct at all would run the other way. As for me, there were lots of things I was afraid of, but that usually didn't keep me from doing what had to be done. I'd once read a definition of courage that called it bravery in the face of fear, and if that were true, I had more than my share.

"Is that what you wanted to tell me, that Grady thinks you're okay with heights?"

"Of course not. But as he looked over at his bodyguard, I had to wonder if he resented the man's presence for a reason different from the one he gave us."

"Such as?"

"If he's up to no good, maybe having a cop trailing him around the clock is more than just inconvenient. How much do we know about what's happened to Grady since we left Charlotte? He could have changed in ways we can't even imagine, and if Grady's on a killing spree, having a police escort isn't the greatest thing in the world for him, is it? Should you tell the officer guarding him that maybe he should watch his own back, too?"

Zach reached for his phone as he said, "It doesn't pay to underestimate that intellect of yours."

"Maybe I'm just jumping at shadows," I said.

"An ounce of prevention, and all of that," Zach said. After being transferred from the switchboard downstairs, I heard him warn the police officer watching Grady without actually saying anything bad about the mayor. It was a fine line he was dancing, and we both knew it, but if it saved someone's life, it was worth it.

After he hung up, I asked, "Where does that leave us now?"

Zach looked at the piles of papers on the tables. "I've got a lot of reading to do. I might be here late tonight."

"Why don't I help? Maybe I can find something in there that could point you in the right direction."

"No offense, Savannah, but I need to ingest this all myself. It's the only way I can wrap my head around it. You know how I work."

"I know; read everything, learn everything, then let your subconscious take over."

"Hey, it's worked in the past."

I nodded. "Then you really don't need me right now, do you?"

"Come on, I always need you," he said with that crooked smile of his that I cherish.

"You know what I mean. If you don't mind, then, I'll head back to the hotel and work on a puzzle."

"I thought you had a few in the bank," Zach said.

"I do, but making a puzzle might take my mind off murder, at least for a little while."

"I'm sorry I dragged you into this," he said.

"Don't be. Whither thou goest, and all of that." I gave him a quick peck, and then added, "Call me when you need a ride."

"I'll have someone here drop me off. Are you sure you'll be okay?"

I smiled brightly. "Don't worry about me. I'm a big girl. I can take care of myself."

"See that you do," he said.

I left my husband with his head buried in a police file. If I'd stayed, I'd be nothing more than a distraction for him, and he had serious work to do. Not that my job wasn't important in its own way, but nobody was going to die if I didn't get my puzzle in on time, whereas he had a great deal more serious things at stake.

As I walked out into the hallway, I found Steve standing there. "You didn't have to wait out here," I said. "We've been finished for a few minutes."

"I didn't want to interrupt anything," he said with a smile.

"Don't worry, if we're canoodling, I'll leave a tie on the door."

"That would be greatly appreciated. I'd hate to walk in on the Chief and do something to merit a chewing out. If you don't mind me saying so, your husband can really drop a hammer on someone if he wants to."

"I've been married to him forever," I said. "Do you honestly think you're telling me anything I don't already know?"

He shrugged. "I'm just saying."

"Go on in," I said as I headed for the elevator. I wasn't sure what Steve could do to help Zach any more than I had, and if that was the case, I knew my husband wouldn't hesitate getting rid of him as quickly as he'd dispatched me.

THOUGH I'D TOLD ZACH I WANTED TO GET BACK TO THE Belmont so I could create another puzzle, there was somewhere else I wanted to go first. I drove to our old Dilsworth neighborhood on autopilot, amazed by how familiar and yet foreign the drive had become. A few shops had closed along the way, and I saw that new tenants had taken their place. An old oak tree I'd always admired had been taken down, and a sapling put in its place. I had to wonder if an ice storm or a lightning bolt had felled it, or if it had been something more mundane, and man-made. Things change, and life goes on, whether I was there to witness it or not. Seeing that tree gone gave me an irrational fear that the house I'd shared with my husband was gone as well. I wasn't sure what kind of catastrophe I was imagining, but in my mind, it was total and complete: where our quaint place had once stood, there was now nothing more than overgrown rubble, from what, I couldn't imagine. The image in my mind was so real that I nearly overlaid it onto the truth when I drove down our street and saw that it hadn't been touched. That wasn't exactly true. The trim was now painted robin's egg blue instead of the moss green I'd preferred, and a few of the bushes in front of the Colonial had been cut back to the point of mutilation, at least in my mind. Still, the house stood just as strong and proud as the day we'd handed the keys over to the Realtor.

I parked on the other side of the street and tried to take it all in. It was the first time I'd been back since we'd sold it, and while I wasn't ordinarily all that sentimental, I was surprised to realize that I was crying softly as I looked at it.

My reverie and introspection were broken when there was a sudden tapping on the passenger window of my car.

I looked up to see the smiling face of Sherry Watts, my longtime neighbor and best friend in Charlotte. Her smile vanished as she saw my tears.

"Savannah, are you all right?"

I wiped the tears from my face, feeling foolish the entire time I was doing it. "Sorry, I just got caught up in it all."

"Well, come out here and give me a hug."

I did as she commanded, and soon found myself wrapped in her embrace. Sherry was what some would call pleasingly plump, with just enough softness around the edges to make her look like someone's mom, which she was, three times over. She had bright red hair, a complexion like milk, and a sharp wit that I'd cherished over the years of our friendship.

"You've lost weight," she said after she pulled away and studied me.

"Trust me, you're wrong."

She shook her head slightly. "Savannah, I know what I'm talking about. The country air must be good for you. How's life treating you?"

"We love it," I said.

Sherry frowned for a moment. "Why didn't you call me? I had no idea you were coming back to the city."

"It just came up," I said. "Zach got a call from the new police chief."

She nodded. "It's been all over the *Observer*. Can you imagine, Charlotte having our very own killer on the loose."

"You don't seem all that worried about it," I said.

She smiled brightly. "Are you kidding? Who'd want to get rid of me? I'm absolutely delightful."

We both laughed at her expression of wonder, and it felt good being in her presence again. I didn't miss much about our move, but losing my friends had to be high on the list of regrets about leaving Charlotte.

She glanced over at my old house. "I just love what they've done with the bushes, don't you?"

"They got kind of aggressive, don't you think?"

Sherry laughed. "Jack hired his seventeen-year-old son to trim them—even though Betsy warned him not to—and knowing Jack, he gave pretty precise instructions. But Justin has a mind of his own, so he ignored them. He's a good kid, but I'm glad I've got girls. Boys seem to have too many hormones."

I frowned for a second before I buried it. I didn't think Sherry saw it, but I was surprised to find that I was jealous that she'd bonded so quickly with my replacements. Life moved on for me. Why shouldn't it for my best friend?

She took my hand and said, "Come on into the kitchen. I've got a pan of sweet rolls that came out two minutes ago, and there's fresh coffee, too."

Sherry was famous for her sourdough bread and rolls, and I knew Zach would be envious when he found out I'd sampled some. I glanced at my watch. "What about the girls? Don't you have to pick them up at school?"

She laughed. "That's right, you don't know. Lindsay got her license, and she persuaded her dad to buy her a car."

"And Bill actually did?" Her husband was notoriously tight with money, and they had a hefty savings account to prove it.

"Come on, you know he's always had a tough time saying no to her. The beauty of it is, she's happy to drive to school, even if it means she has to pick Haley and Jessie up on her way home. I can't tell you how freeing it's been. Now come on, let's get those sweet rolls before the girls get home and demolish the pan."

I followed her inside, forgetting my momentary lapse and trying to enjoy being with my friend again. We'd email and talk on the telephone from time to time, but there was no substitute for personal contact. Though I'd made a few new friends in Parson's Valley, none of the relationships had had the chance to blossom yet. It was true what they said; there were no friendships like old ones.

The three girls came in just as we finished a sweet roll apiece, laughing about something. After hugging each of them and marveling at how much they'd grown, I excused myself.

"Let me walk you out," Sherry said, and turning to her daughters, she added, "Save one for your father."

"Do we have to?" Jessie asked.

"Fine, go ahead and eat his. It's on your head, though, not mine."

Jessie pulled her hand away. "It's not worth it."

"You got that right," Sherry said. "I'll be back in a second."

Back at my car, Sherry hugged me again. As she did, I felt like I was truly home again. "How long are you going to be in town?"

"I'm not really sure," I admitted.

"You could always stay with us, but it might be a little tight," she offered.

"Thanks, but we're staying at the Belmont."

She raised one eyebrow. "My, my, my. We're coming up in the world, aren't we? And don't try to tell me you're paying for it with your puzzle money. I know better."

"If you can believe it, we're guests of the hotel's owner."

"Savannah, you are running in some rarified circles these days." She paused after she said it, looked past me, and then waved her hand in the air. "Betsy, come on over. There's someone you've got to meet."

The last thing I wanted to do was see my replacement, but I turned to see a tall, thin woman with wiry blonde hair coming toward us.

As she neared, Sherry said, "This is Savannah Stone."

"I love your puzzles," she said, absolutely gushing. "I don't know how you do it. They're wonderful."

Sherry grinned. "When I told her whose house she bought, she was thrilled. You've been wondering who your biggest fan was. Well, say hello to her."

I offered her my hand. "It's nice to meet you."

"Stay right here. Don't move," Betsy said.

"Where's she going?" I asked Sherry as the woman hurried quickly back across the street.

"I have no idea. She's a hoot, isn't she?"

"She's something, all right."

A minute later, Betsy came back waving a newspaper in her hand. "I got it. Would you mind signing this for me? It would be such an honor."

"Of course, I'd be delighted," I said. I was rarely asked for an autograph outside of a puzzle convention. There I was treated like some kind of minor celebrity, but in everyday life, no one seemed to know—or care—who I was, or what I did for a living.

After I signed the puzzle, she took it back and stared at my autograph for a few seconds. "You just made my day. Sorry, I'm usually not this ditsy, but I always get this way around famous people."

Sherry and I both laughed, and to Betsy's credit, she smiled back.

I explained, "I'm really not all that much of anything important."

"Trust her, she's telling the truth," Sherry said.

"Well, you are to me."

That got us laughing again.

"Sorry. Old friends, inside jokes," I said.

"Are you kidding? I'm thrilled. You're even nicer than Sherry said you were."

I looked at my old friend. "You've been talking about me?"

"How many neighborhood stories can I tell that you or your husband aren't in? Bring him by, too, okay?"

"No promises. You know how he gets when he's on a case."

"I thought he was retired," Betsy said.

"He's consulting with the Charlotte police," I said.

"Wow, you two must lead pretty exciting lives."

"It's not that different from everyone else," I said.

There was a car honking behind us, and I saw a lanky young man who had to be Justin. "Sorry, I've got to go."

"Is it time for another test?" Sherry asked.

"You know it."

"Tell him I said good luck."

"Will do. It's such a pleasure meeting you," Betsy said as she shook my hand again.

After she was gone, Sherry explained, "Her husband wouldn't let Justin take his driving test until he got a B average in school. You've never seen a boy study so hard. The bad thing is, he was so nervous when he finally did take it, he flunked his first test. It's driving Betsy as crazy as it is him."

"She seems nice."

"She is, but she's not you. I miss you, Savannah."

"I miss you, too," I said. "I'll give you a call later when things settle down a little."

"I won't hold my breath," she said with a grin. "Things never seem to calm down when you're around."

"Is that a crack at me, young lady?"

"Are you kidding? I miss the excitement. Call me."

"I will," I said.

After I got in my car, I drove off quickly, not wanting to linger a moment longer. My life had changed, but there was a part of me that would always be there on that street. It made me a little sad to leave it again, but that was far outweighed by the sense of warmth I'd felt, wrapped up again in my best friend's love. Sherry was one of those friends that life gave us sometimes, but only if we were very, very lucky. It had been as if we hadn't missed a day since the last time we'd seen each other, picking up exactly where we'd left it. I cherished her friendship, and all that she meant to me. I was glad she'd found someone in my old house to be friends with, but even more, that there was still such a big place in her heart for me.

I might not have a lot of money, or ever be famous, but in terms of my friendships and the love my husband and I shared, I was the richest woman in the world.

Chapter 6
...

"WOW, YOU'RE EARLY," I SAID AS MY HUSBAND WALKED into our hotel suite later that evening.

"It's nearly seven," he said as he looked around and whistled. "Man, this place is something else, isn't it?"

"Just wait. Let me give you the grand tour."

"Forget that. Look at that skyline. I can't wait until it gets dark."

"While you're admiring the view, let me order something from room service."

"I thought you wanted to go out," he said, stifling a yawn.

"I've got a feeling you wouldn't be very good company," I said. "We'll eat in tonight, and you can take me somewhere special another night. Did you make any progress since I saw you?"

"You know how it goes. I'm still trying to wrap my head around things now. It will take some time to digest it all."

"Don't push yourself too hard," I said.

He rubbed his eyes. "I would have stayed later tonight, but I kept falling asleep reading the police reports. Order me a steak, would you? I'm going to take a quick shower."

I doubted he'd be able to make it quick. I'd already taken one myself. The shower was like everything else in the hotel, first class all the way. I'd never had a shower with water jetting out from three sides and above, and I doubted that I'd ever be content with a plain overhead nozzle again.

Night was creeping in as I placed our dinner order and settled in on one of the couches facing the bank of windows. I hadn't had a lot of luck with room service in the past, but I had the feeling that the Belmont would be different.

I lost track of time staring out the window at the lights of Charlotte, and I was surprised when Zach came out dressed in one of the hotel's luxurious bathrobes. He wasn't the type of guy to wear robes as a general rule, and after a few failed attempts at giving them at Christmas and one birthday, I gave up trying.

"I didn't think you liked robes," I said.

"Normally I don't, but I could get used to this."

There was a knock at the door, and as I started to answer it, my husband shook his head. "I'll do it."

He pulled his gun out from his bathrobe pocket and moved to the door. I hadn't even known he'd fetched it, but he must have had it in the bathroom with him. This case clearly had him more spooked than I'd realized.

"Who is it?" he called out.

"Room service," I heard the muffled reply.

"What's the order?"

"Two New York Strips, both medium, garlic mashed potatoes, cream spinach, and chocolate mousse for dessert."

He looked at me, and I nodded.

When Zach opened the door, I could see that his gun hand was now in his robe, no doubt holding it on the unsuspecting waiter.

"Would you like me to set it up for you?" the man asked as he pushed the cart into the room.

"We'll take care of it," Zach said. "Hang on, let me get my wallet."

"That won't be necessary," the waiter said. "Everything, including tips for service you receive, has been taken care of."

"Then give the owner our thanks."

The man looked at Zach as if he'd lost his mind, and I understood why. If the manager of the place had only spoken with Barton Lane a handful of times over the years, there wasn't much chance a waiter would be able to talk to him.

He didn't reply, but I could swear he bowed a little as he left the room.

"That smells great," Zach said as he started lifting off lids.

"Did you really think that he might be a bad guy?" I asked.

"Are we talking about the gun? No, I realized he was probably exactly who he said he was, but why take a chance if I don't have to?"

We decided to eat in front of the window, and the food

was just as marvelous as I'd hoped it would be. The steak nearly came apart at the first touch of my fork, and as we ate, I knew exactly what I was going to order tomorrow. With delicious food like this available in our room, why go out and face the crowds?

"Want your mousse?" Zach asked as he uncovered his.

"I doubt I could enjoy it, I'm so full."

"Great. That means there's more for me."

"Hey, hang on a second. I didn't say you could have mine."

He dug into his, and after a quick bite, he said, "You wouldn't like it. It's too rich."

"Not that I don't trust your opinion, but now I'm going to have to try it for myself."

He wasn't eager to give it to me, though. "You're full, remember?"

"There's always room for mousse," I said.

It was everything promised, rich and creamy, with waves of chocolate in every bite. When it was gone, I was surprised to realize that I still wanted more, though I knew I would never be able to eat another bite.

I smiled with contentment. "I hope this place has a first-class spa and gym. If we keep eating like this, I'm going to have to start working out, or I'll never fit into my clothes."

Zach just grinned as he leaned back in his chair. "I hate the reason we're here, but I've got to say, I like the way your friend Barton Lane is treating us."

"He's not my friend," I said. "We've only spoken once."

"Evidently that's more than most folks around here can say. You must have made some kind of impression on him."

"Don't kid yourself. We're getting all this so he can make your life easier and you can focus on who killed his assistant. The man sounded like he was still in shock over losing her when we talked."

"I don't doubt it," Zach said.

I could tell that my husband was distracted as he continued to stare out the window.

"I'm thinking about redoing my hair."

"Good," he said, and then I knew he wasn't listening.

"I'm going to start with a blue base, and then add red and green highlights. It should be nice, don't you think?"

"Nice," he mumbled.

"Zachary Harlan Stone," I snapped.

That got his attention. My husband hated it when I used his full name.

"What?" he asked, meeting my gaze.

"If you want to go back to headquarters, I completely understand. I know how you get when you're getting your teeth into a new case."

He looked tempted—I could see it in his eyes—but he just shook his head. "No, I need some time to digest the facts I've collected so far."

"Would it help to talk about it?"

"Sure, why not?"

"Wow, I can feel the love in the air."

"You know what I mean," Zach said.

"I know; I'm not trying to give you a hard time. Just say your thoughts out loud, and I'll pretend to listen to you."

"Okay, here goes. What I know so far shouldn't take long to tell. The crimes are related, that much is clear."

"From the letters the police got, right?"

"That and the photos the killer sent. This wasn't some casual killing spree. They were planned out pretty thoroughly, and the knife used on the victims was the same type, if not the exact same blade. Both murders occurred in the victims' domiciles, and there were no signs of forced entry in either case."

"What exactly does that tell you?"

"They let their killer in without a struggle."

"So it was someone they both knew," I said. "That doesn't look good for Grady, does it?"

"Not really, but it's not exactly proof we can use, either." Zach tapped his chin, a sure sign he was deep in thought. "There are lots of other reasons Hank Tristan and Cindy Glass could have let someone into their places."

"I can't imagine letting a stranger inside my house," I said.

"How about a delivery man with his hands full? Would you think twice about letting him in? Or a utility repairman looking for a gas leak? If a police officer, or a fireman, came to the door with a plausible story, would you think twice before you unlocked the door? The list goes on and on. You'd be amazed how easy it is to dupe people. I've seen it more than I could ever have imagined before I became a cop."

"But you don't believe that in this case, do you?"

"Savannah, I do my best not to jump to conclusions, no matter what I told Grady. Does it look bad for him right now? Of course it does. Does that mean he's a murderer? I'm a long way from believing that. It will take more than an inkling or an instinct to convince me that a good friend of mine is a killer. I'm going to do my best to figure out who did it. Be sure of one thing, though. If it was Grady, I'm going to nail his hide to a wall."

"But we're hoping it's someone else."

"Of course we are," Zach said.

"Any other clues?"

"Maybe, but I haven't run across them yet. I've got to spend some serious time digging through those files."

"Is Steve any help to you at all?"

"To be honest with you, he's more like a puppy underfoot, but I don't have the heart to throw him out. When he missed out on getting my job, he kind of fell apart for a few months. If I can help him, I will."

"You recommended Davis, didn't you?"

Zach nodded as he took a sip of water. "I had a hard conversation with Steve when I left, and I didn't pull any punches. He's got the makings of being chief someday, but he's going to have to tame that temper of his. I told Grady the same thing and he made the final decision."

"You don't have to tell me about his temper. I heard him talking to his landlord, and he was really laying into him."

"Then you know what I mean. I wasn't sure what to expect when I saw him again, and I was relieved when he volunteered to help me. That's a good sign, as far as I'm concerned."

He yawned, and I matched it without realizing it.

As Zach stood, he said, "It's been a big day, hasn't it."

"It's hard to believe we were home this morning," I said.

"Has coming back to Charlotte made you sentimental for the good old days at all?"

"It was great seeing Sherry and her girls today, but I can't imagine living back here again. I love the mountains."

"Believe it or not, I do, too. We're close enough to Asheville if we need anything, but we're still far enough away so it doesn't feel like we're closed in at all. I forgot what all this car exhaust smelled like, and I don't even want to think about dealing with the traffic."

"But a little excitement now and then is okay, too, right?"

"Everything in moderation, Savannah. Let's call it a night. I'm going to get an early start tomorrow. What are your plans for the day?"

"I've got breakfast with Lorna in the restaurant, and then I'm coming back up here to create a puzzle. It's not going to be a hard one; I can tell you that. My editor isn't crazy about me sending him easy puzzles, but every now and then, I think the readers like them."

"After you're finished tomorrow, come to the station and we'll grab some lunch. You'll be done by then, won't you?"

"I certainly hope so."

As Zach headed for the bedroom, he asked, "Are you coming?"

"I think I'll stay up a little, if you don't mind."

"Of course not. Just don't stay up too long. You've got a big day tomorrow."

"Don't remind me," I said.

He kissed me, and then Zach disappeared into the other room to get some rest. I moved back to the window and stared outside again. Charlotte was at its most beautiful, and I couldn't get enough of the view. Though I loved living in the mountains and had lobbied for the move for years, it was still nice to visit the Queen City now and then. The view from this height made the city look clean and safe, like no harm could befall me there. I knew better, though. There were more murders being committed in the city than Zach was worried about, and I knew that injustices were being done with alarming frequency, but I wasn't about to let that bother me. There was a great deal more good in the city—and the world—than there was bad, and even though Zach's line of work focused on the evil people did to one another, I liked to think instead about the countless acts of unselfish goodness that went unnoticed in the paper and on the evening news.

Chapter 7

...

*E*VERYTHING WAS BEGINNING TO FALL INTO PLACE. THE *killer studied an unfinished puzzle taped to the wall, figuring where each number and letter should go. It was complicated, making up clues to match the final outcome, but a little pain was necessary. If it was easy, anyone could do it, and this was the most complex killing spree that anyone had ever seen. The former police chief was good, that's why he'd been brought in, but he was no match for the murderer's skill. Sending the picture of his wife had been a nice touch, one that would make the game a little more personal.*

That would make the ultimate victory that much sweeter.

It was time to elevate the stakes.

Let them all have a taste of who exactly it was they were dealing with.

Chapter 8

■ ■ ■

IWASN'T SURE HOW MUCH GOOD THE SLEEP ZACH MANAGED
to get did him since he tossed and turned all night, but
I got enough rest to feel somewhat renewed the next
morning. It wasn't much of a shock to see that Zach was
gone when I got up, and I found a note from him on the
mirror.

Savannah,

*I couldn't sleep, so I headed over to the station. Have
fun with Lorna, and good luck with your puzzle. See
you at lunch.*

Love you, babe,
Zach.

My husband wasn't much for traditional romance. Last Valentine's Day, he'd given me a dozen pencils tied together with a bright red ribbon. They weren't just any writing instruments; they were my favorite kind, the only type I could use to create my puzzles. Coming from him, this note was overly gushy, and I folded it carefully and put it somewhere safe. If he had any idea that I cherished every note he'd written me over the years, he would have been surprised. He wasn't all that sentimental, but that was fine. I was sappy enough for both of us.

I glanced at the clock, and I saw that I had half an hour before it was time to meet Lorna for breakfast. I could start a puzzle, but I knew if I did that, I'd never make it downstairs. In my own way, I was as bad as Zach when I was focusing on something.

"LORNA, I'M OVER HERE," I SAID AS I ROSE FROM MY SEAT. I'd taken a table by the window while I was waiting so I could watch people as they scurried about their business. It amazed me how energetic they all seemed, but I couldn't imagine any job or errand worth their harried efforts. I loved being a puzzle creator, and not just because of the intellectual challenge each puzzle presented me with. There was a great deal to be said for any job that allowed me to work in my pajamas.

"Sorry I'm late," she said as she joined me. "I got tied up in traffic. Sometimes I think you and Zach have the right idea. Maybe we should all move to the country and be done with the rat race."

"Don't kid yourself. We have problems there, too; they're just different than the ones you have here."

After we ordered, she said, "I can't imagine what rural crime must look like. Certainly it can't be as exciting as Zach's job was here."

"He's retired," I said.

"But I heard through the grapevine that he's working for the police again."

"Where did you hear that?" I asked her.

"Oh, please; you should know better than anyone that the city's not that big. I was at a party last night, and I overheard someone say that Davis was in over his head, and he had to call your husband in to help with a case."

I knew Zach wouldn't be happy that his presence in Charlotte had already been noticed, but there was no way to lock that particular barn door once the horse had escaped.

"Did you hear what case he was supposed to be working on?"

Lorna grinned. "I was hoping you could tell me."

"I can't talk about Zach's work; I'm sorry."

After they delivered our breakfasts, she asked coyly, "How about a little hint?"

I suddenly remembered that Lorna's name was on the police interview list. Would I really be breaking any family rule by discussing a case she was already involved in, no matter how far on the perimeter it might be?

"You were at the Black-Tie Ball this year, weren't you?"

"You know I never miss it," she said.

"Think about how I'd know that, Lorna."

It took her a second, and then her expression widened. "You mean Zach is investigating Hank's murder?"

"Funny, you didn't use his last name."

She waved a hand in the air. "Come on, everybody knows everyone else at those things. Sometimes it feels as though it's the same party, year after year, with different themes and locales, but all of the same players."

"You must have known Hank Tristan pretty well."

She looked curious. "What makes you say that?"

"You danced with him that night, didn't you?"

"Now you're making me nervous. Were you and Zach there that night? I didn't see you."

"No, but I glanced at the police report yesterday," I admitted.

"Whew, for a second there I thought you were psychic. Yes, I danced with Hank. What a mistake that was."

"Why, wasn't he a good dancer?" I might have sounded a little ditzy, but I was trying really hard to keep our conversation light and airy. If Lorna knew something, she might tell me if I played it right.

Lorna smiled. "No, that wasn't it. He was marvelous, as a matter of fact. Somehow, Hank managed to dance with most of the women there that night. He was a little tipsy when he got around to asking me, and I thought it might make my date jealous enough to take me a little more seriously."

"Did it work?"

She grinned at me. "As a matter of fact, it blew up in my face, just like it usually did before I straightened myself out. Peter wasn't at all pleased with me. Was I actually in the police report? How exciting."

"I don't know how thrilling it is to be the subject of a police investigation, no matter how briefly."

"That's just because you're used to crime. How are the puzzles doing?"

"We're steadily increasing the number of papers they're appearing in."

"I know," she said with a grin. "I've been subscribing to the *Hickory Post* just for your puzzles. Have you ever thought of putting them online?"

"My editor's talked about it, but he's afraid it might eat into our base," I said. "I must say, I'm flattered."

"Savannah, I love your puzzles. They have just the right amount of variation from easy to hard to keep me on my toes. I don't finish all of them, but I'm up to doing three out of four most of the time."

"I'd say that's pretty successful," I said. "You must be getting pretty good."

"They calm my spirit, if that makes any sense. When my mind's racing ten miles a minute, I pull out a puzzle and start working."

"Are you working on anything new now?"

"I'm going to go create one right after we finish here," I admitted.

"I don't suppose there's any way I could watch you do it, is there? I promise I'll be so quiet that you won't even know I'm there."

"There's nothing magical about it," I said. "I sit on the couch, and start playing with numbers. It's a lot like watching a kid do her homework, and just about as exciting."

"You underestimate how wonderful what you do is. You make something out of nothing, and that's an act of pure creation."

"I suppose. I never really thought about it. It's just what I do."

We had finished our meal, and I'd delayed making my puzzle as long as I could.

"Speaking of which, I'd better get to work."

"Thanks for making the time for me. Breakfast is my treat."

"I'd be happy to get it," I said. While I had no compunctions about taking a free room, I still had a little trouble allowing Barton Lane to pick up the tab for everything else.

"You can pay next time," she said.

At least someone was paying. Lorna signaled the waitress for our check, and when the young woman came over, she said, "Your meals today were compliments of the Belmont. I hope you both have a nice day."

Somehow I'd been expecting that, and it was no use arguing with the girl who'd served us so well. "Thank you."

Lorna looked confused. "What just happened here? Did this meal go on your room tab?"

"I suppose you could say that," I said. "Don't worry, it's all settled."

"I honestly would be glad to pay."

How on earth was I going to explain to her that the owner himself was handling it? There was no way I could do it without mentioning Barton's name, something I knew he wouldn't have liked. "You can get it next time," I said. "But perhaps we should go somewhere else tomorrow."

"Why? Breakfast today was lovely."

"Let's just say that it might be nice to get out of the Belmont once in a while."

Lorna looked around the beautifully furnished restaurant. "I don't see how that's possible."

"Trust me," I said, allowing a slight laugh to escape my lips.

"So, I'll see you tomorrow."

I hadn't really agreed on meeting with her the next day, but she was fun company, and I heartily approved of the changes she'd made in her life, and her attitude about the world. "Tomorrow it is. Now, if you'll excuse me, I've got work to do."

"Make it a good one," she said.

I left her, nodding my thanks again to our waitress as I left. She smiled brightly, but there was also an air of curiosity to her expression. I couldn't imagine why she thought the hotel owner was picking up every check in sight for me, but I couldn't exactly tell her, either. For now, I was just going to have to remain a mystery for the staff. I liked thinking of myself that way, Savannah Stone, woman of intrigue.

I couldn't stall anymore, though.

It was time to create a puzzle, and do it in time to have lunch with my husband at the police station.

A FTER I FINISHED THE LATEST BRAINTEASER, IT WAS TIME to write my snippet; a nice little addition to whatever puzzle I'd chosen to create.

Life is full of puzzles, some hard, some easy. Every now and then it's good to revisit the basics, and that's what I've done today. For those of you with Master puzzle-solving skills, remember your joy of solving your first puzzle, and take a moment to relish that sense of accomplishment. For those of you who have

been waiting on the side of the puzzle pool, barely dan-
gling your toes in the water, now's the time to jump in
and try one yourself.

That might mollify my die-hard fans, and still be
enough of a nudge to get others to try a puzzle themselves.
Either way, I was finished for the day, and I could see
what Zach was up to, as soon as I faxed this to my editor.
If I had time, I'd work on a harder one for tomorrow, but
right now, all I cared about was seeing what my husband
had come up with while I'd been playing with numbers.

"**S**TEVE, HAVE YOU SEEN MY HUSBAND?"
The officer looked up at me as I walked into the
hallway in front of the task force headquarters at the police station.

"He's meeting with Davis," he said. "The chief said to
tell you if you showed up, to wait for him."

"It must be odd having Zach back here. He was your
boss a long time, and now you're answering to someone
else."

"Davis is doing the best he can, but he can't hold a
match to your husband." He realized how that must have
sounded, because he quickly amended, "Not that I don't
respect my new boss, too."

"Zach said you were up for the job yourself."

He shrugged. "Sure, I took a stab at it, but I knew it
was a long shot. I'm ten years younger than Davis, and
he's got more seniority on the force than me, too. My time
will come."

"That's the spirit," I said.

Steve's face brightened as he asked, "Did you finish your puzzle?"

"How did you know I was doing one?"

"The chief mentioned it before he had his meeting. I'm a big fan, you know."

"Of my husband? Of course, I understand that. I'm a big fan of his, too."

"No, I mean of you. I do your puzzles every chance I get. Those puzzles are great. I've tried a few others, but I like yours the best."

"Thanks. That's always nice to hear."

"What is?" my husband said as he walked into the hall.

"He was just complimenting me," I said.

"Was he, now? What was the topic?"

"It wasn't anything like that, Chief," Steve said quickly. "I told her how much I liked her puzzles."

Zach frowned for another second, and then laughed. "Relax, I'm just pulling your leg. Savannah's a real wizard with numbers, isn't she?"

"Just like you are with clues," Steve said.

"Not that you could tell that so far." Zach looked at me a second, then added, "Would you mind if we had lunch here again? I'm not fit to be around people today."

"Hey, as long as I don't have to get it, that's fine with me."

"Steve, would you mind?"

"You've got it, Chief. Do you need to see any menus from around here?"

"I haven't been gone that long," my husband said with a smile. "I'll have a cheesesteak from Greg's."

"Make that two," I said, remembering the way the

cheese melted into the sandwich, and the way the peppers and onions had a smoky, grilled flavor.

"You can get something else, if you want."

"I know, but why would anyone want anything else?"

He shrugged. "Beats me. Do you mind, Steve?"

"No, I'm on it. Be back in a flash."

After he was gone, as Zach unlocked the door, I asked, "Is it that bad?"

"What? Steve's doing just fine."

"I'm not talking about that, and you know it." I looked around the room, and noticed that since I'd been there yesterday, a large whiteboard leaned against one wall. It was already filled with my husband's notes, and I knew it was a way he liked to think out loud. "I meant the case."

"It's no surprise Davis called me in," Zach said. "I just had a meeting with him, and it's pretty clear that Grady's breathing down his neck. He wants results, and I'm not sure how fast I can give them to him."

"Why the sudden urgency? We just got here yesterday."

"This is all new to us, but they've been dealing with it for eight days. I don't blame them. I just wish I had something for them."

"Don't worry, you'll solve this."

"Savannah, I wish I had your faith in me," he said.

"You always were your worst critic." Zach looked glum, and I had to do something to snap him out of it if I could.

"It's a beautiful day. Why don't we go outside and wait for Steve? When he brings us our sandwiches, we'll have a picnic across the street."

"I don't know," he said as he looked around the room. "There's a lot of work I still need to do."

"You can't do it if you're focused on how much there is to accomplish. Trust me, you need a break."

He shrugged. "I guess it wouldn't hurt to get out of here for a little while. Let's go."

As we left the room, he pulled out a key and locked the door. "What's wrong, don't you trust your officers?"

"That's the problem, I know them too well. I don't want anyone snooping around and walking through my evidence."

Steve was startled to find us out in front of the station waiting on him. "What's wrong? Did I take too long?"

"No, we decided to eat outside today."

He shrugged, then he handed Zach our lunches. "I'll wait upstairs. There's more work I can do while you're eating."

"Why don't you take off, and I'll catch up with you later."

"You got it, Chief," he said.

Zach and I walked across the street and found a weathered old wooden bench. It wasn't exactly a park, but there was grass and some trees around us, and it felt like we were getting away from it all.

Zach immediately dove into the bag and pulled out a sandwich. To his credit, he handed the first one to me before he retrieved the other one for himself. As we ate, we enjoyed the day and tried not to talk about murder. After we finished, Zach collected our trash, but he made no move to leave.

"This sunshine feels great, doesn't it?"

"I bet it's not as humid at home," I said.

Zach laughed. "You don't have to sell me on it, Savannah. I wouldn't mind being back there myself right now."

"I thought you were looking for a little excitement in your life."

"I would at least like to have a chance to solve this," he said. "The problem with investigating these murders is that I have to push some powerful people to get answers, and I still can't be sure they're telling me the truth. Hank and Cindy deserve better than that."

It wasn't odd to hear my husband talk about the victims as though he knew them personally. He'd been trained by a woman who was an expert in the criminal thought process, and she'd stressed the need for the detective to distance himself from the victims, but it went against Zach's nature. By personalizing the victims, he worked that much harder to find their killers.

I just hoped he could do it before the murderer struck again.

Chapter 9

. . .

WHEN WE WALKED BACK INTO THE POLICE STATION, Davis was waiting for us by the front door.

"What's going on, Chief?" my husband asked. "You're not going to bust my chops about taking a lunch break with my wife, are you?"

Davis frowned. "Zach, while you were gone, we got another note from the killer."

"It wasn't about me, was it?" I asked, suddenly getting the insane impulse that I was the killer's next victim, even though I had no real ties to the case. I didn't know either victim, though we had a mutual friend in Grady. The photo the killer had sent of me in Grady's truck had shaken me more than I'd realized.

Davis said, "Of course not. Why, did something happen today?"

"No, I had breakfast with Lorna Gaither, and then I created a puzzle and faxed it to my editor from the hotel. I haven't even had time to get into trouble yet."

"Let's see the note," Zach said.

"It's in my office."

We walked back to Davis's office, where Zach had spent so much time over the years. It had been completely redecorated since his time there, and while my husband had enjoyed dark woodwork and muted colors, Davis had redone the place into a bright and airy space with modern furniture, something I never would have pegged him for liking. Though mostly neat, I saw an open newspaper on one corner of his desk. As I glanced at it, I saw that there was a puzzle open, though not one of my own. It was partially completed, and I had to smile when I realized that he'd been working in pen.

"What do you think?" Davis asked as he watched Zach's expression as he took the changes in.

"It looks good," Zach said. "It suits you."

I looked at my husband to see if he was teasing, but his expression was serious.

"Thanks." It was clear that Davis had been holding his breath a little, and he released it with my husband's approval.

"Here's a copy," Davis said as he handed a sheet of paper to Zach.

"Could I see the original?" my husband asked. "I can't get a solid feel for copies."

I thought about the photocopied sheets upstairs, and wondered about that statement. Zach must have seen something on my face, though I could have sworn I'd hidden my puzzlement.

"I like copies for display so I can get a handle on how things fit into the puzzle, but when it comes to getting a feel for something, I have to hold it in my hand."

"That makes sense to me," Davis said as he handed a clear plastic envelope to my husband, who took it as if it were loaded with poison. "There's something else you need to know before you read it."

"What's that?" Zach asked, clearly distracted by wondering about the contents of the letter.

"Usually they come here without any routing, but this time it was addressed directly to you."

Zach frowned as he took the letter, but I felt a chill run through me. It was one thing having my husband investigate the murders from the safety of that room upstairs in police headquarters, but when I realized that the killer was aware of what Zach was doing, it made my heart freeze.

"This isn't happening," I said.

Zach read it, then handed it to me.

"Should I?"

"He mentions you, too," my husband said.

I took the letter and read.

Finally, a worthy adversary. I thought it was going to take another execution before they were smart enough to call you. You and your wife make such a nice looking couple. It would be a shame to break up the set. But I'm getting ahead of myself. By all means, do your best to catch me. I will strike again, and there's nothing you can do to stop me. I'm as safe as if I were in Parson's Valley. That's probably where you should have stayed, but I'm looking forward to seeing if you can puzzle out my next move before it's too late.

"He's clearly nuts," Davis said. "Why would he taunt you? What does it possibly gain him?"

I turned the letter over and saw "4O" written in delicate script on the back. "We've got another clue here," I said.

Zach took it from me, studied it, and then said, "Evidently I'm not as smart as he thinks I am. I have no idea what it means. Does anyone else? Does forty mean anything to anyone?"

"It's part of a puzzle," I said without thinking.

"This isn't one of your creations," Zach said. "Real killers don't send clues through the puzzle page."

"I didn't say it was," I replied. "But it's clear that this guy is intelligent."

"Not from the way he committed the murders," Davis said. "He stabbed both victims in their homes. That doesn't exactly take a rocket scientist."

"Did you find any clues at either of the murder scenes? Did anyone see the victims with the killer? Has he made one single mistake you can point to?"

"No," Davis reluctantly admitted. "He's been lucky so far."

"That, or very good."

Zach asked, "So, what's your point?"

I wanted to see something before I pushed my theory any harder. "Let's go upstairs, and I'll tell you."

Davis started to follow us, but he got a call on his phone. "I've got to take this."

"We'll see you up there," Zach said.

"Don't wait for me. This might take awhile."

After we left his office, Zach said, "This better be good."

"Trust me, okay?"

Steve was waiting outside the task force room, and I saw he was using his time to work one of my puzzles. He saw that I'd caught him. "Don't you ever do any easy puzzles anymore? It might be nice to have a no-brainer once in a while."

"As a matter of fact, I made a simple one this morning."

"When's it going to show up?"

"I'm guessing sometime next week."

He looked puzzled. "You don't know when your puzzles are going to run in the papers?"

"The exact date? No, not usually. If I do a themed puzzle summary, they'll usually run it when I ask them to, but I have to have those in a month early."

"If you two are finished discussing number puzzles, I've got work to do," Zach said as he unlocked the door.

"You know, it would make it a lot simpler if you gave me a key, too," Steve said as we all walked inside.

"Not even Davis has a key to this room," Zach said. "As long as I've got evidence stored in here, I'm going to keep it that way. No offense, Steve."

"None taken. I don't mind hanging around waiting for you to get back." He grinned and slapped his newspaper against his leg. "I'm on the clock either way, Chief."

"Don't you think it's time you started calling me Zach? I haven't been the chief for a while."

"I'm not sure it's a habit I can break," Steve said with a smile. "Or even want to."

"Do you have a problem with Davis?" Zach asked softly, and I knew Steve was treading on dangerous ground.

"No, sir. He's my boss. I'm behind him a thousand percent. Grady made his choice and I can live with it."

Zach was clearly tired of that particular conversation; I could see it in his eyes.

Zach took the original of the note we'd just gotten and stored it in a locked box where he kept all of the other letters the police had received from the killer. Once that was safely put away, he pinned the front copy on the foam board with the rest of the copied notes, and then placed the back copy on the other side of the room. I didn't know why he'd separated them so entirely, and then suddenly, I realized he was giving me my own space to work out my theory.

"It seems that there has to be a code here somewhere, don't you think?" I asked.

"What makes you say that?"

I smiled at him. "If I told you it was woman's intuition, you wouldn't believe me."

"You're right, I wouldn't."

I walked over to the back copies.

"If we only knew for certain what they meant," I said as I studied them. I was sure the numbers on the backs of the photos and letters were related to some kind of puzzle, a format the killer was using to map out the murders in his mind. But beyond that, I had no idea how it all came together.

"What do you want me to do, Ch—, I mean, Zach?"

Zach smiled at Steve. "I know it's going to be tough, but you can do it." He pointed to a pile of boxes in one corner of the room. "Those are notes from the two crime scenes. I need you to make a list of everything they have in common for me." As Steve moved toward the boxes, Zach added, "Don't include just what you see. Try to dig a little deeper and tell me what's not there."

"It sounds like I'm looking for a white dog in a snow-storm," Steve said.

"Something like that. Are you up to it?"

"You bet," he said as he moved away from us.

"How about you?" Zach asked. "Do you mind spending some of your time here to work on that theory of yours?"

"You can have all I've got."

Zach nodded, and then to my surprise, he kissed me briefly on the lips. It was about as public as he ever got with his displays of affection. "You're my kind of gal, you know that, don't you?"

"That's handy, since you're my kind of guy."

He winked at me, and then Zach walked over to the locked box and opened it again. When he was examining direct physical evidence, it was like he was channeling someone else, he got so lost in his thoughts. I had no idea what was going through his mind, but I'd seen that look in his eyes enough to know that I could set off a firecracker under his nose and he wouldn't even notice it.

I looked back at the board full of copied clues, and studied the mishmash of letters and numbers. I was about to ask Zach for their order of appearance when I thought to turn the copies over. As I'd hoped, these were two-sided copies, with the crime scenes depicted on one side and the letters the killer had written matched to their codes on the other. That still didn't tell me what I wanted to know, though.

"What order did these come in?" I asked, forgetting for a second that Zach could be on the moon for all the chance I had to get an answer from him.

Steve looked around, and then he said, "If you're talk-ing to me, there's a log over on that table."

I walked over to the spot he'd pointed to, and after digging through some of the paperwork, I found a master list of the mailings. Taking it back with me, I glanced at the board and saw that my husband had pinned them up randomly. I arranged the four entries in the order they were received until I had a good idea of how the mailings should be organized. Taking out my cell phone, I snapped a quick picture so I'd have a reference to carry with me, and then I turned the codes over and snapped a photo of the fronts. The two crime scene images were disturbing, but if I was going to help with the case, I had to steel myself for what I might see. Once I had the front pages in my phone, I turned the copies back over, and started recording the number sequences on a notepad. There were four sequences so far, two matching crime scene photos and two notes, including the latest entry.

3A, 5A, 2E, 4A, 1E, 4O.

I stared at it for what felt like an hour, hoping for some kind of breakthrough.

Nothing. If the forty meant anything, I'd have to figure it out later. For now, I had to focus on just the letter-number combinations.

Did the repeating pattern mean anything? A A E A E. Did that mean the next letter would be an E? Would it match the pattern? Even if it did, I still didn't know what that might mean.

Okay, forget about the letters. How about the numbers? 3, 5, 2, 4, 1.

3, 5, 2, 4, represented a pattern, especially if the next entry was a 3. It was something to consider, but I couldn't do anything with it yet. They added up to 15, and when they were added together, it made 6. Again, so what? 3

times 5 divided by 2 multiplied by 4 divided by 1 totaled 30, which added up to 3. Even though it was true, what could it mean?

I didn't see any significance to any of the sequences I'd come up with so far. What else could they represent? How about if I took the letters and numbers and charted them on an x-y axis? Would that yield me anything? I took out a pad of paper from my purse and drew a rough graph, with numbers going vertically and letters horizontally.

```
5    *
4    *
3    *
2          *
1          *
     A B C D E F G H I J K L M N O P Q R S T U V W X Y Z
```

There was a pattern there only if the next note was 6A or 6E. That would create a stair-step segment, but so what? So far, I had a 1E, 2E, 3A, 4A, and 5A. Why had 5E been skipped? Was there a missing note, one that the police misfiled or accidentally threw away before anyone realized the significance of it?

I had another thought, and redrew my grid, this time substituting numbers in the order of the notes received where the stars now stood.

```
5    2
4    4
3    1
2          3
1          5
     A B C D E F G H I J K L M N O P Q R S T U V W X Y Z
```

No, that didn't make any sense, either. Had something been missed, perhaps a vital clue to the whole thing?

I finally gave up. If there was a pattern of any significance there, I couldn't see it. Most likely I didn't have enough information to solve the puzzle yet. Given time, and enough entries, I should have more of a chance to see what the killer was trying to tell us. Or was there any hidden message there at all? Was it a prank, a ruse to make the police work harder than they should on nothing more than a nonsensical set of letters and numbers that in reality meant nothing? No, I couldn't believe that. Each entry had been painstakingly drawn, as if the murderer was proud of what the segments represented.

There was a message there.

I just hadn't figured it out yet.

I looked up from my pad to find my husband staring at me, a broad smile on his face.

"What's so funny?" Steve was far enough away and so focused on his work that he probably couldn't hear us, but I kept my voice low just in case. I knew how it was to be interrupted in the middle of a thought, and I didn't want to do anything to disturb the investigation.

Zach matched my soft tone. "You look so intense when you're working. It's just like you're creating a puzzle."

"I wish that's what it was. There's a logic to my puzzles, but this is all just a jumble."

"Well, you gave it your best shot," he said. "Thanks for trying."

"Are you kidding? I'm not giving up that easily. I've got a couple of ideas, but I need more information."

"We may not get it," Zach said. "Do you have anything so far?"

I looked at my sheets, and kept coming back to 5E. "I think there's a chance that the police missed a note."

"What do you mean?" The smile was suddenly gone from my husband's face.

I showed him what I'd done, and he caught the missing 5E faster than I had, but to my credit, I'd laid it out for him. "There should be a 5E, but how do we know that's not what the next note will have on it?"

"If that's true, we'll just have to wait until another one arrives. But what would it hurt to go through the stack of letters no one's had a chance to really dig into yet? Couldn't there be something there that was missed the first time around?"

Zach frowned, and then he called Steve over to us. It took him two tries to get the man's attention, and I smiled when I realized I'd been right about his sharp focus. "I need you to go down to records and search through everything we've gotten since the first murder. Then again, go back a week before that, in case there's something there."

"Absolutely. What exactly is it that I'm looking for?"

Zach pointed to the wall. "Hunt for anything that looks like it came from the killer. Study these for a few minutes before you go."

"I don't have to," he said. "I've already stared at them for hours."

After Steve was gone, I said, "It's a long shot, and he's probably not going to be able to come up with anything."

"It doesn't cost a thing to have him check," Zach said. "That was a good spot, Savannah."

"It could be nothing."

"Or it could mean everything. I'd hate to tell you how much of my time I've burned over the years looking for clues that weren't there. This is part of the procedure. You keep digging into things, no matter how unrelated or impossible they might seem at times, and every now and then you hit pay dirt."

"I don't know how you do it," I said.

Zach laughed. "Do you think I could make a puzzle?"

"Don't sell yourself short."

"Only if you promise not to do the same thing yourself. There's real skill in what you do. You've got a mind that works in ways mine never could."

I stifled a yawn. "I'm beat."

"It's just past five," Zach said.

"The level of my exhaustion has nothing to do with the hands of a clock. I made up a puzzle this morning, and I've been working on this all afternoon. My brain's fried."

"Why don't you go back to the hotel? I'll be along later."

"You could always come with me," I suggested.

"Sorry, but I quit early yesterday. If I do it again, Davis is going to think I've gone soft on him. Go ahead. Take a long shower, order up some room service, and I'll call you a little later."

"I know I should argue with you, but I'm too tired. Don't forget to call."

I grabbed my things, and I was just about to leave when the door burst open. Steve looked excited as he showed us an envelope in his hand.

It appeared that I'd been right about something, at least.

We suddenly had another clue.

* * *

ZACH CAREFULLY REMOVED THE NOTE FROM ITS ENVE-lope, slid it into a clear plastic sleeve, copied both sides, and then handed the duplicates to me.

The note simply said, *"The game's afoot. Try to catch me. I dare you."*

And that was all that was written on the front.

As I was turning to the copy of the back, Steve asked Zach, "How did you know it would be there?"

"Don't give me any credit. It was all Savannah's idea."

Steve nodded. "That's good police work."

"It just made sense that something was missing," I explained.

"Trust me, it's a lot harder to see what's not there than what is."

I shrugged as I studied the copy in my hands.

There was no number or letter sequence there, and aside from a smudge or two, the paper was blank.

"It's not from him."

Zach looked surprised. "What are you talking about? It matches his handwriting perfectly."

"But there's no sequence on the back."

Zach looked at my copy, and then retrieved the original. After a moment of silence, he said, "It's there, but the copier missed it. The paper must have buckled."

I took the offered plastic sleeve from him and flipped it over. I didn't know if it was my imagination, but I could swear I felt an electric shock when I touched it. I had to look hard, but I finally found the missing entry, so softly written that it had been easy for the copier to miss.

I walked to the machine, set the darkness to its fullest setting, and then made another copy of the original.

Faint, but clearly there, I saw a letter and number sequence on the paper as if I'd willed it to be there.

5E.

It was our missing letter.

But I still didn't know what it meant.

Chapter 10

■ ■ ■

"SAVANNAH, YOU'RE A HARD WOMAN TO TRACK DOWN."
I'd gone back to my hotel, enjoyed a long and hot shower under those lustrous jets of water, and I was waiting on my room service order to arrive when my phone rang.

"Uncle Thomas, how are you?" My uncle, my mother's little brother, was all the family I had left besides my husband and his clan. He lived in Hickory, about an hour and a half drive from Charlotte, and oddly enough, about the same distance from Parson's Valley, the central point of two ends of a line.

"I'm better, now that I know you're safe. Don't you ever check the messages on that answering machine of yours?"

"We haven't been home the past couple of days. What's up?"

"I was wondering if you might be coming this way anytime soon. There's something I need to discuss with you."

I didn't admit that we'd passed the Hickory exits off I-40 just the day before, and though I'd thought of him briefly as we'd driven past, there had been no time to stop.

"Is something wrong?"

"It's nothing, really. It can wait until we see each other again."

I knew my uncle wouldn't have kept calling unless it was important. He avoided every bit of modern technology he could, and for him to call me on my cell phone number, I realized that it was likely more important than he was letting on. "Come on, don't try to kid a kidder. What's happening?"

"I went to the doctor the other day," he said, and a wave of dread raced through me. I couldn't bear losing my uncle. He was the last real tie I had to my family, at least as far as I knew. My mother's only other brother, Jeffrey, had left North Carolina the day he'd turned eighteen, and no one had heard from him since. There had been rumors that he'd gotten rich, but just as many that he was in prison serving a life sentence. As far as I was concerned, Uncle Thomas was all I had left.

"It's nothing, but I realized that I'm starting to get older, and there are a few things that need to be settled now."

"Is it serious?"

"I just told you, it's nothing. But every now and then,

a man has to take stock of his life, and there are a few things I need to get off my chest." He sighed deeply, and then added, "I'm probably just being a silly old fool. Forget I said anything."

"Honestly, I was thinking about driving over to see you sometime soon. We're in Charlotte right now."

"You didn't move back there, did you? I love your place in Parson's Valley. It suits you, Savannah."

"Don't worry, we're just visiting. Actually, Zach's working on a case."

"He's still freelancing, is he? They just can't seem to let him go."

"What can I say, my husband's good at what he does." I glanced at the clock. It was just after seven, and though the shower had helped some, I was still tired from my mental exercises all day, but I couldn't let that stop me. "Let me get dressed, and I can be there in an hour and a half."

"Hang on, I didn't mean you had to come tonight."

"I don't mind. Honestly. You're not going to bed anytime soon, are you?"

He chuckled. "I don't sleep much more than six or seven hours a night. I put it off as long as I can, usually."

"Then I'm coming right now," I said.

"Take it easy. There's no hurry."

"It will be fun," I said when there was a knock on the door. I'd forgotten all about my dinner. "Hang on one second."

I opened the door without quizzing the hotel employee as Zach had done, and I was certain he would have disapproved, but I found it awkward to do. The same man who'd delivered food to us the night before smiled briefly as I let him in, and after he was gone, I returned to the phone. "Sorry about that."

"Is Zach there? Do you need to go?"

"No, it was just room service," I admitted.

"Then eat your dinner, and get some rest. It would be foolish to drive up here at night."

"It's summer; the sun won't go down until after I get there."

"But then you'd have to drive back in the dark, wouldn't you?"

I laughed. "Okay, you got me. But I'm coming up first thing in the morning. I'll leave early enough so we can have breakfast together."

Uncle Thomas laughed. "Then you'd better head out by four thirty, because I always eat at six."

That was too early for my tastes, by at least an hour. "Why don't we make it lunch, then?"

"I eat at eleven," he said. "But I can push it back an hour for you."

"Don't be silly, eleven sounds fine. I'll try to get there earlier so we can hang out a little. And Uncle Thomas?"

"Yes, Savannah?"

"Are you sure nothing's wrong?"

"Not a thing that can't be fixed. I'll see you tomorrow, child."

"Bye."

As I ate my dinner—a chicken taco salad this time—I wondered what had brought on the need for Uncle Thomas to see me. He was normally a loner, quite content to be left alone, even by those of us who loved him. For him to make a concerted effort to see me had me more than a little worried. I knew there was no use fretting over it tonight, so I tried to get my mind off it. I briefly considered getting back to the puzzle of the number and letter sequences that I was working on for Zach, but the futility of that was too depressing. If I weren't so tired after I finished eating, I could jump on tomorrow's submission, but puzzles were the last thing on my mind at the moment.

Zach came in half an hour after I'd finished my meal.

"You look wiped out," I said.

"I'm not used to this grind," he admitted. "Sometimes I forget just how hard I used to work."

As he rubbed his chest, I asked, "Is your scar hurting?"

"Truthfully, I think it's all in my head."

I hugged him. "Zach, I saw you on that hospital bed with bandages on your chest and tubes coming out of you. It wasn't your imagination."

"You know what I mean." He looked over at the cart I'd been too tired to shove out the door. "What did you eat?"

"Chicken taco salad," I answered. "Would you like me to order you something for dinner?"

"I'm too beat to care about eating right now. I think I'll just grab a shower and go to bed."

"I'm going to see Uncle Thomas tomorrow," I blurted out.

"I know I'm not paying enough attention to you, but you don't have to take off on me."

"He's been trying to call me for two days. He wants to see me, and for him, it sounds urgent."

"Is there anything wrong?" Zach and Uncle Thomas

got along incredibly well, and there were times when the three of us were together that *I* felt like the third wheel.

"He went to the doctor, but he swears there's nothing wrong with him."

"Then why the sudden urge for company? Should we go right now? I'm game if you are."

I kissed him, and then I said, "Thanks for offering, but we're both exhausted. I'm going to see him at lunch tomorrow, if you can spare me."

Zach frowned, and then he said, "I could probably get away, too."

"That's crazy, and we both know it. I don't need to stay here, but you do. You've got a case you have to work on."

"Family comes first," Zach said resolutely.

"I love you for saying it, but we both know what our priorities are. I won't be gone long. You won't even have a chance to miss me."

"There you're wrong," he said as he hugged me tightly. "Now, if you're sure you don't want to go tonight, I'm going to hit the shower."

"Go," I said.

After I heard the water running, I ordered him a dinner of stir-fried beef tips, despite his earlier protest that he was too tired to eat. Once Zach smelled the food, I knew he wouldn't be able to resist it any more than I could say no to a chocolate cupcake.

When the food arrived, he was still in the shower, and I was about to go get him when he came out wearing a robe.

"What smells so good?"

"Room service," I answered.

"Savannah, I told you that I wasn't hungry."

"Then don't eat it. I might peck at it a little myself, if you're sure you aren't going to have any." I was full from my salad, so at least for the moment, I was bluffing.

Zach walked over and lifted off the lid. "Stir fry. That looks great. Maybe I'll have a bite or two after all."

He took the plate, along with a bottled water on ice, and moved to the window. "Care to join me?"

"Sure thing," I said as I took a seat.

As Zach ate, he nodded a few times, but conversation was kept at a minimum. When he finished, I saw him looking longingly back at the cart. "Wasn't there enough for you?" I asked.

"I was just thinking some dessert might be nice."

I laughed. "I thought you were too tired to eat."

"What can I say; I just got my second wind."

"If you're serious, we could always order something else."

He clearly thought about it for a few seconds, then said, "No, I'd better not. You can if you want to, though."

"Maybe later. Were you able to make any more progress after I left?"

"Nothing worth talking about. I need to let things percolate a little right now."

"In other words, you don't want to discuss it."

"If you don't mind," Zach said a little apologetically. "You know how I get."

"Better than anyone else in the world. We could watch a movie, or some television, if you'd like."

"To be honest with you, I'd rather just sit here and watch night fall on Charlotte. We're never going to get a view like this again, and I want to memorize it as much as I can."

"I think that sounds perfect."

As we sat there in relative silence, I marveled at how lucky I'd been to find someone who matched me so well. There were no awkward silences between us, or words spoken just to fill the emptiness. Zach and I were in sync enough to let those quiet times envelop us, and to enjoy the lack of chatter like the gift that it was. When we went to sleep later that night, I felt as though my center was calm again, just as it had been in Parson's Valley. It was my new home, and I loved it, but wherever Zach was, that was truly where I belonged, and everything else was just a matter of geography.

W HEN I WOKE UP THE NEXT MORNING, THE BED WAS empty. I started searching for a note or something from my husband when I realized that I'd forgotten all about my scheduled breakfast with Lorna. It was too early to call her, so I'd have to phone her from the road. I'd been looking forward to seeing her again, but if I waited to leave until after we had breakfast and chatted a little, it would cost me too much time. I was sure she'd understand, and if she was free, I'd have to try to reschedule for the next day.

I found Zach in the shower when I walked into the bathroom.

"I thought you'd already be gone," I said.

"Hey, it's only seven."

"I know, but you get obsessed when you're working, and don't try to deny it."

"I went for a run," Zach admitted. "You know how sometimes it helps clear my head."

As the shower stopped and I handed him a towel, I asked, "Did you have nightmares again?" When my husband was wrapped up in a case, he often had bad dreams from trying to put himself into a killer's mind. It was no wonder he reacted that way, though he didn't want anyone else to know that he wasn't always the calm, levelheaded guy he presented to the world.

"Yeah, they were pretty tough." He frowned for a second, then said, "You've got a big day today. Breakfast with Lorna, and then a drive to Hickory."

"I'm canceling breakfast," I said as I took over the shower. "From the sound of Uncle Thomas's voice, I'm not delaying my visit by an hour."

"Are you afraid he's not telling you everything?"

"He's a man," I said. "Most of you seem to be reticent by nature when it comes to talking about your health. I'm amazed he even went to the doctor in the first place. That alone tells me it must be serious."

"We think we're bulletproof most of the time," Zach admitted. "When we're not, we try to deny it until we can't."

"I don't get you," I said.

There was no response.

"Zach? Did you hear me?"

From the bedroom, I heard him ask, "Were you talking to me?"

"No, but you could tell me when you leave the room."

He chuckled. "Sure I could, but what fun would that be?"

I stepped out of the shower, and my husband handed me a towel in turn. "I could get used to this."

"What, fresh towel service every morning?"

"Sure, that, too, but I mean you handing me a towel every day when I get out of the shower."

"I'll see what I can do," he said. In the short time I'd been in the shower, my husband had dressed, combed his hair, and was ready for work. He gave me a quick kiss, and then said, "Say hello to Tom for me."

"I will. Zach, while I'm gone, you be careful, do you hear me?"

"Savannah, what trouble will I be able to get into when I'm locked up in that command center? I'm safer than the mayor up there."

"Speaking of Grady, are you going to talk to him again today?"

"Why, because our last chat went so well? No, I'm probably not going to brace him again until I have something a little more substantial to say."

As I dried my hair, I asked, "Do you think you'll find something on him?"

"You can bet that if it's there, I'll find it," he said.

"I know you will. Not that I'm not flattered, but shouldn't you be going to work now?"

"Are you trying to get rid of me?"

"No way. I just don't want to keep you from your investigation."

"It will wait a little bit."

There was a knock at the door, and I asked my husband, "Were you expecting someone?"

"I called room service while you were in the shower,"

he said with a grin. "I thought we could have a quick bite together before you go. What do you think?"

"I think that's a great idea. Give me a second and I'll join you."

I got dressed quickly, and then met Zach out in the living room of the suite. Dining in front of that spectacular view was quickly becoming a habit for me, and I knew I'd miss it once we were back in Parson's Valley.

"Wow, this is really nice."

"Hey, nothing but the best for my wife," Zach said.

"Especially when we're not footing the bill. I hate to admit it, but I feel a little guilty about all of this."

As we started to eat, Zach shrugged. "I never could have accepted any of this if I was still on the force, but as a consultant, I don't have any problem with it."

That surprised me. "You honestly don't mind?"

"Savannah, this man lost someone he cared about. It's helping him knowing that he's making my life easier so I can focus on finding the killer. If it's a good thing for him, and it doesn't cost me anything, why shouldn't I accept his generous offer?"

"It sounds good to me. Do you have any new leads for today?"

"I've got a couple of angles I want to check out," he said.

"Go on, I'm listening."

"You know I can't talk about my thought process," he said.

"I was just wondering if that changed, too."

"Not a chance."

I smiled at him. "Just checking."

He took a bite of toast, and then said, "Davis wants a

progress report first thing this morning, but I don't know what I'm going to tell him. Maybe I need to pop in on Grady after all and see if I can catch him off guard. I don't know; I'm not sure what I'm going to do just yet."

I pushed my plate away, too full to finish the omelet my husband had ordered for me. "That was great. Are you ready to go?"

"Are you rushing me?"

"No, stay as long as you like, but I need to get on the road."

He pushed away from his plate. "Hang on a second, I'm almost ready."

As we left the suite and rode down in the elevator, I said, "I still can't believe we're here."

"In the Belmont?"

"Sure, but mostly just being back in Charlotte. I wasn't sure that it was that great of an idea coming back, but as much as I'm enjoying it, I can't wait to get home."

"I know just what you mean."

When we got to the lobby, there was a uniformed officer standing beside a large plant. He was trying his best to look inconspicuous in his uniform, but he was failing epically.

"Where's Steve?" I asked Zach. "I thought he was your ride."

"He's taking a personal day," my husband explained.

"I could always drop you off at the station on my way out of town."

"It's out of your way, and you know it. This will be fine." He gave me a quick peck, and then added, "Have a safe drive, and don't forget to call me when you get there."

"Okay. I'll see you tonight."

After my husband was gone, I headed for the parking

garage and collected our car. I glanced at the clock on the dashboard when I got in and saw that if I didn't hit too much traffic, I should be at Uncle Thomas's a little after nine. I was excited to see him, but I also had a sense of dread about what he was about to tell me.

There was only one way to find out, though.

Chapter 11

...

AS SOON AS I GOT A LITTLE WAYS UP I-77 AND OUT OF THE main part of town, I dialed Lorna's number.

"Hey, there. You just caught me. I was getting ready to leave the house," she said.

"I'm glad I called, then. Something's come up, so I'm going to have to cancel on you this morning."

"Really? I could make it later, if that would be more convenient for you." The disappointment was clear in her voice. "I've really missed chatting with you, Savannah."

"I've missed you, too," I said, "but I'm on my way to Hickory, and I'm not sure when I'm going to be back."

"What on earth are you going to do up there?"

"I'm visiting family," I said.

"I know what that's like," she said. "Could we do it tomorrow?"

"I don't see why not, if nothing else comes up."

"Wow, I feel so special," she said with a laugh.

"I didn't mean anything by that. It's just that with Zach's job, I'm not sure what's going to happen the next hour, let alone the next day."

"That's fine. I was just teasing. Tell you what. Let's plan on tomorrow, but if something comes up, just give me a call."

"Will do," I said, and hung up. I'd always liked Lorna, but the changes in her had made her even nicer to be around.

As I drove toward Hickory, I found myself enjoying the scenery. The interstate going to Statesville cut through a corner of Lake Norman, and I saw a cluster of sailboats docked by a complex situated right on the water, and a few Jet Skis were already out enjoying the day. It must be nice to be able to spend time on the lake every day, though Zach and I could never have afforded property anywhere near the water. When I glanced through my rearview mirror back toward the lake, I saw a black car with heavily tinted windows two vehicles behind mine, but I didn't think much of it.

At Statesville, I switched from I-77 North and took I-40 West. It was the same direction I would have driven if I was going home, but I wasn't making that trip, at least not today.

Out of habit from Zach's many lectures on personal safety, I looked back, and sure enough, the black car was still there. I tried to tell myself that it was a coincidence. After all, anyone leaving Charlotte when I had who

headed to Hickory a little above the speed limit would
be close to me all the way there. But it still left me a little uneasy. I thought about speeding up a little to see if
they'd still follow me, but Zach wouldn't be happy if I
got a speeding ticket. I decided to ignore it and go on my
way.

Half an hour later, I took the exit for Uncle Thomas's
house, and ten minutes after that, I was at his place. The
black car had taken my exit, and I'd felt my stomach
tighten, but whoever it was had pulled into a convenience
store to get gas, and I had laughed a little self-consciously
at myself.

Uncle Thomas was half a mile from Lake Hickory, really just a wide stretch of the Catawba River. While I'd
never seen a sailboat there, there were usually plenty of
fishing boats, ski boats, and Jet Skis on the water. Uncle
Thomas had a kayak, and he always put it in the water at
Geitner Park on a small creek that led out onto the lake.
The two of us had gone kayaking every summer whenever
my folks and I would visit him, and I'd loved that quiet
time we spent together on the calm water. There was always something to see, from herons taking off to turtles
sunning themselves on floating logs.

I found my uncle in the front yard of his house, tending
a raised-bed garden that was about the size of a sheet of
plywood. Though his hair had whitened over the years, it
was still full, and there was no brilliance lost in his smile.
Looking at him again, I felt the comfort and safety of my
childhood sweep over me. Whenever Uncle Thomas was
around, I knew in my heart that nothing could ever be
wrong.

After I got out, we hugged, and then I looked carefully

at his garden. "Wow, you've really downsized, haven't you? I remember when half your yard was full of your vegetable garden."

He smiled. "Ever since your aunt died, I haven't needed that many plants. She was a demon freezer and canner, but I have no interest in doing any of that. I just grow a few things every year to keep my hand in it."

I looked at the bed, a twelve-inch high wooden box sitting on the ground, filled with rich, black soil. In that compact space, he was growing three tomato plants, two rows of potatoes, a block of onions, and a block of green beans. "How did you manage to fit so much into such a small space?"

"What can I say? When I get started, I have a hard time stopping."

"You could always build another bed," I said.

"Then I'd just fill it up, too, and we both know it." His smile faded as he added, "I'm finished up here. Why don't we go onto the porch?"

I nodded. While his house wasn't really anything that special, he had a screened-in porch that I'd always adored. When I'd been a kid, I could remember having slumber parties out there, hearing the crickets and watching the fireflies doing their nightly dances. While my uncle's place was still technically in the city of Hickory limits, he had nearly an acre of land, with trees all around him. It was a little like his own slice of heaven.

After Uncle Thomas washed up at the spigot outside, he asked me, "Would you like some lemonade?"

"You wouldn't be stalling, would you?" I asked him.

"Me? Would I do something like that? How's that husband of yours? Is he still treating you right?"

"You know it. He's fine, and he sends his love. He's working on a pretty bad case for the Charlotte police at the moment. They're in a jam, so they called him in."

"How's the consulting business going?"

"It comes in spurts. Anything else you want to talk about? How are the Crawdads doing?" That was our local Single-A professional baseball team, and my uncle rarely missed a home game.

"It's too soon to tell," he said. "Okay, you're right. I've been beating around the bush, but I called you up here, so I should get to it."

Now that he was getting ready to tell me something, I found myself wishing that I'd been the one stalling, instead of him. Uncle Thomas was more important to me than I'd even realized, and the prospect of losing him was enough to break my heart.

"You don't have to tell me," I said suddenly. "We can just sit out here and enjoy the day."

"No, you're a busy woman, and I've got things to do myself. I'm sure you have a puzzle due today."

"There's a puzzle due just about every day," I said. "If I don't get around to it today, I have some saved up. If they run through those, they can always use old ones."

"I hate repeats," he said. "I feel like I'm being cheated."

"Hang on a second. You do my puzzles?"

He nodded. "Ever since the Hickory paper started carrying them. I'm getting pretty good at them, too."

"That is the sweetest thing I've heard in ages," I said, truly touched by his admission.

"Why wouldn't I do them? I'm proud of you, Savannah, and so was your mother." He frowned, and then said, "I'll be right back."

What was he getting? Were there test results he wanted me to look over? Was it even worse than I'd feared?

To my surprise, a full five minutes later, he came out onto the porch with a small wooden box clutched firmly in his wrinkled hands. It was big enough to hold a packet of letters four inches thick, or just about anything else that would fit into that space.

"Those aren't test results," I said.

He looked surprised by the declaration. "Of course they aren't. Why would you think they were?"

"You told me you went to the doctor, remember?"

"Savannah, I also remember telling you that everything was fine. Sure, my blood pressure's higher than he'd like, and I could stand to lose ten or fifteen pounds, but there's nothing dire."

"That's a relief," I said, suddenly feeling a weight lift from me. I knew I wouldn't have my uncle around forever, but that didn't mean I was ready to let him go just yet, either. "What's in the box?"

"It was your mother's," he said as he handed it to me.

"I thought I cleaned everything out after she and dad died," I said. It had been a painful process going through their things after the accident, but I'd forced myself to do it, along with help from Zach and Uncle Thomas.

"You did, as far as you knew. Astrid asked me to keep this for her, and I didn't have any way to say no. She told me to give it back to her in five years, and if she wasn't around, I was supposed to give it to you then. Well, I'm not waiting another two years. You deserve to have it now."

"What's inside? Do you have any idea?"

"I never peeked, if that's what you're asking. It could be full of gold doubloons for all I know." He hefted it in the air, and then said, "Strike that. Gold would be heavier than that."

He offered it to me, but I had a difficult time taking it from him. "Maybe you should look first."

Uncle Thomas shook his head. "Your mother was clear. I was not to look inside, no matter what the circumstances. I didn't break my word to her when she was alive, and I'm not about to start now."

"You're not breaking your word," I said. "You'd be doing it as a favor to me."

"Savannah, I couldn't love you any more if you were my own daughter, but there are some things I can't do for you, and breaking my word is one of them. I'm sorry, I truly am, but I won't do that."

"I understand," I said. I reluctantly took the box from him, and saw that while it had a certain heft to it, there wasn't any gold inside, at least not literally. I couldn't imagine what might be inside, but I was in no hurry to find out. I put it on the table beside my chair, still unopened.

"Aren't you the least bit curious?" Uncle Thomas asked.

"Yes, but I'm not ready to see what's in there yet. I think I'll wait until Zach can see what's inside with me." Many times, my husband was a source of strength for me, and whatever was in that box, I knew that I'd be better suited to handle it with him by my side.

"That sounds like the right thing to do," my uncle said.

I looked around at the beauty outside. "What would you like for lunch? Should I make something for us?"

He grinned. "I've already taken care of it. There's a pot roast in the oven that should be ready in about an hour."

"We're eating roast at ten thirty in the morning?" I asked, not able to keep the amusement out of my voice.

"I've become a fairly good cook, but I'm lousy at timing meals to come out when I want them. I don't know how your aunt managed it all those years. If it's too early, I understand completely. I guess I got excited that you were coming, so I kind of jumped the gun a little."

"Ten thirty sounds perfect," I said. "Can we eat out here?"

"We can eat wherever you want to, child," he said with a grin. Had a weight been lifted off him as well? Uncle Thomas seemed relieved to have passed my mother's box on to me, no doubt from fulfilling one of his last obligations to her. He'd loved my mother, and had shown her even more care when my uncle Jeffrey had left. He and my mom had been close, so the stories went, and when Jeffrey disappeared on his eighteenth birthday without a word to any of them, it had nearly broken her heart. That was when Thomas and his sister had formed such a tight bond.

We chatted for a while, and I heard the timer go off in the kitchen.

Uncle Thomas grinned at me. "It's showtime. You grab the place settings and I'll fetch the food."

I was getting the plates in the kitchen cupboard when my uncle lifted the lid from the roast. It smelled divine, and I was surprised to realize that my mouth was watering, despite the time of day and the relatively full state of my stomach.

*   *   *

AFTER WE ATE, I NOTICED THAT IT WAS BARELY ELEVEN o'clock.

I started carrying dirty dishes into the kitchen, and asked my uncle, "What would you like to do now?"

"After eating that much roast, I'd like to take a nap," he said.

"Go on. I can occupy myself while you're sleeping."

Uncle Thomas laughed. "I was joking, Savannah. I'm not that old, at least not yet. I would love to have you stay with me all day, but I know you've got things to do, so you don't have to keep me company."

"Anything I've got on my plate can wait," I said.

"Do you mean that?"

"I do," I said. "I don't have to leave for hours yet."

"Then what do you say? Should we get the kayaks out and take a little trip on the water?"

I hadn't been in a kayak forever, and I wasn't even sure I could still paddle one, but the hope in his gaze was something I couldn't bring myself to crush. "Let's go."

We loaded the kayaks into the back of his old brown Ford pickup, and I noticed large spots on the hood where the paint had peeled off, leaving a chalky gray surface exposed. "You should get that painted before it rusts."

"I know, but I can't find the right shade of spray paint to match it," he said as we drove to the park. For an instant, I could swear I saw the black car again on the road, but it could just as easily have been my imagination. There was no doubt about it; I was starting to jump at shadows after spending so much time thinking about murder.

I tried to put that aside and get back to my uncle. "They have people who do professional paint jobs, you know."

"Savannah, I'm not going to spend five hundred dollars

getting an eight hundred dollar truck painted. This suits me just fine."

It was true, too. There was something about that old pickup truck that matched my uncle's personality. Though they were both tattered a little around the edges, there was a strength underneath that was undeniable.

We put the kayaks into the creek at the landing and glided through the water beside the path that ran around the perimeter of the park. Fishing bobbers hung from the trees like Christmas ornaments, lost to overly enthusiastic anglers, and logs from a recent storm were scattered in the water. As we turned a bend, a handful of ducklings and their mother paddled for shore. Uncle Thomas and I went all the way to the highway bridge, and as was our custom, we stopped underneath, listening to the cars thudding away overhead.

"Are you ready to head back?" he asked me after ten minutes.

"I am, if you are."

"Let's go then. I'll race you to the landing."

"I doubt I could beat you," I admitted.

"Come on. You can do it. I have faith in you." And then he took off like a shot in the water. I had no choice but to race after him, laughing so hard I could barely hold my paddle. Being with my uncle out on the water brought back a sense of joy to me that I hadn't had in a long time. For those few moments, it was like being a kid again, and I reveled in what his presence could do for me.

THANKFULLY, I DIDN'T SEE ANY BLACK CARS ON THE WAY back to his house. After we stowed the kayaks away under the deck, he said, "Girl, you're really good for me. I haven't felt this young in ages."

"Neither have I," I said. I glanced at my watch and saw that the afternoon was quickly slipping away. "I hate to say it, but I should probably head back to Charlotte."

"Thanks for coming. You made my day something special."

"I'll try not to stay away so long next time," I said as I headed for my car.

"Aren't you forgetting something?" he asked.

Then I remembered my mother's box, still sitting on the screened porch by my chair. "That's right."

"Hang on, I'll get it for you."

He did just that, and a few seconds later, Uncle Thomas handed the box to me. "I don't know what's inside, but I do know one thing. Having you was your mother's greatest joy in life. She told me that many times."

"Thank you. For everything."

I kissed his cheek, then hugged him like I was never going to let go. When I pulled away from him, I was startled to find a tear tracking down my cheek.

"Hey, there's no reason to be sad," he said softly, "Wherever you go, a part of me will go with you."

I said my good-byes, and as I drove away, I looked back at him. Every time we parted, I knew it could be the last time we saw each other, but his words did offer me a bit of comfort. He would live on in my heart as long as I took a single breath, and though we were many miles apart, in another—and very real way—we were always together. I'd loved my mother, but we'd had our share of tumult over the years. With my uncle, things had always been uncomplicated. One for all, and all for one, and no mercy for anyone who tried to interfere with that. As I headed back toward Hickory, I was startled to realize that I hadn't married a man much like my father, but I had found someone who shared many of his traits with my uncle. It was no wonder the two men got along so well.

They both had a part of me.

As I drove back to Charlotte, I kept glancing at the box on the seat beside me. What secrets had my mother entrusted her brother to hold for me, and why was he giving them to me now? Would it be something awful, or wonderful?

And did I have the courage to open it, even with Zach by my side?

AS I TOOK THE EXIT FROM I-40 EAST TO I-77 SOUTH, I RE-alized that I was too tired to make anything but a simple puzzle, and there was no way my publisher was going to put up with that. I wasn't all that thrilled with calling him, but I really didn't have much choice.

"Derrick, it's Savannah," I said when I got him on the line.

"Would that be Simple Savannah, the easy puzzle maker?" he asked with that smart-aleck tone of voice he loved to use with me.

"Hey, sometimes folks like to remember how far they've come, and for others, it gives them a chance to get started."

"I read your snippet, you don't have to repeat it over the phone. I trust you have something a bit more challenging today."

"That's the thing. I need you to use one of the puzzles you have in my backup file."

"Savannah, you need fresh puzzles every day, you know that, don't you?"

"I would if I could, but I don't have time right now."

There was a long pause, and then he said, "If this is too much for you, maybe you should go ahead and retire like that husband of yours did."

My puzzles were popular with the readers, and Derrick knew that, but since I'd gotten my work into more and more newspapers, he regretted the original deal we'd signed. His syndicate had one-time publishing rights to my puzzles, and he got a flat fifteen percent commission each time I got a check. Since we'd signed that deal, he came to find out that it was too generous on my end, at least in the opinion of some of his colleagues. Since then, he'd been trying to get me to sign another deal under terms more favorable to him, or if that didn't work, he wanted me to quit so he could replace me with someone else. It was a constant struggle dealing with him, and it was one reason I was rarely late with a puzzle. If everything went as expected, the main contact I had with Derrick was my growing bank account.

"There's no chance in the world I'm quitting. Besides, they love my little snippets, as you call them. I'd be harder to replace than you might think."

He didn't answer that, a clear indicator that he suspected that I was right.

"Fine, we'll use one of your old ones. Just don't make a habit of it."

The way he said it was insulting, and I wasn't in the

mood to take any grief from him today. "They aren't old to the readers, remember that."

I could hear him riffling through a file on his desk. "You only have three left after I distribute this one; you know that, don't you? That means you're just three days away from being in breach of your contract. If that happens, all bets are off."

I hadn't realized my cache of backup puzzles had gotten that low. One bout of the flu and I'd have to renegotiate my contract with him, and that was something I wasn't willing to do.

"Don't worry; I'll have a handful more by the end of the month."

He sounded disappointed as he replied, "If you think you can do it, but I don't want any more of those tiny little submissions like you sent yesterday. For what they're paying you, the papers expect more complex math and logic puzzles from you."

"I'll see what I can do," I said, though I had no intention of creating a puzzle that was too complex for my average reader. There might be puzzlemakers out there who could run circles around my computational challenges, but I had something they could never replace. The snippets that Derrick disliked too much as "homey" were something that came from me, and no one else in the world could come up with them just the way I did.

"I need a new puzzle tomorrow, Savannah."

"Good-bye, Derrick," I said, and hung up on him before he could reply.

I hated to call him, since every conversation we had always led me to feel like I needed a shower, but I wasn't about to let his sour disposition ruin my mood. My time with Uncle Thomas, especially out on the water, had been too dear for me to let anything else ruin it. I'd buckle down and crank out more puzzles, and get enough breathing room to keep Derrick off my back.

Just not tonight.

Chapter 12

...

I WAS ACTUALLY FEELING BETTER AN HOUR LATER. AFTER A long shower and a fresh outfit, I was ready to tackle a puzzle after all. I'd just settled onto the couch with a pad of paper and a pencil when there was a knock at the door.

I thought about ignoring it, but it was like a ringing telephone. I just had to answer it.

"Yes?" I called out before I opened the door. Zach's warnings were starting to sink in, especially after I had the feeling that someone had followed me from Charlotte to Hickory, even though I still wasn't certain if I'd been right or not.

"Savannah, I'd like a moment of your time, if I could."

Just because the man knew my name didn't mean I had to open the door. "I'm sorry, but I don't know you."

"Of course you don't," he said. "I could show you some identification if you'd open the door. I happen to own this hotel. "

"How do I know that's true?" I asked.

"I suppose you can't." After a moment's pause, he added, "It appears that we're at a stalemate. Is there anyone at the hotel that you trust?"

I thought about it, and realized that there was one person who fit that bill. "Garrett," I said.

"Excellent."

I could hear him speak briefly into his telephone, and a minute later, the manager arrived. "Ms. Stone, it's Garrett."

That was certainly a voice I'd come to recognize. I opened the door, and there were two men standing in the hallway. Garrett smiled at me, but the man with him was a stranger to me. Then I realized that there was something familiar about him, though I had no idea what it was. The inkling was gone as quickly as it had come.

"Sorry about that, but you can't be too careful," I said.

"Your prudence is admirable," the man said. "Allow me to introduce myself in person. I'm Barton Lane."

I wasn't sure what he was expecting, but the hug I gave him was clearly a surprise. I thought Garrett, as cool and calm as he'd been with me before, looked as though he was going to pass out.

"Barton, thank you for everything. I've never felt so pampered in my life."

When I pulled away, I saw that he was smiling. "It's my pleasure." The hotel owner turned to his employee and added, "You may go."

"Of course, sir," Garrett said. As he walked to the elevator, I saw him turn back slightly and look at me with an expression of complete awe.

"Won't you come in?" I asked, moving aside so he could step into his suite. The place was immaculate, except for the pad and pencil still on the couch. He took it in instantly.

"Forgive me. I've disrupted your work."

"I haven't even gotten started yet," I admitted, "so you're not disturbing anything. Can I get you anything?"

I suddenly realized how insane the offer was, since he had everything at the hotel at his disposal.

"No, I'm fine, but thank you for offering. I trust the accommodations have been suitable."

"They've been more than that," I replied.

"Good." He frowned as he stared at his feet, then said, "Let me get to the point. I need a favor from you."

"Anything," I said, and I meant it. The man had spared no expense making us comfortable, and if there was a favor I could grant him, I would do it gladly.

"I'm afraid it's a lot to ask, but I was wondering if you would help me go through Cindy's things. The poor girl had no one else in the world but me, and I find that I can't bear to do it alone. After our conversation the other day, I felt I had found a kindred spirit in you." The poor man looked as though he was about to cry. "I know it's a great deal to ask, but there's no one else I could approach."

It was humbling to know that this multi-millionaire had no one but me to aid him in doing such an uncomfortable task. "I'm glad to help, but isn't there someone on your staff you could have do it?" I couldn't imagine how many employees he had at this hotel alone, and I knew it was just one of his many holdings.

"I'm sure there are countless people I could pay to perform this service for me, but this is personal, and I'm afraid I've been rather remiss in allowing anyone into my life. I know it's too much to ask. Forgive me."

He started to leave, and without realizing what I was doing, I reached out and grabbed his arm. Barton was clearly surprised by it, but I couldn't exactly take it back. "I'd be honored to help you."

"Honestly?" There was a sliver of hope in his eyes as he looked at me.

"Just let me call my husband first."

He nodded. "I have a few calls to make myself. Meet me downstairs when you're finished, and I'll have a car take us there."

"I'd be glad to drive," I said.

That got a smile. "Thank you, but that won't be necessary."

"I'll just be a minute."

He turned to go, and then hesitated. "Thank you, Savannah."

"That's what friends are for. No thanks are necessary."

I called Zach the second the door closed.

"Stone," he said when he answered, his voice sounding like the cop he used to be.

"You're not going to believe what just happened," I said.

"Are you still in Hickory?"

"No, I'm back in Charlotte."

"How was Tom? Is he all right?"

"He says he is, and I believe him. Zachary, would you let me talk?"

"Sorry. Go ahead."

"Barton Lane asked me for a favor, and I'm going to do it."

That got the silence I'd been looking for. "Well? You don't have any problem with that, do you?"

"What kind of favor are we talking about here?" he asked.

"He wants me to help him clean out Cindy Glass's apartment."

"Savannah, that's not funny. I'm beat, and I'm not in the mood for one of your jokes."

"Zach, he just left our hotel suite, and now he's waiting downstairs for me in the lobby."

"Are you serious? He really asked you for help? Can't he get one of his minions to do it?"

"This is personal," I said.

"Why you? Surely he's known more folks a lot longer, and better."

"I don't think he has," I admitted. "Is there a problem with us doing it?"

"No, it's been released as a crime scene. I was there this morning, and I didn't see anything of value to the investigation."

"You didn't tell me. You aren't holding out on me, are you?"

"We haven't talked since this morning, Savannah."

"Okay, you're forgiven. So, is it okay?"

"It's fine with me, but it's a little surreal having someone with that much money asking you for a favor, don't you think?"

I stared out the window before I replied. "I'm trying not to think about how much money and power he has. Barton is someone who needs my help, and I'm going to give it. And, you never know, I may find something that you all missed."

Zach's voice lowered, and I knew he meant business. "Savannah, you've helped me in the past, and we both know it. There's something about the way your mind works that allows you to reach conclusions that I can't see. You've got a gift. Just be careful. Call me when you get back to the hotel," he said.

"I will, but I have no idea how late it will be. You might beat me back here."

"I wouldn't count on it. I'm pushing myself through the last of these files tonight so I can actually start detecting. I'm afraid that it's going to be a long night."

"For both of us," I said. "Love you."

"Love you, too," he said as he hung up.

At least I was ready for cleaning, since I was wearing my typical outfit of blue jeans and a T-shirt. That was one thing I loved about my job; there was no dress code.

I FOUND GARRETT WAITING FOR ME DOWNSTAIRS WHEN I entered the lobby. "If you'll come with me," he said.

"Sure thing."

He wanted to say something else to me as we walked to the front of the building, it was clear in his eyes, but he held back. The poor man looked tortured, so I finally asked him, "Is there something on your mind?"

The manager stopped and looked at me. "I know it's not my place, but I hope you'll be gentle with him. He's a good man in some serious pain right now."

It was clear Garrett cared about his boss. "I'm doing all that I can to help him."

"We all know that, and we're most grateful," he said.

We started walking toward the front door again. Parked outside was a shiny black limousine. I hadn't been in one since my wedding day, and I honestly hadn't expected to be in one again. The driver was standing by the door, and he opened it the second I approached. Garrett bowed toward me as I got in, and I winked at him. Barton appeared to be in a deep conversation on the phone with someone, and as we started to drive off, he hung up.

"What was that about?" he asked.

"What do you mean?"

"I saw the way Garrett bowed to you. That's out of character for him."

How had the man caught such a subtle move out of the corner of his eye while he was on the telephone with someone else? He had to have greater powers of focus and concentration than most people did. Maybe that was one of the sources of his ability to acquire wealth.

"Your employees care about you," I said. "It should make you feel good."

"I hardly know the man, and he's my only contact there," Barton said.

"They know you're a good boss, and it's pretty clear you're hurting over your loss."

Barton looked genuinely surprised by that. "Am I that transparent? I thought I hid my grief better than that."

"It's okay to be sad," I said. "You lost someone you cared about."

"More than I can say," he admitted.

As we drove across town, Barton said, "I tried to get her to move into the Belmont where there was at least a modicum of security, but she refused. Cindy prized her

freedom more than that. When she was off work, she liked
to live her own life. Here, she could lift a finger and have
anything she wanted, but in her own place, she had autonomy."

"I like her already," I said.

He nodded. "I approve of strong, independent women,
but I should have insisted. If I'd only known . . ."

"You can't play that game," I said, putting my hand on
his arm. "Second-guessing yourself is worse than cruel;
it's pointless."

"You're right. I embrace that philosophy in business,
but I can't seem to accept it in my personal life."

"Don't think about her loss," I said. "Celebrate who
she was. Tell me about her." I needed to get his mind focused on the good rather than the bad. If I could do that,
he might be able to get through the painful task we had
ahead of ourselves. There was also the slight chance I
might learn something new about Zach's case.

"She was sunshine personified," he said simply. "The
room lit up whenever she walked in, and faded a little
when she left it. Not that she was some kind of Polly-
anna," he added hastily. "Cindy had a temper that could be
quite fierce when she was challenged. There was spirit
under that soft demeanor, and anyone who crossed her had
to be sure they were right. She clashed with me more than
a few times over the years, and I knew when she challenged me that I needed to rethink my position. I trusted her
as my moral compass on tough decisions, and I changed
my mind more than once when she pushed me."

"She sounds like a great person," I said.

"I never had a wife, or children of my own," Barton
said softly. "She was as close to family as I had since I

was a teenager." There were gentle tears tracking down his cheeks, and I could see that the topic of his own family was too painful to discuss. "I felt better having her be a part of my life," he added. "Is there anything more you can ask of someone?"

"Not in my book," I admitted. "I couldn't imagine living if my husband was gone."

"Nearly losing him must have been devastating for you. It was a miracle he survived that gunshot."

"How did you know about that?"

"It was in all of the newspapers," Barton said. "I just have to imagine how you must have felt."

"Worse than I can ever describe," I admitted. "But enough about me. What exactly are we going to do at Cindy's place?"

"I want to collect a few personal things, and then I'll have someone else go through the rest of it." His voice choked a little. "This is probably a bad idea from every angle you examine it, but it's something that I have to do. Thank you for going with me."

"I'm honored you asked me," I said.

He started to reach out to pat my hand, pulled back for a moment, and then lightly touched my fingers. No words were spoken, but a great deal was understood in that instant.

We reached an ordinary-looking apartment complex, and as the driver stopped the car and opened our door, Barton hesitated before getting out.

"I'll do it myself, if it would help," I said. "It can't be easy for you to go inside."

He took a deep breath, and then said, "No, I can manage it. I'm not at all certain how long I'll be able to keep up my nerve, so let's get this over with."

I followed him out of the car, and as we stood at the apartment door, I saw that his hands were shaking as he held the key out toward the lock.

"Let me do that," I said as I took the key from him.

"Thanks," he answered, his voice barely above a whisper.

When I opened the door, a wave of disinfectant smell swept over me. I wasn't sure that the odor was better than what it had disguised, but then again, I didn't have any experience with dead bodies.

It was a typical young single woman's place, decorated with a wide palette of oranges, browns, and greens. She had a framed Monet poster over her couch.

"I have the original at home," he said softly as he studied it. "If I'd known she loved it, I would have given it to her." He wiped away his tears, and then he said, "I'm being ridiculous, I know. I've got hundreds of people who work for me."

"She was a lot more than just an employee to you. It hurts losing someone you care about."

He nodded. "This is more difficult than I ever imagined. I'm sorry, Savannah. I just can't do it."

I hugged him, and though it was clear he wasn't all that comfortable with anyone embracing him, he let me. When he pulled away, I said, "You don't need to be here. I'll go through and collect anything that looks like it might have sentimental value to you, and then I'll bring it back to the hotel."

"There was a necklace, sterling silver, with a cow pendant on it in black and white. She loved it, but it wasn't found when her body was discovered."

"I'll keep my eyes open," I said.

He nodded numbly, and then left without saying another word. After the car pulled away, I dead-bolted the door behind me and started digging into the apartment, and more importantly, Cindy Glass's life.

CINDY WAS NEAT, WHICH WAS A REAL PLUS FOR ME, GIVEN the search I had ahead of me. Checking out her place was a lot easier because of it, but at the same time, it made me sad to think that this tidy young woman's life was cut so short.

There was no way around it; I was going to have to pry into her most personal things if I was going to help Barton.

The first place I looked was her lingerie drawer, knowing that many women liked to hide things there. She had a great deal of conservatively cut panties for the week, but there were also a few brightly colored pairs that had to be reserved for the weekend. Under it all, wedged into the back of the drawer, I found a photograph of Cindy and a young man that couldn't be identified by the snapshot. They'd been skiing, and he had a fit build, but his face had been haphazardly torn out of the photograph, leaving nothing really identifying in what was left behind. Who had it been, I wondered, and how long ago had she and he broken up? From the way the photograph was torn, I was guessing that the breakup hadn't been Cindy's decision. I took the picture and put it on the bed where I was starting a pile of things to take to Barton. I'd have to go over everything I collected again to make sure it wasn't a clue before I turned anything over to him. Barton had asked me to take my time, and I was going to honor that request.

There were a few more photographs scattered throughout the apartment, mostly of Cindy and her friends, and then I found one I was certain Barton would want. It showed the two of them together, standing side by side and smiling broadly. In the background was a sign hanging from the ceiling proclaiming "Happy St. Patrick's Day." I wasn't sure where it had been taken, but I put it on the growing pile and moved on.

As I searched the small apartment, I kept my eyes open for the cow pendant necklace Barton had mentioned. There wasn't much in the place in the way of jewelry, just some oversized earrings and a few glittering peace symbol necklaces housed in a small wooden box that appeared to have been made at summer camp a long time ago. Cindy had retro tastes in her jewelry as well as her curtains and bedspread. The material in her bedroom for both sported a matching pattern of brown, gold, and green rings on an orange background. I wondered what her clothes were like. As I opened the small closet door, I found mostly work clothes, but among her prim business suits, I found another section of the closet filled with flared blue jeans and bright tops. Cindy was clearly button-down at work, but when she played, it was obvious that she enjoyed casual comfort. In the kitchen, I searched each drawer and cabinet in turn, but it was so generic that it could have been anyone's place, so there was nothing to add to the pile. The living room, the only other room in the apartment besides the tiny bathroom, had few things of a personal nature in it. All I could come up with was a half-finished crossword puzzle, and a well-read copy of *Fahrenheit 451* by Ray Bradbury. I was about to leave it on the table, but then I spontaneously added it to the pile.

As I walked back into the living room, I saw that there was a blinking light on her answering machine. Out of habit, I hit the play button and heard a man's voice say, "Cin? Are you there? Call me, this fight is ridiculous." Who was she fighting with, and why? Hadn't he heard that she was dead?

This sounded like something Zach should know. I picked up my cell phone and dialed my husband's number.

He picked up on the fourth ring, just before it went to voice mail. "'Lo?"

"Hey, did I call at a bad time?" I asked.

"No, I was digging into one of the last boxes of evidence, and I couldn't hear my phone. What's up? Are you still at the Glass place?"

"I am," I said. "I promised Barton I'd stay as long as I needed to."

"Is he there with you?"

"No, he came in with me, but he couldn't take it. I'm collecting a few things for him, and I was walking past the answering machine when I noticed that the light was blinking, so I hit the play button."

"You shouldn't have done that," he said. "We're in the middle of an active police investigation."

"You're the one who gave me permission to come here, remember?" If he was going to use that tone of voice with me, he was going to get it right back.

"Sorry. You're right. I shouldn't have snapped at you like that. I'm just tired, I guess. What did it say?"

"Evidently she was fighting with someone, and he called to make up with her."

"If he killed her, he had to know she wouldn't be getting the message."

"I thought of that." I said. "But what if he's trying to make it look like he's innocent? That call might help him, if a jury hears it. Shouldn't you trace it?"

"It's probably innocent enough, but I'll have Joe look into it. He's the guy who drove me over here today. Hang on." He covered the mouthpiece, but I could still hear some of his conversation.

A minute later, he asked, "Is there anything else?"

"I'm not sure I want to share the rest of it with you," I said.

"Come on, give me a break, Savannah. I'm up against the wall here."

My voice softened. "Did Davis give you a hard time today?"

Zach snorted. "He never showed up for our meeting, and no one's seen him around here all day."

"That's a good thing then, isn't it?"

"I don't know about that. When the police chief bails out on you, it can't be good."

"How about Grady? Have you spoken with him?"

"Nobody knows where he is, either. He told his assistant that he was taking the day off. Who knows, maybe the two of them are off somewhere conspiring."

"Slow down, Zach. Don't let the paranoia get to you."

He sighed. "I know. I'm just whipped."

"I am, too. I found a photo of Cindy and a man in her lingerie drawer."

"Really? I looked there, but I didn't see anything."

I kept my comment about my husband going through a woman's lingerie drawer to myself. He didn't need to hear me teasing him at the moment. "It was in the back, wedged in. I'm not sure it means anything. The guy's face has been ripped out of the picture."

"Wrap it up in your handkerchief and don't touch it any more than you have to. I'll get it from you tonight. What else did you find?"

"It's what I didn't find that's bothering me. Do you know if the investigating officers collected any personal correspondence from her place?"

"Sure, I don't even have to look. There's a box of letters she kept, along with some photos that might be significant, and a few other things. Why?"

"Did they find a silver chain with a cow pendant on it?"

He paused, and then said, "I don't think so. Hang on; let me grab the inventory list." I could hear him pull out some papers, and then he said, "No, nothing here about that. They took some photos of her jewelry box, but they didn't take it as evidence. Does it matter?"

"It must to Barton. It's the main reason he wanted to come here tonight."

"Well, we don't have it," Zach said. "How much longer are you going to be?"

"I'm just about finished. Why? Are you ready to come back to the hotel?"

"I wish I were, but I'm afraid I'll be here half the night."

"Should I come join you?" I asked.

"No, I'm not going to be very good company. Why

don't you go back to the hotel, and I'll see you sometime later?"

I thought about telling him about the box Uncle Thomas had given me, but if I did that, I knew Zach would insist on being by my side when I opened it, and he was needed right where he was. I'd deal with it—or not—by myself, one way or the other.

"Don't stay there too late," I said.

"I'll try not to fall asleep on the table, but I'm not making any promises. Call me later, okay?"

"You know I will."

After I got off the telephone with Zach, I took one last look around the apartment. There might be something there that had value to Barton, but without knowing what it was, I couldn't say. I was certain he'd have a crew come in after me and bag, tag, and catalogue the apartment's contents, so I didn't worry too much about missing anything.

That wasn't why I'd been there.

I looked at the paltry selection and frowned. What was I missing? Cindy hadn't been all that sentimental, if the limited personalized things before me were any indication.

I hated to go back to Barton so empty-handed, but I didn't have much choice. I couldn't manufacture sentiment out of thin air.

I finally picked up my cell phone and called the hotel.

"Garrett, it's Savannah Stone. I'm ready for my ride back to the hotel."

"Yes, ma'am. The driver is waiting for you outside."

I hadn't expected that. "Barton's not still here, is he?"

"No, he's in his penthouse suite here. As soon as you arrive, I'll escort you there."

"I thought we had the top floor."

"Of the public rooms, yes, but there is one more floor above you."

"Then I'll see you in a few minutes," I said.

I found the driver out front, but before I walked to the limousine, I locked the door to Cindy's apartment behind me.

"I'll take the key, if you don't mind," the driver said.

"Oh. Of course," I answered as I handed it to him. "I'm Savannah."

"I'm Henry," he replied, and then he smiled brightly. "It's a pleasure to meet you."

"Don't tell me you're a puzzle fan, too."

He looked surprised by the question. "No, ma'am, I'm not exactly sure what that is, but you've done a service for my employer, and I greatly appreciate it. He hasn't asked anyone for help as long as I've known him. You should feel honored."

"I do, but I'm not sure I did much good." I had collected the few things I'd managed to find in a paper grocery bag, and it felt too light in my hands.

"You helped, trust me."

As he drove us back to the hotel, I asked from the back, "Did you know Cindy Glass?"

He nodded, and I could see a tear in the corner of one eye. "She was special; there was no doubt about that. I can't imagine why anyone would want to harm her. I thought it was going to kill Mr. Lane. He didn't leave the penthouse for five days, but talking to you on the telephone when you and your husband first arrived seemed to revive him. Today, I finally believe that he is beginning to mend."

"I wish I could take credit for it, but I haven't really done anything."

Henry shrugged. "Sometimes three quarters of the battle is just showing up and trying your best. At least that's what my grandmother used to say."

"She was a smart lady," I said.

As we drove through traffic to the hotel, I leaned back in my seat, trying to get a handle on what I'd seen. I wanted to go through the letters the police had taken from Cindy Glass's apartment. More than that, I needed to. Before, she'd just been a name to me.

Now she was a real person.

And if there was anything I could do to help Zach find her killer, I was going to do it.

Chapter 13

■ ■ ■

"SAVANNAH. WELCOME BACK."

Garrett had evidently been waiting for me by the front of the Belmont, and he opened the door to the limo for me, but I didn't leave until I spoke to Henry first. "Thank you for the ride."

"It was my pleasure."

"Mine, too," I said.

"Ms. Stone, would you do me a kindness?"

"If I can," I replied.

"Tell your husband a great many people are pulling for him. He's got an army at his disposal. All he need do is ask."

"I'll let him know."

Garrett raised an eyebrow as I got out.

"Something to say, Garrett?" I asked him.

"You seem to make friends wherever you go," he said.

"I just listen to people when they talk to me," I said.

"That explains a great deal. You have a tendency to make the person you're with the center of your universe. It's quite intoxicating."

That wasn't the first time I'd been told that I was a good listener. "My mom always told me that there was more skill in listening than there was in speaking, and that she never learned anything by running her mouth."

"It's an admirable ability, but one that I'm afraid is becoming a lost art in this day of technology."

"There are always people behind emails and text messages," I said. "It just takes a different kind of listening to hear what's being said."

"True."

As we walked through the lobby, I noticed several of the staff watching us surreptitiously. When I caught a glance or two, there was always a smile backing it. I wasn't sure what I'd done to merit their goodwill, but I wasn't about to rebuff it.

I walked toward the main elevator, but Garrett touched my arm to stop me.

"It's this way," he directed. He showed me to a nondescript nook in the lobby that I hadn't noticed before. Garrett opened a door to reveal a private elevator. He held the door open, swiped his card, and then started to get out.

"Aren't you going with me?"

"It's Mr. Lane's orders. No one is allowed upstairs without his direct consent. If there's anything you need, at any time, it is yours to ask."

"Thanks," I said, but the doors were already sliding

closed. I didn't know why I was so nervous about seeing Barton Lane again, but I was. Perhaps it was because I was seeing him on his home turf. Maybe it was due to the light bag of memories I was taking him. Whatever the reason, I was as nervous as a teenage girl on her first date.

I wasn't sure what I was expecting when the elevator doors opened. Our suite was elegant, so I couldn't imagine how nice the penthouse must be. It didn't let me down, either. The floors were tiled with marble, and the furniture looked to be all antiques. The ceiling in the entryway was at least twenty feet high, and there was a crystal chandelier hanging that looked like it would fit in a presidential palace. I took all of that in in a moment, because the second I saw Barton Lane's face, I knew that the man was in some serious pain, and I didn't have time to look around at my surroundings anymore.

"Did you find her necklace?" he choked out.

"No, I'm sorry. I didn't, and I checked with my husband on the way over here. The police have no idea where it is, either."

He physically sagged at the news, and I had to step in to hold him up. What significance could that little cow pendant have for him?

"Was it important?"

"She loved cows, so I bought it for her on her twenty-third birthday. Cindy never went anywhere without it."

No wonder it had so much sentimental value to him. I had to do something.

"I did find a few things that looked like they might hold memories for you," I said.

Barton nodded absently. "Let's go into the study."

Wow, his suite had its own study. I had no idea this was how the wealthy lived. I couldn't imagine the square footage Barton had in his home. As we walked through the foyer and past the formal dining room, it was like moving through a movie set. The only difference here was that everything was real.

We entered a comfortable room the size of our living room at home, and I was suddenly surrounded by a timber-frame structure, a distressed old-growth pine floor, and a stone fireplace tucked neatly into one corner. There was oversized furniture in the room that made it look like a cozy retreat from the world. "I love this. It's Timberlake, isn't it?" Zach and I had been to the Bob Timberlake furniture gallery in Lexington, NC, an hour's drive from Charlotte. We'd even met Bob there once, an artist of world renown who'd turned his talents to furniture as well.

"Yes, he designed this set for me." It was clear that Barton didn't want to discuss furniture.

I opened the bag in my lap so I could start pulling out its contents, but my host stopped me. "One item at a time, if you don't mind."

I agreed, and reached in to withdraw the copy of *Fahrenheit 451*. "I wasn't sure if this was significant or not."

He took it from me. "She told me a month ago that she'd never read it when she spied a signed hardcover in my library. I tried to give it to her, but she just laughed and insisted a used paperback copy would be fine. I kept her busy here, so she was reading it in bits and pieces, and we discussed it whenever she finished a new chapter." He rubbed the cover of that book as if it were gilded in gold.

After a moment, Barton set it aside and looked expectantly at me. My hand touched the wrapped photograph, and I paused to explain its presence before I brought it out.

"My husband believes this might be significant," I said, "so it's important that no more fingerprints get on it. I have to hold it. I'm sorry, but he was most insistent."

"I understand," Barton said.

I took it out, carefully unwrapped the picture, and then held it so he could see it. I saw Barton frown, so I asked, "Do you know the man she's with?"

"It's difficult to say, isn't it? It surprises me, though."

"Why's that?"

"If Cindy had wanted to remove his image, she would have cut him out with scissors. I can't imagine the circumstances where she would just tear it like that."

"Maybe she was angry about the breakup. Do you happen to know who she was dating at the time she died?"

Barton sighed. "She was adamant about keeping her personal life and her work with me separate, so I never pried. Honestly, though I always thought of her more as a daughter than an employee, I wanted to respect her privacy." He smiled softly as he added, "At least I decided to after the first time I asked her something personal. She may have looked serene on the outside, but the young lady had a spirit of fire."

I set the photograph aside, and retrieved the next picture. It was one of Barton and Cindy together, and as I handed it to him, I saw tears start to form in his eyes.

"I'd forgotten she had a copy of this."

"When was it taken?"

"Two years ago. We were in Chicago on business at one of my other hotels, and as we were walking through the lobby during the St. Patrick's Day celebration, my manager took the photograph. I wasn't pleased at the time—I dislike having my picture taken—but Cindy decided she wanted one of us together, and I had to be smiling. I did as she asked, and had a copy made for her. Excuse me a moment."

He left me alone in the study, and I wondered if he was stepping away to collect himself. It was clear he was being tortured by my little show-and-tell, but it was at his request, so I wasn't going to stop unless he asked me to.

When he came back, he was holding an oil painting, and its subject matter startled me. It was the same image as the photograph I'd found, carefully reproduced by someone very good with a paintbrush. "This hangs in my bedroom hallway," he said. "I never showed it to Cindy."

"I'm sure she would have liked it," I said.

"I doubt it," he said with a smile. "She would have thought I was indulging a whim. That's why I kept it to myself."

He leaned the painting against the wall, and then took his seat. I pulled out the jewelry box, and Barton reached for it.

"She made this herself," he said as he stroked the wood. He opened it, looked through the jewelry, and then set it aside. "I'll go through it later. Is there anything else?"

I pulled out the last photograph, one clearly taken several years ago. Barton studied it a moment, and then he explained, "This was taken before she came to work for me." He pointed to the two other girls in the photograph. "This is Samantha, and her name is Kayla."

"Have you met them?"

"Absolutely. They came to my Christmas party every year. Two delightful young women, I must say."

"So, the three of them stayed in touch?"

"Yes. In particular, Cindy and Samantha spoke every week, and they often took their vacations together."

"Where can my husband find Samantha?"

"Do you think she might know something?" he asked, intent on my reply.

"I can't say, but Zach always says that police work is asking a lot of questions, and then boiling down the answers until something significant occurs to him. It might be nothing, but I'm sure my husband would like to speak with her."

"I'll get you her address," he said.

He picked up the telephone, whispered into it, and after a brief pause, he handed it to me.

"Samantha Riggins can be reached at the following number and address." It was a local area code, and I knew the address as being in the South End, one of Charlotte's neighborhoods. At least Zach wouldn't have to fly across the country to interview her.

I handed the telephone back to Barton, and then looked back into the bag. "Sorry, that's all that I could find. The police have a few items they're holding for the investigation, but as I said, the necklace didn't turn up."

"Perhaps the cleaning crew will find it." He glanced at his watch. "I'll send my best maids to work on her apartment right now. When they're finished, I'll go through anything else they might find."

I frowned at that, and Barton quickly added, "Don't think what you did tonight didn't matter. You walked in with me, and when I couldn't take it, you carried out my wishes. These things you found," he said as he swept a hand toward the coffee table, "mean more to me than this hotel, or any of my other holdings. You've done me a great service tonight. Is there any way I can repay you?"

"You're already putting us up in your nicest suite," I said. "That's thanks enough."

"Nonsense. That was to aid your husband in helping me, more than anything else. The debt I owe you is personal, Savannah, and I always pay my debts."

"Then you can be my friend," I said.

"That's all you ask?"

"It's all I want."

"Then that's what you shall have, my friend."

He stood, and I followed suit.

As we walked out of the study, Barton asked, "Have you eaten yet?"

"No, I haven't had time," I admitted.

"I expect your husband will be eagerly waiting for you downstairs."

"The last time we spoke, he told me he'd probably be working half the night."

"Then may I be so bold to ask you to join me for dinner? I can't promise much, but I make the best pancakes in the world, and I'd be pleased if you'd join me."

I laughed. "Pancakes? Really?" I hadn't meant to sound so incredulous, but I couldn't help myself. Being in the nicest luxury suite in one of the best hotels in Charlotte with the owner, and having him offer to make me a dinner-breakfast, was just a little too surreal for me.

"My mother couldn't cook much, but she was an excellent pancake maker, and she passed on her knowledge to me before I left home."

"That's funny."

"Why's that?"

"We have a pancake dinner tradition in our family, too."

"It must be a southern thing," he said lightly. "Would you care to join me?"

"That sounds great."

We moved into his kitchen, with its cherrywood cabinets and industrial oven. There was a griddle imbedded in the marble-topped island, and stainless steel appliances were everywhere.

As he mixed the batter and began pouring rounds onto the griddle top, I said, "I'll set the table."

"Don't bother. Why don't we eat here at the island?"

"Sounds good to me," I said.

"The plates are over there, and the silver is in that drawer."

I retrieved fine bone china from the cabinet, and sterling silver knives and forks. With the linen napkins he retrieved, I set our places, and added crystal goblets.

"There's milk and orange juice in the refrigerator," he said.

"Which would you prefer?"

"I'd like milk myself."

I poured two glasses, found the butter as well, and turned to see that Barton had the syrup out, in crystal as well.

When the first pancake was finished, he flipped it onto my plate. I waited for him, but he waved his spatula in the air. "Go on, they're too good to eat when they're right off the griddle to wait."

I added a little butter and a tad too much syrup, and

then tasted it. He was looking expectantly, so I smiled as I said, "Delicious. These may be the best pancakes I've ever had, and that's saying something."

"I add a touch of cinnamon to the batter," he said. "It makes all the difference in the world, in my opinion."

We alternated eating pancakes after that, and after we were finished, I said, "I'd be glad to do the dishes."

"Thank you, but I have someone who does that for me." He stared at me a second, and then asked, "Would you like to see my secret vice?"

I wasn't sure I wanted to. I was just warming up to the man. "Okay," I said hesitantly.

He laughed at my reluctance. "It's nothing like that. We have to go on the roof, though."

I decided if I told him about my fear of heights, it would ruin the nice evening we'd shared. But there was no way I was going close to the edge. "Lead on."

To my surprise, we walked out to our common stairwell. "I keep this unlocked," he explained as we walked up the short flight to the door. "No one has access to it but the top two floors, so you have my blessing to come and go as you please."

I couldn't imagine the circumstances that I'd take him up on it, but I kept that to myself.

Once we were on the roof, I changed my mind. The space, lit with gentle illumination, sported some chairs and a table, but what really caught my eye was a raised-bed garden, filled with tomatoes, beans, onions, and potatoes. "It's great," I said. "In fact, my uncle has something a lot like this."

"It's the only way I can indulge my green thumb without leaving the hotel," he explained. "There's something about getting my hands dirty that I've never forgotten. It was one of my favorite childhood memories."

"I can tell that you really love it."

He smiled. "It's the most calming thing I have in my life. Coming up here renews me somehow."

"How nice that must be," I said as I stifled a yawn.

"You must be exhausted after the day you've had."

During our meal, I'd regaled him with tales of my day in Hickory with Uncle Thomas, and he'd hung on every word. "I am beat," I said. "Sorry I'm not better company."

"Savannah, you've been delightful. Let me walk you back downstairs."

We moved to the stairwell, and returned to Barton's floor. He explained, "I'd let you back in through the stairwell on your floor, but the doors lock automatically. I'll have that taken care of tomorrow, so you can come and go as you please."

"Thanks, I appreciate that."

Barton summoned the elevator. "I'm afraid this is an express elevator, so you'll have to ride downstairs to the lobby before you can go to your suite."

"I don't mind," I said.

He hesitated at the door, and then said, "Thank you for making something so painful bearable for me."

"I just hope I helped."

"More than I can tell you."

"Good night, then," I said as I walked into the elevator.

"Good night."

As I rode downstairs, I wondered how a man as wealthy as Barton Lane could be so lonely. It must be hard to have everything in the world at your disposal, and not have anyone to share any of it with. Had Cindy been that person for him? It would explain why he was taking her death so hard, and why he was so insistent that my husband find her killer. I wondered if Zach had made any progress, and as I rode down the elevator, I thought about calling him. If nothing else, he would be fascinated to hear that a multi-millionaire had made me dinner. There wouldn't be the slightest twinge of jealousy there, something I was thankful for. My husband was secure in the knowledge that I loved him with all my heart, and that there wasn't a man on the planet I'd prefer over him, regardless of how much money he had. I put my phone away instead of calling him, though. I knew when he was digging into the case, a distraction could cost him a train of thought, and it was more important now than ever that Zach focus on catching Cindy Glass's killer.

BACK IN MY SUITE, IT WAS HARD TO BELIEVE THE EXPERI-ences I'd had that day. I wanted, more than anything else, to share them all with Zach.

A flashing light on the telephone caught my eye, and I picked up and replayed my messages.

The first was from Uncle Thomas, wanting to make sure that I'd arrived back to Charlotte safely. It was amazing. I was a grown woman, and yet my uncle still worried about me. In a way, it felt good knowing that there was someone out there thinking of me beyond my husband. I didn't have a fraction of the money Barton Lane had, but I had something he coveted nonetheless. There were people in my life who loved me, and that was something I couldn't put a price tag on. I hit the pause button on the telephone, and then called Uncle Thomas.

He picked up on the first ring. Instead of a normal greeting, he asked, "Savannah?"

"It's me," I said. "I'm sorry. I should have called you when I got back. I just got wrapped up in a few things here."

"Nonsense, I know you're too old to check in. I just had a bad feeling about you, so I wanted to talk to you."

"Don't tell me you're having premonitions," I said.

"No, it's nothing like that, but I dumped that box on you, and then I felt guilty about it. I'm not sure what your mother was thinking. I'm not a big fan of messages from beyond the grave."

"I'm sure it's nothing like that."

"You haven't opened it yet?"

"No," I said as I looked at it, still sitting in its place on the coffee table. "I was planning to wait for Zach, and he's going to be tied up most of the night."

"We should have opened it together. Knowing Astrid, it's hard to tell what she put in there."

"Are there any family skeletons she could be telling me about?" I was honestly intrigued by the idea, but that didn't mean I wanted to find out anything bad about my kinfolk. The South was long known for burying its secrets instead of exposing them to the light of day, but sooner or later, they almost always came out.

"Not that I know of. The oddest thing that ever happened to us was Jeffrey taking off like he did."

"You never heard from him, did you?"

"No, but to be honest with you, I never expected to. We fought all of the time growing up, and your mom usually took his side. Looking back now, I can't remember anything significant we ever argued about. Our personalities just didn't mesh. I never really missed him, but I'm sure your mother did. I wonder."

"What?"

He paused, and then said, "I can't help speculating if Astrid knew where he was all along. No, that's nonsense. She would have told someone. I'm sure that box is nothing more than old photographs and keepsakes she wanted you to have. I don't have to tell you how sentimental your mother was."

I had boxes in storage at home with third grade book reports and macaroni artwork, so I didn't need a reminder. "No, I've got all the proof of that I ever needed."

"She had a real fascination with things, didn't she?"

"I think it was more about the memories they evoked," I said, surprising myself with the answer. The way Barton Lane had held that paperback had struck a chord with me, and I could remember my mom doing the same thing with the Christmas ornaments my grandmother had made for her.

"You're right. I never really put that together. You've grown into quite a woman, you know that, don't you?"

"Sometimes I wonder," I said.

"Well, you can stop. I'm proud of you, Savannah. I never told you that enough growing up, but I mean to do it now."

"I'm proud of you, too," I said.

That elicited a laugh. "And why is that?"

"You've endured more than your share of hardships over the years, and yet you haven't let any of it beat you down."

"Losing my Celia almost killed me," he admitted.

"But you pulled yourself through."

"With the help of family and friends and the Good Lord above." He paused, and then said, "I'll let you go, but thanks for calling me. I love you, Savannah."

"I love you, too, Uncle Thomas."

After we hung up, I nearly forgot about my other message. I hit the play button again, and was happy to hear Zach's voice.

"I don't care what time it is when you get this, or what you think I might be doing. Call me. I miss you, if you can believe that. I know it's just been a handful of hours since we saw each other, but what can I say? I'm kind of used to having you around."

I hit the save button on the phone so I could replay that sweet message whenever I wanted to. I'd been reticent to call him before, but with his blessing, I couldn't dial my husband's telephone number fast enough.

"Can you talk?" I asked after he grunted his name.

"Savannah. Hey, how are you?"

"I'm well. Are you at a stopping place?"

"Sure," he said with a sigh. "That's as nice a way as any to say I've hit a dead end."

"I didn't mean anything by it."

"Trust me, it's not you. I keep pounding my head against the wall, but all I'm getting is banged up and bruised."

"Then maybe you should stop doing that," I said with a laugh.

"Could be. How did the meeting with Barton Lane go?"

"We had dinner together after I gave him what I'd

found in Cindy's apartment, except for the skiing photograph, of course. You're not jealous, are you?"

"That depends."

"On what?"

"What did you have? I'm starving."

I laughed at his response. "You should order a sandwich."

"Yeah, I probably should before I collapse from hunger. Thinking's hard work. Hang on." After a minute, he got back on. "I sent Joe out. He's a nice enough guy, but he's not Steve."

"Any idea when your helper will be back?"

"He's supposed to pick me up tomorrow morning at the hotel, but we'll see. You know I was just teasing you about the food. I trust you with my heart and my life, Savannah." There was another pause, and then he asked, "Nothing happened, did it?"

"Of course it didn't. He made me pancakes."

"You mean he ordered them from room service," Zach said.

"No, he mixed up the batter and cooked them for me himself."

"Okay, now I'm jealous. It's one thing to order room service, but I can't imagine him waiting on you."

That was better. It was good to hear a twinge in his voice, regardless of how much I loved him.

"Relax, he's old enough to be my father."

"It's not like that hasn't happened before with rich, older men."

It was my turn to laugh. "Zachary Stone, I'm many things, but a trophy wife candidate is surely not among them."

"I don't know about that. I think you're a prize," he said.

"Right back at you. Have you had any luck so far?"

The frustration in his voice was clear as he said, "Not that you could tell. We know these murders are connected, but other than through Grady, I can't find a single common denominator between them. There has to be something else tying her to Hank Tristan's life. Grady might know of something, but we can't ask him, can we?"

"He's AWOL at the worst possible time, isn't he?"

"That's right, I didn't tell you. I found him. He says he had to get away from things, so he spent the day hiking on the parkway." The Blue Ridge Parkway was a couple of hours away, and I knew Grady liked to hike, especially the loop trail around Price Lake. It was secluded up there, and Zach and I had joined him a few times in the past.

"Is he being any nicer to you than he was before?"

"He's settled down some. He told me he's had some time to cool off, so we're getting together for breakfast. Sorry, but I'm going to have to bail out on you tomorrow."

"That's fine. I'm eating with Lorna, remember? Should we make it a double date?"

"I don't think so. Their breakup wasn't all that friendly, was it?"

"Lorna seems to be completely over it," I said. "But maybe you should tackle his honor by yourself."

"I was just thinking the same thing. Could we at least have lunch together? I miss you, Savannah."

"It's a date," I said.

I heard a commotion on the other end of the line. "Is everything okay?"

"It's nothing. Joe just got back with our sandwiches."

"That was fast."

"He went across the street, and I doubt they're very busy this time of night. It's not pancakes fresh off the griddle, but it will have to do."

"You don't mind, do you? Really."

"No, but you can't blame me for wishing it was me making pancakes for you instead of a man I haven't met."

"We'll have to fix that then, won't we? Do you have any idea when you'll be back here?"

"Not a clue. I might have to stay all night."

"Do whatever you have to," I said. "Your work is important."

"Thanks, Savannah."

I thought of something. "Zach, did you run across a woman named Samantha in your reading?"

He paused, and then said, "The name's familiar, but I can't remember where I read it."

"Could it have been in Cindy's address book?"

"How did you know that? That's exactly where it was." I could hear him leafing through something.

I read her address to him off the information I'd been given in Barton's apartment.

"That's it. Do you want to tell me how you know about her?"

"Barton said she was Cindy's closest friend. He believes that if Cindy was seeing anyone, Samantha would know about it."

"I'll talk to her tomorrow."

"Is there any chance I could go with you?"

"Why?"

"Maybe she'll be more likely to disclose facts about Cindy's love life if there's another woman there."

"Maybe."

"Maybe I'm right, or maybe I can go?"

"Maybe both," he said with a hint of laughter in his voice.

After we hung up, I got out a pad and pencil and moved to the couch. I thought it might not be a bad idea to get a jump on tomorrow's puzzle. Besides, I was too wired up from everything that had happened to get to sleep, and late night television usually bored me to tears.

After half an hour, I gave up. I believed that I woke up brilliant, and got duller with each passing moment. My puzzle would have to wait until morning.

There was something I'd put off, but I couldn't postpone it anymore.

It was time to open the box Uncle Thomas had given me from my mother. It would have been nice to have Zach there with me, but that wasn't going to happen anytime soon, and I had to face it tonight, or I wouldn't be able to sleep a wink.

I retrieved the box, moved to a seat by the windows, and, after I took one last deep breath, I opened it.

Chapter 14

###

MY HANDS WERE SHAKING AS I PULLED OUT THE FIRST item from the box my mother had left for me. It was a photograph, and I recognized my mother and father immediately, though they'd been teenagers when it had been taken. My mother was wearing blue jeans and an old flannel shirt. Her hair was pulled back into a ponytail of ash blonde hair, while my father was wearing gym shorts and an old T-shirt. His hair was long, nearly touching his shoulders. It wasn't the man I'd known growing up. Whenever his hair touched the tops of his ears, it was time for a haircut. In the photo, he had a cocky arrogance to his stance that showed me a little bit why my mother had fallen for him.

The next photograph was older still. It showed two young boys and a little girl sitting around a campfire. My grandfather was behind them, the gleam in his eye apparent even across the years. When I studied the photograph closer, I saw that it was my mother's family. Uncle Thomas was there, and eating a roasted marshmallow was my other uncle, Jeffrey. There was something about Jeffrey that looked familiar, but I couldn't see all of his face in the poor light of the fire. From what I could make out, his resemblance was stronger to my grandmother, who sat quietly beside him. Uncle Thomas and Mom were more like their father. I kept staring at my unknown uncle, wondering where he was right now, or even if he was still alive.

Setting it aside for a moment, I removed the next item. It was a heart-shaped locket, and I wondered if my mother had received it from my dad. It took a few seconds to get the locket open, and I was surprised to find another man's picture inside, clearly not my dad. Why had she kept it all those years, and more importantly, why was she handing it down to me? He didn't look at all familiar, and I didn't have a clue how I might find out who he was. And then I realized that I'd just spent the day with my best chance of knowing. I'd have to go back and see Uncle Thomas to ask him if the man looked familiar to him. If he didn't know, I wasn't sure how I was ever going to find out.

After the photographs, there was a stack of letters, all neatly tied together with a faded red ribbon. I opened the first one, and saw that it was a love letter from my father to my mother. It just took a few sentences for me to feel like some kind of voyeur, even though Mom had supplied them to me herself. I folded the letter back up and slipped it into its envelope. I wasn't sure if I'd ever read them, but somehow, it felt good possessing a piece of my past before I even existed.

Beneath the letters, I was getting to the bottom of the box. I wasn't sure what I'd find, but a safety deposit box key was the last thing I imagined.

Even more startling was the note that it was taped to.

Savannah, if you're reading this, I'm not around anymore. I didn't know what to do with the contents of this safety deposit box, so I'm dumping it in your lap. I shouldn't do it, I know that, but I plan to deal with it someday and hopefully you'll never have to see this letter, or what I've hidden from you.

I just can't deal with it today.

If you are reading this letter, I hope you are well. I often regretted not having more children so you'd have someone in your life once your father and I were gone, but I was thrilled to have you. In many ways, you were my greatest achievement, my legacy, my bid for immortality.

Don't think badly of me when you open the box.

I didn't know what else to do.

I hope you do.

Forgive me. I love you.

Mom

I picked up the telephone and dialed my uncle's number, even though I knew that it was past his bedtime.

"Hello?" he answered after several rings.

"Uncle Thomas, it's Savannah."

I could hear the weariness in his voice. "I was hoping you'd call. Just not this late."

"Sorry, but it couldn't wait. Do you know anything about a safety deposit box my mother had?"

There was a long pause, so I asked, "Uncle Thomas? Are you still there? I need you to wake up. This is important."

"I'm awake, trust me. I honestly never put the two things together."

"What are you talking about?"

"I got a notice last year that a safety deposit box at the old Southern National Bank in your mother's name had lapsed, and I was named as the other signatory. They asked me if I wanted to renew it, or collect the contents of the box. I went to the bank, and I paid fifty dollars to have them drill it, since I had no idea where the key was. When they got it opened, they put me in a room by myself, and I opened it. Inside was another box, with a note to me."

"What did it say?"

"That I was supposed to hold it for you until you asked me about it, and not turn it over until then. I wanted to give it to you right away, but I didn't want to break my word to your mother, either."

"So you've still got it."

"Not anymore."

I felt my spirit sink. "What happened to it?"

"When I went to get the first box, I slipped out to your car and put the second one in the backseat under an old blanket. I kept trying to tell you about it, but your mother's note haunted me. I didn't know what to do."

"So, I've got it? What's inside?"

"I didn't look in either box," he said. "They were both for you."

"You shouldn't have sneaked it into my car," I said.

"Darlin', the list of things I shouldn't have done would fill up a notebook the size of Texas. If I wronged you or your mother, I'm sorry, and that's the truth."

"You did the right thing. I just wish you would have told me about it sooner."

"I'm truly sorry."

"You're forgiven," I said. "Now if you'll excuse me, I've got another box to open."

"At least you won't have to come back here and go to the bank."

"I'll call you tomorrow and tell you what I found."

"You don't have to do that," he said. "I lost that right."

"Not on your life."

He sighed. "Then call me tonight."

"No matter how late it is?"

"Not even if it takes an hour."

I hung up and grabbed my car keys.

I was panting as I reached the car, and my hands shook as I retrieved the box. A part of me had worried that someone might have taken it since I'd arrived back in Charlotte, but it was still where my uncle had put it.

I thought about opening it right there, but though the parking garage was well lit, it still didn't feel very secure. Tucking it under my arm, I headed back upstairs to see what was so important that my mother had locked it away from the world.

Back in my suite, my hands were shaking as I opened the box.

Inside were stacks of hundred-dollar bills.

My mouth fell open as I counted them, and I was shocked when I realized there were a hundred of them.

My mother had stuffed ten thousand dollars in a safety deposit box, and she'd asked me for her forgiveness when she dumped it into my lap.

Beneath the money was a brief handwritten note.

And as I read it, I was more shocked than I'd been when I'd found the cash.

Astrid,

I shouldn't have left you, or the family. More importantly, I never should have taken the money.

I hope you can find it in your heart to forgive this fool.

Use this money to buy yourself a little happiness.
You deserve it.

J.B.

J.B. had to be my uncle. After all, the note said as much, didn't it? But why hadn't she spent the money? Had she held a grudge that long over my uncle's desertion of her and their family?

I was more confused than ever, and I thought about calling Zach, but the man I really wanted to speak with was my uncle.

"Good, you're still awake," I said when Uncle Thomas answered his telephone.

"Are you kidding? I've been dying to find out what I've been holding onto the last two years."

"Would you believe ten grand in hundred-dollar bills?"

"Not likely. What was inside?"

"Ten grand in hundred-dollar bills," I said.

There was a pause, and then my uncle said, "You're not kidding, are you? What was she doing with that kind of cash?"

"You didn't get a packet of money yourself, did you?"

"Not hardly," he said. "Why, should I have?"

"That's not up to me to say. From what I can tell, your brother sent Mom that money and asked for her forgiveness."

I hated to tell my uncle that his brother hadn't cared all that much for him, but it was pretty clear he wasn't surprised by the news.

"That makes sense," he said. "They were always close."

"What am I going to do with all of this money?"

"What did the note say?" he asked.

"It told her to spend it on something that would bring her some happiness."

"Then that's what you should do," Uncle Thomas said.

"If she couldn't bring herself to do it, why should I?"

"Savannah, I don't have to tell you what a complicated woman your mother was. I'm sure she had her reasons. If you're not comfortable spending it, maybe you could donate it to your favorite charity."

"Maybe. I honestly don't have a clue what I'm going to do with it."

"Then put it in the hotel safe until you do," he said. "You can't just leave that kind of money lying around."

"You're right about that. I'm sorry I called you so late."

"No, I wouldn't have been able to sleep anyway." He paused, then asked, "Did J.B. say anything else?"

"That's strange. I always heard everyone refer to him as Jeffrey," I said. "And yet the note was signed J.B."

"My brother always was an odd bird. Sometimes he went by his first name, and sometimes he would only answer to his middle name, but most of the time, among the family, he was just plain J.B." Uncle Thomas stifled a yawn, and then he said, "I'm going to be up in a few hours, so I should probably try to get a little rest. Thanks for calling me back."

On an impulse, I asked him, "Uncle Thomas, do you want the money?"

He seemed shocked by the question. "Of course not. It's not mine."

"It doesn't belong to me, either," I said.

"According to your mother it does. You inherited everything she had when she and your father died, right?"

"Right."

"Then that money, and any problem she had with it, is yours now."

"Gee, thanks for the support," I said with a laugh.

"If your worst problem today is figuring out what to do with ten grand, I wouldn't mind trading with you. Good night."

After we hung up, I called the front desk and was surprised to hear Garrett answer. "Don't you ever go home?"

"Tonight I've been catching up on paperwork. How may I assist you?"

"I've got some cash I need you to keep for me in your safe."

"I'll send someone right up," he said.

"I hate to ask, but could you come here yourself? It's not that I don't trust your employees, but if it's not too much trouble, I'd rather deal directly with you."

"Say no more. I'll be there in two minutes."

He was as good as his word, and within ninety seconds, there was a discreet tap at my door.

I asked him to identify himself, and after he did, I opened the door for him. "Thanks for doing this."

"It's my pleasure. You have some cash you wish to keep with us? There's a safe in your suite, you know."

I'd considered the idea, but then I'd rejected it. It wasn't that I didn't trust it. I would just feel better having it out of easy reach, in case I got tempted before I figured out what I was going to do with it.

"I'd rather you take it," I said.

He nodded, and I handed him the stack. Garrett counted out the bills, wrote me a receipt, and then put the cash in an attaché he'd brought with him.

"You have access to this around the clock," he said. "Is there anything else you need?"

"Not tonight."

"Then I'll bid you a good evening," he said.

After he was gone, I felt better not having the cash with me. There was something about my mother's note, and her reluctance to spend the money, that made me glad I didn't have it in my hands.

I was going to have to tell Zach, though.

But not tonight.

He was still working, and I was so exhausted, I could barely keep my eyes open.

Tomorrow would be soon enough to tell Zach what I'd found. Knowing my husband, I was certain his instincts would help guide me, but ultimately, the decisions were mine to make.

* * *

I WOKE UP TO A NOISE IN THE OTHER ROOM. MY FIRST IN-stinct was that it was Zach, but the bed beside me was empty. I doubted it was the cleaning crew; they never came in unless they had my verbal approval.

I looked frantically around the room for some kind of weapon, but the closest thing I could find was a table lamp. I quietly unplugged it, pulled off the shade, and opened the bedroom door.

There was no one there, but then I heard someone moving around in the bathroom down the hall. It was a large suite, and Zach and I had just used the bathroom that was connected to the master bedroom.

I should have called the front desk—I realized that later—but at the moment, I was experiencing a surge in adrenaline. I crept up to the door, and then shouted, "I've called the police. Stay right where you are."

Against my orders, the door opened, and I saw Zach peek out. I hadn't even realized that I'd raised the lamp in the air and pulled it back, ready to strike.

"Thanks, but the light's fine in here," he said as he pointed to the lamp in my hands, still poised to strike. His hair was wet, and he was wearing one of the hotel's luxury robes.

"You nit. Why didn't you use the master bath?"

"I didn't want to wake you, if you can believe that." He gestured to the lamp, which was now on the table. "Did you really call the police?"

"No, I didn't," I admitted. "But I was going to."

"Savannah, if you thought there was a prowler in here,

you should have locked yourself in the bedroom and called the cops, or at least hotel security."

"I panicked, okay?"

"Fine, but learn from it. If it happens again, don't try to handle it yourself."

"You would have," I said a little petulantly. "I don't always need a big, strong man around to protect me."

"In the first place, I was a cop for a lot of years. In the second place, I'm armed. And in the third place, if I weren't either one of those things, I would have done the exact same thing."

"As I did?" I asked, hopefully.

"No, that was just nuts. I would have stayed in the bedroom and called someone for backup."

"I don't believe you."

He smiled broadly at me. "Well, shame on you, then."

"When did you get in?" I asked my husband as I followed him into the master bedroom.

"Ten minutes ago."

"Did you get any sleep at all last night?"

"There's a great couch in Davis's office," he said with a grin as he got dressed. "I crashed there for about three hours."

"That's not much sleep."

"I've gotten less in the past when I was working on a case, and we both know it." He slipped on his shoes, completing his outfit. "I'm starving. Any chance you can have breakfast with me?"

"Sure. Let me make a phone call first."

"Hang on a second. You're meeting Lorna downstairs, aren't you?"

I nodded. "I was, but I can cancel it. I'd much rather eat with you."

"You canceled yesterday, didn't you?"

"Yes, but it wasn't exactly in concrete."

He shook his head. "I won't ask you to do it on my account. Tell you what. Why don't I order a huge breakfast from room service, and you can keep me company. I want to hear about your day yesterday. Do we have time?"

I looked at the clock and saw that I had forty minutes before I was due downstairs. "We should be fine."

He grinned. "Then I'll place my order."

After he got off the phone, I asked, "You did hear that I wasn't eating with you, right?"

"I heard, but if I know you, you'll graze anyway, and I wanted to be sure I'd have enough to eat."

We walked out into the living room and took our usual seats by the windows. The city was overcast today, and rain tapped at the windows. It wasn't a perfect postcard filled with sunshine, but it was still beautiful. There were days when I enjoyed a good gloomy overcast sky, and today was going to be one of them.

"How's Thomas?" Zach asked.

"Confusing," I said.

"That's an interesting answer. What happened?"

"He gave me a box from my mother that he's been holding onto since she died."

"Why's he giving it to you now?" Zach asked, the investigator's stare in his eyes.

"He was supposed to wait longer, but I think something shook him up, and he wanted to get rid of it."

"Did you look inside yet?"

"I checked it last night. There were some photographs,

some old love letters from my dad, and a key to a safety deposit box. That's not all. There was a note with it, too."

I got the box from the end table, opened it, and handed him the note from my mother.

The second he finished reading it, he stood and said, "What's Lorna's phone number?"

"Why?"

"I'm canceling your breakfast and we're driving to Hickory."

"There's no need to."

"Savannah, I don't know how you even slept after reading that note. What's inside the box? Why didn't Tom tell you about it sooner? It raises a lot of questions, doesn't it?"

"Sit down," I said. "I've got the contents of the safety deposit box, too."

"You didn't mention that your uncle gave that to you, as well."

"I didn't know it the last time we talked. He had to clean the safety deposit box out, but all he found was another box. Uncle Thomas hid it in the backseat of the car while I was there yesterday. He wanted me to have it, but I don't think he knew how to tell me."

"So? Don't keep me in suspense. What was this great secret your mother was keeping from the world?"

"There was ten thousand dollars in the box, all in hundreds, and a note from my uncle."

"Why would Tom give your mother that kind of money?"

"Not that uncle. The other one."

"Jeffrey? I thought he was lost forever."

"Evidently he contacted my mother, and he wrote her a note along with the cash. This is it."

I handed him the second note.

After he read it, he said, "No wonder you were jumpy when you heard me in the bathroom. Having ten grand in your room will make you paranoid if anything will."

"It's not here. I put it in the hotel's main safe downstairs as soon as I knew what I had."

"That's smart thinking," he said. Zach tapped the second note. "That answers at least some of my questions."

"I don't see how. Why didn't my mother spend the money? Why did she leave it to me? And why did she ask for my forgiveness?"

"It's obvious, isn't it?" Zach said as there was a knock on the door.

After the bellman identified himself, Zach let him in. He directed that the cart be set up by the window, and as soon as the worker was gone, he started lifting lids.

"This looks great. You can have a bite or two, but most of it is mine."

I moved between him and his food, a dangerous maneuver even when my husband wasn't starving. "You don't get a bite until you explain what you just meant."

"What are you talking about?" he asked as he looked at the food.

"You said it answered questions, but all I can see are more things I don't understand."

He held up his index finger. "Think about it, Savannah. Your mother didn't forgive her brother. She didn't even get back in contact with him, and she felt bad about cutting you off from your family."

"How do you know that?"

"The money was still there, so she didn't forgive him. If she had, there was no way Astrid wouldn't spend it. Your mom knew how you felt about your Uncle Thomas. Do you honestly think she didn't agonize over keeping Jeffrey out of your life? She had to be really conflicted by all of it, and lastly, she dumped it all in your lap."

"She didn't want me to contact J.B., did she?"

Zach smiled. "You noticed that the envelope with a return address wasn't with the letter, didn't you? I'll make a detective out of you yet." His stomach grumbled as he looked at the food. "Can I eat now?"

"Go on. Sorry, I didn't mean to get in your way."

"Feel free to join me," he said as he dug in. I was tempted; it looked awfully good, but if I ate a big meal now, I would never be able to have breakfast again in fifteen minutes with Lorna.

"Maybe I'll have one cinnamon stick," I said, taking one from his plate and dunking it in maple syrup.

"They're great, aren't they?"

After I ate one, I was debating about grabbing another when I asked Zach, "What do you think I should do?"

"I definitely think you should stop eating those cinnamon sticks. You wouldn't want to spoil your appetite."

"You saw me eyeing them?"

"Hey, I'm a trained detective. Not much gets past me."

"Well, I wasn't talking about the food," I said. "I mean the money."

"Beats me," he said after a moment's thought.

"You're a lot of help."

"This has to be your decision. You can't really contact your uncle, since you still don't know where he is. Unless Tom knows. Have you asked him?"

"He denies having any contact with his brother since the day he walked out."

"Could he be lying?"

I was surprised to hear my husband ask that about Uncle Thomas. "Why would he possibly do that?"

"Think about it. If he was trying to protect you, I can see it, can't you? After all, those boxes have been in his hands for a while, but you're just getting them now, aren't you?"

"I'm sure he had his reasons."

"Okay, let's say he has no more idea than you do about how to find Jeffrey. That means you couldn't return the money, even if you wanted to. The way I see it, you have three options."

"Go on, I'm listening."

"You can keep it, spend it, or give it away. If you choose the last option, I'd be more than willing to take it off your hands."

I grinned at him. "Thanks for that generous offer."

"Hey, you know me. I'm all heart." Zach glanced at his watch. "I'm not trying to get rid of you, but aren't you going to be late for your breakfast appointment?"

"I've got another minute. I didn't mean to take up all of our time together this morning. Have you made any more progress on the case?"

He finished another bite. "Not ready to talk about it yet," he said, and then polished off the last cinnamon stick. At least he'd removed the temptation from me. "Maybe by lunch."

I looked at the ruins of what was left of his breakfast. "Seriously? Do you honestly think you're going to be able to eat again today?"

"Hey, thinking's hard work. You know that better than most folks do."

It was true. Though making puzzles didn't seem like hard work, creating them often left me tired and hungry, and not necessarily in that order.

"Lunch it is. Where would you like to go?"

"Give me a call, and we'll see what we can work out. In the meantime, you'd better scat."

"I'm going," I said as I kissed him, and then smacked my lips. "Um, maple syrup."

"No extra charge," he said with a grin.

I left him, and headed down the elevator. By the time I arrived at the lobby, I was feeling good about my life.

And then a woman moved directly in front of me as I stepped off, staring at me like she wanted to kill me.

Chapter 15

...

"**Y**OU'RE SAVANNAH STONE," SHE SAID. THERE WAS NO question in her inflection.

"Guilty as charged," I said. "Is there something I can help you with?" I was surreptitiously looking around the lobby, trying to spot Garrett or one of his security guards. I knew I probably should have denied who I really was, but she'd caught me with my guard down.

"You can tell your husband to find out who killed my brother," she said. The woman was about my age, but she'd done nothing to make herself anything other than severe, both in clothing and expression. She was bone-thin, as if she had lost all interest in eating, and her graying blonde hair looked dry and brittle, like withered hay. Almost as an afterthought, she added, "Don't trouble yourself finding security. I've said what I needed to say, and I never had any intention of harming you."

She started to leave, but I grabbed her arm before she could get away. "Hang on a second."

She started to pull away, but I wasn't about to let go yet. "I'm finished here. I said what needed to be said."

"That's all well and good, but I haven't had a chance to talk yet. Now, why don't we try this again?"

She looked perplexed as I released her arm, and then I held out my hand. "My name's Savannah Stone. And you are?"

Almost without conscious effort, she took my hand as she said, "I'm Julia Tristan."

"I'm pleased to meet you, Julia. Let me start by saying that I'm sorry for your loss."

She looked at me a moment, and then the poor woman started to cry. We were getting the attention of some of the staff now, as well as a few of the hotel's guests.

I didn't care. I put my arms around her, and then let Julia cry herself out. In three minutes, she pulled away from me, wiping her cheeks and eyes with an old linen handkerchief.

"Feel better?" I asked her.

"Much. Thank you. You're the first person I've spoken with since Hank was murdered who actually seems to care."

"That's because you haven't met my husband yet. He's the reason I know so much about your brother. Zach tries to get to know the subjects of his investigation." I'd almost said "victims," but I'd caught myself just in time. I didn't want to be responsible for another crying jag.

"If he's anything like you, I believe you. Please, tell him that I'm counting on his help."

"Is there anything else you'd like me to pass on to him?"

"No, not that I can think of," she said. "I spoke with an officer earlier, but he barely seemed to pay attention to my answers. What else does your husband need to know?"

"I was wondering if there was anyone in particular that your brother was close to before he died."

"Was murdered, you mean." Her words were as strong as black coffee.

"Murdered," I corrected.

She nodded, and appeared to be pleased by my acquiescence. "The first person I'd look at would be the mayor, unless your husband is intimidated by him like everyone else in this town seems to be."

"He's aware of their confrontation," I said. "Anyone else?"

"How about the new chief of police?" Julia asked as she looked around the lobby. I wasn't sure if she was looking for police officers, or just random spies, but the action made me wonder if she was a little bit unhinged.

"What did Davis Rawles have to do with your brother?"

She looked at me carefully. "Do you know him? Of course you do. Your husband chose him as his replacement."

"My husband had nothing to do with that," I said, though that wasn't strictly true. He'd made a recommendation, and it had to have carried some weight, but the ultimate decision hadn't been his. "Trust me, my husband isn't influenced by his friendships. If anything, he's harder on people he knows than he is on perfect strangers. Why did you bring up Davis's name?"

"He and my brother went in together on a little business venture, and when it failed, Davis threatened to kill him. Is that motive enough?"

"What happened?"

"Davis and Hank bought some land in the mountains together on the speculation that a resort would be built nearby. Hank had his hands in a lot of different businesses. He wasn't just a land speculator, but no one really knew every one of his sources of income. When the parent company dropped out on the development deal, they both lost a sizeable amount of money. Evidently it was bigger for the police chief than it was for Hank."

"I didn't know that," I said.

"Does your husband?"

"If he doesn't yet, he will soon, and that's a promise," I said. "Any other names I should add to the list?"

"There were a few other officers who were minor investors, but I don't know their names."

"Tell you what. Find out, and then leave me a message at the front desk. I'll tell my husband as soon as you tell me. Anyone else?"

She frowned, bit her lip, and then said, "I've gone over that night a thousand times in my mind, and the only other reason I can think that someone would want to kill my brother was that dance. Every woman he danced with should be interviewed, along with their significant others."

"I know for a fact that my husband is going painstakingly through the files, and he's reading the police interviews right now."

Julia was about to say something else when I saw her face go cold. "What just happened?"

"She was one of them," Julia whispered, and then quickly dashed away.

I turned to see who the mystery woman was, and was startled to see Lorna heading toward me.

* * *

"**W**HO WAS THAT, SAVANNAH? SHE LOOKED AS THOUGH she'd just seen a ghost when I walked up."

"To be honest with you, I just ran into her. I can't think of her name right off the top of my head." I was lying, but I didn't really want Lorna to know what Julia Tristan had just told me. "I'm sorry, I know I'm late."

"That's fine," she said, apparently dismissing Julia from her mind. "Are we still having breakfast?"

"You know it," I said. "Let's go. I'm starving."

While not technically true, I *was* hungry. In particular, I was going to order cinnamon sticks. I hadn't been able to forget the sample I'd gotten of Zach's, and now I wanted some for myself.

After we placed our orders, she asked, "How was Hickory?"

"It was good. I love catching up with my uncle."

"Family's important. Speaking of that, have you been seeing much of your husband lately? I imagine the investigation's keeping him pretty busy."

"We spend some time together every day," I said. "Maybe not as much as I'd like to, but that's the way it goes when he's working."

"Has he made any progress?"

"He has some ideas," I said, not really wanting to get into it with her.

"Any suspects yet?"

"Lorna, I really don't feel comfortable discussing it." I looked around the dining room, but no one seemed to be paying any attention to us. "Why are you so interested, anyway?"

"I knew one of the victims, remember? It's so creepy. One minute we were dancing together, and the next minute he was dead."

"It wasn't a matter of minutes," I corrected her. "It was more like hours."

"Still, it makes you think."

"Yes, I suppose it does."

Our food arrived, and as we started eating, Lorna said, "I've got something for you, but I forgot to bring it."

"What is it?"

She smiled at me. "It's a surprise, actually. Can I drop it off at the hotel tonight?"

"I'm not really sure what our plans are, but you can leave it at the front desk."

"No, I'd rather deliver it to you in person. How about tomorrow at breakfast?"

"I'll have to see. I might not know if I'm free until the last minute."

She smiled. "Taking another trip to Hickory?"

"I'm not planning to, but you never know. If you don't mind taking a chance that I won't make it, we can pencil tomorrow in."

"That's all I can ask." She laughed gently, and then added, "Trust me, my date book isn't exactly full these days."

"Aren't you seeing anyone special?"

"That depends on your definition. They're all special, aren't they?" she said with a smile.

"I don't know how you do it. I can't keep up with the one man I've got, let alone deal with a string of them."

"Practice, practice, practice," she said.

After we were finished eating, I said, "I hate to eat and run, but my dance card's pretty full today."

"I'm just glad we had a chance to get together," Lorna said as we started to walk out of the restaurant.

"Me, too."

"Until tomorrow."

"Maybe," I said.

"That's good enough for me." Lorna could be demanding in her friendship; I knew that from past experience.

Back in the lobby, I looked around for Julia Tristan, just in case she'd lingered, but the woman was gone. I needed to talk to Zach about her, and it couldn't wait until lunch.

The second I was back upstairs in our suite, I dialed his number.

To my surprise, his assistant Steve answered.

"May I speak with Zach?"

In a lowered voice, he said, "Sorry, but he can't be disturbed."

"Is he sitting in a corner, staring at the junction where the walls meet? Are his feet up on something? His hands are locked behind his head, aren't they?"

Steve sounded agitated when he answered. "How could you possibly know that? Were you just here?"

"No, but I've seen it often enough. He's got a thread he's following in his head, and you could set off an M-80 under his chair and I doubt he'd notice it."

"You two are something, have I told you that?"

"You did. When he comes out of his trance, have him call me, okay?"

"Will do."

After we hung up, I paced around the room. I had a lot to talk to Zach about, but it would be less than productive doing it while he was on a track of his own. I knew better than to try to break through to him when he was that deep in thought. It would just have to wait, and I was going to have to deal with it.

In the meantime, I had a puzzle to create, and not an easy one, either.

I STARTED PLAYING WITH IDEAS FOR MY NEXT PUZZLE, RE-membering that I'd promised Derrick something more complicated than I'd been doing lately. I hadn't promised him anything much more difficult though, so I decided to do a sequencing puzzle this time.

After an hour and a half of erasing pairings and changing the numbers, I finally had a puzzle I was happy with.

Now I just had to write the snippet, and I'd have Derrick off my back for another day.

Puzzles are like people. Some are easy to figure out the second you see them, while others are more complicated from the start. But over time, I've found the most interesting people, as well as puzzles, appear to be simple initially, but are in fact much more complex once you get below the surface.

I read it again, and still wasn't exactly sure what I'd meant by it. Some snippets were like that, coming to my conscious mind unbidden, as if I were channeling them as I typed, if I believed in that kind of thing. Though the horoscopes appeared close to my puzzles in many of the newspapers that carried them, the two were worlds apart. My puzzles were based on logic, and used the ability to take a limited amount of information to solve a conundrum. However horoscopes were inspired by the authors and how they perceived the stars and planets, I was pretty sure that even they would agree they weren't based on my particular brand of mathematical reasoning.

I checked the puzzle again, solving it myself, and thought it was okay. Not great, but good enough. And until things settled back down in my life, that was going to have to suffice.

I WAS IN THE CAR ON MY WAY TO MEET ZACH FOR LUNCH when my cell phone rang. I fumbled for it in my purse, and said, "Hello?"

"Is this a bad time?" Sherry asked.

"Are you kidding? It's never a bad time to talk to you." I was just starting to realize that what I'd missed most about Charlotte were not the beautiful architecture or the advantages to the big city like restaurants and culture, but the people I'd known there.

And my former neighbor was at the top of the list.

"I don't want to interrupt any deep puzzle thoughts," she said.

"I just finished it and faxed it to my editor."

"Good. You made quite an impression on your visit back."

"Don't I always? You make it sound as if it's hit or miss."

"I'm not talking about me, you goof. I mean Betsy. She

keeps gabbing on and on about what a thrill it was to meet you. I've got to be honest with you. If I didn't love you already, I'd be sick of the sound of your name." I could hear the smile in her voice as she said it.

"What can I say? I may have just three fans, but they're all very vocal about it."

"You've got more than that, and you know it."

I pulled into the police station parking lot and shut off the engine. "Is that why you were calling, or was there something else on your mind?"

"I don't know what your schedule's like, but could you swing by the house tomorrow after the kids go to school? They only have four more days, and then they're with me all summer."

"You love it, and you know it."

"I do," she admitted, "but when my free time is winding down, I try to jam as much living into it as I can. What do you say? Will you throw your old friend a life preserver?"

"Absolutely. Hey, if you'd like, we could have breakfast in the hotel restaurant. You can order anything on the menu."

I was about to tell her about my open tab when she interrupted. "I was thinking more along the lines of eggs and toast at my kitchen table. That's not too mundane for you these days, is it?"

"Are you kidding? It sounds like paradise."

"Great. I'll see you around eight."

"Let me guess. The kids are gone by seven fifty-five."

She laughed, and I enjoyed the warmth of it for a moment. "You got me. See you tomorrow."

"Till then."

I got out of the car and headed toward the front entrance. I suddenly realized that I needed to call Lorna and cancel our breakfast date tomorrow. I was just punching her phone number in when I ran into Davis on the steps outside.

"Hey, Chief," I said as I killed the phone call.

"I still can't get used to being called that," he admitted.

"Don't worry; you'll get used to it. Is Zach upstairs?"

Davis shrugged. "I have no idea. I've been barred from the task force room, if you can believe that. In my own building!"

"It shouldn't come as some kind of big surprise. You know how Zach works."

"I realize that the man likes his privacy, but Steve Sanders comes and goes as he pleases."

"Don't be so sure about that," I said as I tucked my phone back into my purse. "Zach's the only one with a key. If he's not there, Steve has to wait outside the door in the hallway like everyone else."

That made Davis smile, so I had to ask, "What's so amusing about that?"

After a moment's hesitation, the police chief said, "You know he was expecting to get my job, don't you?"

"I heard he was being considered for it," I admitted.

"Well, he jumped the gun and started making promises he couldn't keep. When he lost out to me, he made a lot of people mad at him around here. To be honest with you, I was kind of surprised when Zach chose him to help out on this case."

"That's not the way it happened at all. Steve volunteered, and I think Zach didn't have the heart to say no."

Davis nodded. "That makes more sense." He paused a moment, and then asked, "So, tell me. What exactly is going on up there? You've got more access to the investigation than I do."

"He's still collecting information," I said.

"I heard he's left the building a few times. Any idea about exactly where he went?"

What was going on here? Even if I knew, I wasn't about to tell anyone what my husband was doing in his investigation, even if it was his boss asking the questions. "You'd need to ask him that. I'm just a simple puzzle maker."

"We both know better than that, Savannah." His phone went off as he was getting ready to tell me something else, and after a moment of whispering, he said, "Sorry, I've got to take this. I'll catch up with you later."

"See you," I said.

I walked upstairs and found my husband still in his corner, with his feet propped up and a blank stare on his face. I tried to back out of the door silently, but my elbow hit it and rattled it in its frame.

That brought him out of his thought process.

"Sorry," I said.

"Don't be. I was just about finished anyway."

"I hope that's true, and that I didn't wreck anything for you." I looked around the room. "Where's your minion?"

"I didn't need him today, so I sent him back to the squad room."

"I bet he wasn't too happy about that."

"No, not so much. How did you know that?"

I put my purse down on one of the tables. "I just had a chat with your boss."

"Funny, I thought that was your title," he said with a grin.

"No matter how hard I wish it, it still hasn't come true," I replied with a smile of my own.

"If it's not you, then I assume you were chatting with Davis. What did he have to say?"

"It's funny, but if I didn't know better, I would think he was grilling me for information about your investigation."

Zach shook his head, and his smile was replaced with a scowl. "He shouldn't have done that. When I wouldn't tell him, he came to you."

"Well, it's a cinch he didn't go to Steve."

Zach looked intently at me. "What do you mean by that?"

"There's more bad blood between them than I realized. I've got the feeling that neither man likes the other, regardless of what they might say."

"Not all personalities get along."

"It goes deeper than that," I said.

"Woman's intuition?"

"No, keen observation skills honed over the years."

"Isn't it the same thing?" Zach asked.

"Maybe," I admitted. "Are you at a place you can get away for lunch?"

"Honestly, I can be gone longer than that. I've squeezed about all I can out of this information. It's time to do some fieldwork."

"All right. Now you're talking. Before you decide the order we interrogate suspects in, there's new information you need to know."

"Slow down, Savannah. I never said you'd be a part of the active investigation."

"Zach, I know a lot of the players, and some of these people won't talk to you if it's a part of your investigation. Trust me, we'll get more out of them if I'm there with you."

"And why do you say that?"

"Look at me. Am I the least bit intimidating?"

"Are you kidding me? I'd rather face an angry mob than take you on sometimes."

I touched his arm lightly. "Thanks, I appreciate that, but these people don't know me. You're this big and dark bruiser of a man, and sometimes when you ask questions, it's like you've got a hammer behind your back. Me, I overwhelm them with softness, and then I move in for the kill."

"Maybe. But even if it's true, I'm not about to put your life in danger."

"I was the one the killer took a photograph of, remember? Don't you think it's safe to say that I'm already in a little bit of trouble here? Why not take advantage of my offer?"

He paused for a second, and then said, "Okay. You're right."

I nearly questioned what I was hearing, but I knew if I got cute at that moment, I'd lose the tiny foothold I'd worked so hard to attain. "I appreciate that."

"No gloating? No celebratory dance?"

"No, sir. Just my thanks."

He whistled softly under his breath.

"What?" I asked.

"Just when I think I have the game figured out, you change the playing field on me."

I shrugged. "What can I say? I like to keep things interesting. Now come on; let's go eat."

"I know better than to try to argue with you." He smiled, and then added, "Besides, I'm hungry, too."

"Then what are we waiting for?"

Chapter 16

...

"I'VE MISSED THIS," I SAID AS I TOOK ANOTHER BITE OF heavenly pizza.

"There are things to be said for civilization," Zach agreed as he tackled another slice. There was no way we were going to be able to eat the whole thing, but we were going to give it our best shot.

We were eating at our all-time favorite pizza haunt in Charlotte, Luigi's on South Tryon near Whitehall on the Southside of town. Try as we had, we had found nothing in our new hometown that even came close to their particular take on New York–style pizza.

After we were finished eating, we grabbed refills of our drinks and decided to discuss the case out in our car. The pizzeria was jammed, as it should be, given the great food they served, and Zach didn't want anyone to overhear our conversation.

"Oh, man, I need a nap," Zach said as we walked back to our car.

"We could always head back to the hotel for an hour, if you wanted."

"I'd love to, but we both know that's not going to happen. Tell me more about Julia Tristan."

I'd started to tell him what Hank's sister had told me, but he'd asked me to wait until we could discuss it without anyone overhearing us.

"Well, the first thing she did was break down and cry," I admitted. "I told her I was sorry for her loss, and that made her fall apart. It appears that no one else has offered her any sympathy for losing her brother."

"What else did she say?"

I bit my lower lip, and then I began to tell him what I'd heard. "She has Grady at the top of her suspect list after the fight they had."

"No surprise, there. A great many people saw that fight. Did she have anything else?"

I'd hesitated telling him about his friend, but I really had no choice. "She said that Davis and Hank were business partners in a land speculation deal that went bad. Evidently Davis lost a lot of money, a great deal more than he could afford to lose. Did you know about that?"

"No, this is the first I'm hearing about it."

"What are you going to do? Julia thinks Davis and Grady aren't going to be investigated, because of who they are."

"We both know better than that. I hope that's what you told her."

"Oh, yes, I assured her that no one was going to get a free pass on this. Is it true?"

"About Davis? It could be. He was always looking for ways to double his money. I can see him going into business with Hank. He had a reputation for turning things into gold with every venture he became involved with."

"So, you'll talk to him?"

"I'll talk to him," Zach said as he added a few notes to the book he always carried with him, whether he was on a case or not. I knew that once a note went in there, it would be explored from all angles until Zach was satisfied with the answer enough to strike it out. It might have seemed arcane to people used to BlackBerries, cell phones, and laptop computers, but it worked for him, and I wasn't about to suggest he change. He'd been too successful in the past for that to happen.

"Who else did she bring up?"

"The women at the ball, as well as their dates. She thinks there's a chance that Hank stepped on somebody's toes when he danced with every willing female at the party."

"Anybody in particular?" Zach asked.

"You should have seen Julia's face when Lorna walked toward us. It was as though she'd seen a ghost."

"Did she say anything?"

"Something like, 'She was one of them,' I think. She took off before Lorna had a chance to get to us."

Zach nodded, and then made another note in his book.

"Seriously? You're putting Lorna's name down in your Suspect column?"

"Savannah, she was there that night, and she danced with Hank."

"From what I've heard, Hank danced with a lot of women."

"She also used to date Grady. That ties her to one suspect and one victim. I'd be a fool not to put her name down just because she's a friend of yours."

"She's not that good of a friend," I said, "but I still don't think she's a killer."

"You know as well as I do that most killers don't seem like the type."

Zach put the car in gear, and I noticed that we were heading in the opposite direction of the police station. "Aren't you going to go talk to Davis?"

"I can find the chief of police whenever I need to," Zach said.

"You couldn't yesterday," I pointed out.

"That's true, but we've got a better chance of knowing where he is than where Samantha Riggins might be. I want to focus on Cindy Glass's murder for the moment."

"But you're not going to forget about Hank Tristan, are you?"

"There's not a chance in the world of that happening. We'll deal with Davis after we've had an opportunity to talk with Samantha. I just hope she's home."

"If she's not, you'll be able to track her down. I have faith in you."

"It's nice that at least one of us does," he said.

"Come on, you know you're good at what you do without me telling you."

"I have my moments, but this case has more twists and turns than a mountain highway. I'm not afraid to interview my suspects just because they have power in this town, but the chances are good that I'm going to alienate at least one of my friends before this is over, and I don't have that many to spare."

I rubbed his shoulder. "No matter what, I know I can trust you to do the right thing."

"You bet you can," he said, adding a small smile.

We pulled up in front of an apartment complex in the South End, and I asked, "Are we here already?"

"What can I say? Time flies when we're together. Besides, that was one of the reasons I wanted to go to Luigi's. It's not that far from Samantha Riggins's place."

"But not the only reason," I said.

"Not by a long shot. Lunch was so good, we might have to head back there tomorrow."

"I'm game if you are," I said.

We got out of the car and walked up to the complex. It didn't take long to find Samantha Riggins's apartment, and I started to knock on the door when Zach stopped me.

"What are you doing?" I asked him.

"I'm taking the lead in my investigation," he said. "I shouldn't have to remind you that you are here as a consultant, and I expect you to let me conduct this interview without interference. Are we clear?"

"If you're asking me if I understand you, I do. On the other hand, if you want to know if I accept it, you're out of your mind."

"Then maybe you should wait in the car. I'm serious, Savannah."

After a moment's thought, I asked, "Would it be proper for me to ask a question, if I see a direction you might not see?"

"I suppose that would be all right. Just let me lead the investigation. Okay?"

"Fine," I said.

I took a step back, and he rapped on the door. After thirty seconds, a tall and thin, very fit blonde in her mid-twenties answered the door. I could tell she was in shape because it was clear she'd just gotten back home from a run.

"Can I help you?" she asked as she toweled off the back of her neck.

"Samantha Riggins?" my husband asked.

"Yes," she replied, looking a little nervous, which was understandable, given the circumstances.

"I'm working with the police on the Cindy Glass murder," he said.

She didn't budge from the door. "I'd like to see some identification, if you don't mind."

"Of course," he said. I knew he didn't have a badge anymore, but he did still carry around his credentials from being the police chief.

She studied the photo ID card for a moment, looked at Zach while ignoring me, and then said, "One minute."

She ducked back into her apartment, and I could hear the dead bolt slide into place.

"You have a way with women; you know that, don't you?"

Zach just shrugged without replying. When he was working, he changed into a totally different man, one I had trouble recognizing sometimes. It was almost as if he was slipping on a mask that fit him perfectly, and yet it still managed to change everything about him.

A minute later, the door opened, and Samantha invited us inside.

"Did you call the police to check on me?" Zach asked.

Samantha grinned. "No, I did better than that. I

Googled you. Sorry about you getting shot. That must have been awful."

"It was," I said, not realizing I'd spoken it aloud.

Zach pointed to me and said, "This is my wife, Savannah."

"It's nice to meet you," she said as she offered me her hand.

I took it and then I started to ask her about Cindy, when I looked over at my husband. He was frowning slightly, and I knew this was no time to overstep my bounds.

"Nice to meet you, too," I said, and then I did my best to fade into the background.

Samantha studied us both with a polite glance, and then she asked, "Can I get you something to drink? I'm sorry, but all I've got is herbal tea and diet soda."

"Thanks, but we're good," Zach said. "Do you have a minute to talk about Cindy Glass? I understand you two were close."

"We were like sisters," Samantha said.

"That's what we heard," Zach answered.

Before he could say another word, I said, "We're sorry for your loss. It must have been terrible for you."

Samantha's eyes glazed for a few seconds. "It's the craziest thing. I picked up the phone this morning and started to call her to see if she'd like to run with me. I didn't even get her answering machine."

"Her place has been cleaned out," I said.

"Man, it didn't take the vultures long to move in, did it?"

"Actually, it was her boss's idea," I said. "I was there yesterday helping him go through her things. Evidently he was designated as her executor."

"Yeah, Barton's okay with me. He asked me if I wanted anything of hers, but everything I need of Cindy's, I have."

I couldn't help myself. I asked, "What exactly would that be? A sterling silver chain with a cow pendant, perhaps?"

"No, I mean personal things that were between the two of us, like cards she's given me over the years, and the silliest hat you've ever seen. Things like that."

"Then you don't know where the necklace might be?"

Samantha frowned. "Barton asked me the same thing. No, I haven't seen it. Why, is it important?"

"It's hard to say at this point," Zach said. "I'm still gathering information." Zach studied his notebook for a second, and then he asked her, "What exactly was her relationship with her employer?"

I looked oddly at Zach, trying to figure out where that question had come from. He hadn't even met Barton Lane. Was he really a suspect? I tried to catch his gaze, but he was staring hard at Samantha.

"She loved him."

"Was there anything romantic about their relationship?" Zach asked.

I started to say something, but Zach offered me a split-second glare that was enough to shut me up.

"Of course not," Samantha said. "He was like a father to her, in just about every respect. Cindy's dad took off when she was a kid, and she focused on Barton, but there wasn't anything creepy about it. He's a good guy, and he always looked out for her."

"Fine," Zach said as he jotted that down. "Then who was she romantically involved with? Would she tell you?"

"Trust me, Chief, if there was a man in her life, I knew about him from the start."

"Anyone lately?"

Samantha frowned. "That's a hard question."

"It shouldn't be; not if you two were as close as you claim."

I didn't like my husband's tone of voice at all, but I couldn't say anything to him at the moment. That didn't mean I couldn't rip into him once we were alone again.

"We were close, but there was someone she'd been seeing over the past month that she wouldn't talk about. He was older, and Cindy didn't want to admit it to me."

"How much older?"

"I couldn't say. The age wasn't the only thing, though. The guy had a high profile in Charlotte, I know that much."

"But you don't know anything more than that?"

Samantha looked as though she wanted to cry, and I wanted to step in and stop my husband from what looked like bullying to me, but I knew if I did, Zach would never let me tag along with him again.

"Hang on a second," she said, and Samantha got up and went into the other room.

Here was my chance.

"What do you think you're doing?" I hissed at him.

"I'm conducting an official police investigation," he said. "What does it look like?"

"Do you have to be so mean?"

He looked genuinely shocked by the question. "I have to be gruff and abrupt to let them know that I'm not kidding around here. Two people have been murdered, and for all we know, someone else is next on this murderer's list. I don't have time for niceties."

"Does it really take all that much more time to be civil?"

"Savannah, let me handle this my way."

I didn't say anything in response, and we sat in silence until Samantha walked back into the room carrying a newspaper with her. She held it as if it were the Holy Grail.

"What's that?" Zach asked, and I noticed his tone was just a little nicer. Truthfully, maybe it was just my imagination, but I liked to think I was making a difference.

"Nine days before she died, I was over at Cindy's, and I saw her staring at a newspaper."

"That one in particular?" Zach asked as he leaned forward.

"Let me tell this, okay?" Good for her. I was proud that she had some snap to her words.

"Sorry," Zach said, though it was pretty clear the apology was tepid at best.

"Anyway, we were having breakfast in her kitchen, and I saw her looking at a photo in the *Charlotte Observer*. When I asked her about it, she said wistfully, 'Isn't he handsome?'

"Which one, I asked her, since there were two photographs on that particular page. In one of them, two men were standing on some kind of platform shaking hands. The other was a headshot of a businessman, at least that's what he looked like to me from the suit he was wearing. Cindy suddenly looked at me as though she'd said too much, and before I could get a better look, she folded the paper, and threw it in the trash. Cindy is a . . . was a demon at recycling, and she never would have thrown that away if she hadn't been hiding something."

"So, you dug it out of her trash?"

"Don't be disgusting. I bought a paper the second I left her, and I found the photos she was pointing out."

"May I see that?" Zach asked.

Samantha nodded, and handed him the paper. I looked over his shoulder when he opened it, and I saw something that shook me to the core. The photo of the two men together showed Grady and Davis. The other photo showed Hank Tristan, and was accompanied by a story on a business he was building in Ballantyne.

Zach appeared too focused on the photo of Davis and Grady, so I tapped the headshot of Hank Tristan. He nodded, brushing me off, but I didn't let it bother me. If I'd pointed it out to him first, he'd give me full credit for the discovery. There wasn't an ounce of macho pride in my husband. He'd publicly thank a nine-year-old girl if she helped him solve a case. Results were all Zach cared about, and that was just one more reason why I loved him.

He started to hand the paper back to Samantha when I said, "Hold on a second."

"What is it?" my husband asked me.

"Let me see that."

He handed the paper to me, and as I looked at the photo of the two men, I saw another familiar face standing just behind them. I showed it to Zach and pointed it out. "That's Steve Sanders, isn't it?"

Zach studied it a second, and then said, "Yeah, but it's not much of a photo of him."

"It's possible though, isn't it?"

"I suppose. That was a good spot." He glanced at the paper, and then at Samantha. "May I keep this?"

"If it helps you find out who killed Cindy, you can have everything I own."

"Just the paper, at least for now," Zach said, and offered her a gentle smile. Samantha responded to it with a smile of her own, and I wondered if telling my husband to be nicer to his interview subjects had been the best idea, especially when they were prettier, younger, and skinnier than I was.

Zach stood, and to his credit, my dear husband turned to me and asked, "Is there anything else you'd like to ask?"

"No, you covered everything perfectly."

Samantha led us to the door, and she lingered there as we left. "If there's anything I can do to help, just let me know. I miss her so much."

"I'm sure you do," I said, my heart instantly softening to her. After all, who could blame her for returning one of my husband's smiles? He was a good-looking guy, after all. "We'll let you know if we think of anything else."

As we headed back to the car, I said, "She liked you. You know that, don't you?"

"What can I say? I'm a likeable guy."

"Come on, you were a detective once upon a time. You had to notice the way she smiled at you."

"Savannah, don't be ridiculous. I'm an old married man. No woman in her twenties is going to be interested in me."

"And if they were?"

"I'd tell them that my heart belongs to another." Zach

surprised me then by picking me up off my feet and hugging me.

"Put me down, you big lug," I said, laughing with every word.

"Fine, but you know that I never cared about looking like a fool. I love my wife. Arrest me."

"If they do, they'll have to arrest me, too."

He winked. "Maybe if we ask Davis nicely, he'll put us in the same cell."

"You're in an awfully good mood all of a sudden," I said.

"I know I shouldn't be; this is serious business. But I can't let it kill my spirit, can I? We're narrowing things down, Savannah. I don't like the direction the investigation's taking, but I have to admit it; I enjoy it when the puzzle pieces start to fit together."

"Did I miss something? Which pieces are you talking about?"

"Come on, it's too big a coincidence that the first murder victim was tied to Hank, Davis, and Grady."

"And Steve," I added.

"And Steve," he agreed. "Let's play with some possibilities. If Cindy was having an affair with Hank, it could explain why she was murdered, and it would tie the two homicides in together."

"What if she was seeing Grady before he admitted to dating her? Remember, the photos in the newspaper appeared at least a week before they met, according to Grady. How about Davis? It's easy to see how he or Steve would be attracted to her. Cindy was a pretty girl." In one of the photographs I'd seen of her, she'd looked so full of spirit, so alive, that it was hard for me to believe that she was dead.

"Then she could have been killed out of jealousy, and Hank saw something or knew something that got him killed."

"All of those lives are so tangled together; I don't know how you're ever going to straighten it all out. How are you handling all of the things you're learning?"

Zach frowned. "I hate that three of my friends are involved in this mess, but if one of them is a murderer, I'll see him hang for it."

"I know you will. It's what you do."

"It's more than that, Savannah. It's who I am. I'm tough on the bad guys, and if any of my friends are involved, I'm going to be even harder on them."

WHEN WE GOT BACK TO POLICE HEADQUARTERS, I was still happy about Zach's rare public display of affection.

But the second we got off the elevator, that happiness vanished in an instant.

Something bad was happening in front of the task force room, and I wasn't sure if even my husband was going to be able to fix it.

Chapter 17

■ ■ ■

"**S**TEP OUT OF THE WAY OR I'LL HAVE YOU THROWN OFF the force," Davis was yelling when we hurried to him. Steve Sanders was standing his ground, and so far neither one of them had seen us.

"The Chief said that no one goes inside without him."

"I'm the only chief of police around here," Davis roared.

"What's going on?" Zach asked. He hadn't shouted, but there was an edge to his words that neither man could ignore. My husband might not have still been the acting chief, but he hadn't lost that edge of authority in his voice.

"Good, you're here," Davis said, much calmer than he had spoken before. "You need to let me in this room, and I mean right now. I don't know how you got Sanders to defy me, but I'll see that he pays for it."

"You told me I could have any assistant I wanted," Zach said. "I chose Steve. Nobody can have two bosses, Davis. You can't just overrule me like this, not after giving me autonomy on this case."

"You work for me, too. Remember?"

"If you're going to act like this, maybe that's not such a good idea anymore." Zach turned to me. "Come on, Savannah. We're going home."

"Back to the hotel?"

"No, to Parson's Valley. It appears that I've just been fired."

"You quit," Davis said, his voice a whine now.

"Call it what you will. But I won't have you trying to impede my active investigation."

We were at the elevator when Davis came to us. "I'm sorry," he said softly.

"What was that?" Zach asked.

"I said I was sorry," Davis repeated, clearly not at all happy about having to do it. "I shouldn't have snapped at you like that."

"Are you saying that it's my investigation? No matter what happens?"

He shrugged. "That's what we hired you to do."

"Then I need to interview you," Zach said.

"About what?"

"The murders."

"**T**HAT'S NOT FUNNY, ZACH," DAVIS SAID.
          "Do I look like I'm laughing? We can do this now, or I can wait until you take the time to get an attorney."

Davis shook his head. "You're serious, aren't you?"

"Completely."

"I don't need an attorney. Ask away."

"Not out here."

We headed toward the task force room, and I saw that Steve Sanders was grinning, though I wasn't sure the other men saw it.

"Go downstairs until I call you," Zach told him, and Steve looked disappointed as he started for the elevator. With all that my husband had on his mind, he'd still seen that grin.

In a softer voice, he said, "Savannah, you shouldn't be here, either."

I was about to protest when Davis said, "I don't have anything to hide. She can stay."

Zach shrugged, and I took it as an engraved invitation.

Once we were inside, Zach and Davis took seats at one of the tables, and I found a spot where I could watch them both and hear everything that was said, but still be out of the line of fire.

Zach pulled out his notebook, scanned it for a few moments, and then dove right in. "How well did you know Hank Tristan?"

"We had several mutual friends in the community," Davis said.

Zach pushed his chair away and stood. "If you're not going to be completely honest with me, there's no need for us to have this conversation."

"What are you talking about?" Davis looked clearly puzzled by my husband's behavior.

"You were more than acquaintances," Zach said. "You were business partners."

"How did you hear about that?" Davis asked.

"That's not important right now. What matters is whether it's true or not. Don't hold out on me, Davis. I mean it."

The new chief seemed to take it all in, and after a moment, he seemed to sink into his chair. "We were investors in a deal to develop some mountain land. I wasn't the only cop in on it. Sanders had a stake in it, too."

"But I'm willing to bet that it wasn't anywhere near the amount you lost."

Davis looked a little pale. "I sunk everything but my pension into it. When the planned resort went to Tennessee instead, I lost it all."

"You must have been mad enough to kill someone," Zach said softly.

"It was a blow, but we all took a beating on it. Sometimes in life you have to take a chance. I thought it was a sure thing, but I turned out to be wrong. A lot of people lost money on that deal."

"Even Hank? I heard he protected himself somehow."

Davis looked at my husband as though he had a crystal ball, or maybe even a Ouija board. "All I know is that he lost money, too. Not as much as I did, but he still felt it."

Zach shrugged, and then made a note in his book. "How well did you know Cindy Glass?"

"What are you talking about? I didn't know her at all."

"Come on, Davis."

Zach waited, and finally, the new police chief said, "I don't care who you have as a source. I didn't know the young lady."

Zach nodded, made another note, and then asked, "Why did you want to get into this room? What was so important?"

"I'm getting a lot of pressure from high up. I wanted to see if you'd made any progress yet."

"Who's pressuring you? Grady?"

"You play things close to the vest, so I can, too." He stood. "Are we finished here?"

"For now."

Davis clearly didn't like that answer, and it looked as though he was going to say something, but he thought better of it and left.

"What do you think?" I asked Zach the second Davis was gone.

"I'm still not sure. The fact that I can't rule him out is bad enough though, don't you think?"

"Were you really going to walk away?"

Zach grinned at me. "Not on your life. I was bluffing, plain and simple."

"You had me fooled. I was starting to get excited about going back home."

He touched my shoulder lightly. "Is it really all that bad here?"

"No, it's been nice coming back, but it's not home anymore, is it?"

"Not so much. I wish I could tell you that this will all be over soon, but I can't. I've got a feeling this killer isn't going to stop on his own."

"Then you need to figure out who it is before he kills someone else."

"I'm doing the best I can," he said as he reached for the phone. "Send Sanders to the task force room," he ordered, and then he hung up before he could have possibly gotten a reply.

"You're good at giving orders; you know that, don't you?"

"That wasn't an order. It was a request."

I laughed. "You might think you formed that as a question, but trust me, it was a direct order."

"I guess old habits are hard to break."

"Sometimes."

He stood and started pacing around the room. "There's something here. I can feel it. It's so frustrating knowing that there's a clue I'm missing out on completely."

"It will come to you. Give it some time."

"I'm afraid that's one thing we don't have a great deal of left."

I saw the concern in his eyes. "Do you think he's going to do something soon?"

"What do you think? You read the note, too."

Zach walked over to the board, and then read the last communication to us aloud. "He's taunting me. I can't believe he threatened you, and I didn't send you away."

"Even if you could get rid of me, which you can't, where could I go? He knows where we live, Zach. The only way either one of us will ever be safe is if you catch him."

"Any luck with this code?"

"I'm stuck," I admitted. "There's got to be a pattern to it, but I don't know what it is."

"So, we're both having trouble seeing the truth. The question is, is he really that good at hiding his intentions, or are these notes and codes just part of one big lie?"

"I wish I knew."

"That makes two of us."

I could see that Zach was getting into a funk, and I had

to help him stop it before it took over. If he began to doubt himself, and his abilities, I knew there would be no chance of stopping the killer.

"What do we do next?" I asked.

"What? What do you mean?"

I waved a hand around the room. "We're stuck when we look at these walls. Let's get out and talk to more people. You always said that if all else failed, it was a good idea to stir the pot. So, let's go stir."

He frowned for a few moments, and then nodded. "You're right."

"Of course I am," I said with a smile. "Who should we talk to first?"

"Is there anyone more involved with this case than Grady? It's time we had another chat."

We were walking out of the room as Steve Sanders showed up. "I thought you needed me."

"I changed my mind."

"That's fine," Steve said. "If there's anything I can do, all you have to do is ask."

"How much did you lose on that mountain land deal?" I asked impulsively.

"What? How'd you hear about that?" He frowned, and then Steve said, "Strike that. Davis told you. I lost five grand. It wasn't a fortune, but I wasn't happy to see it go, either."

"Five thousand dollars is a great deal of money," I said.

"Yeah, but Davis lost ten times that. It's the only thing that lets me sleep at night."

"Did you know Cindy Glass very well?"

"Who?" Steve asked.

"The murder victim."

"Oh, yeah, I blanked out on her name for a second. No, not really. Why, what have you heard?"

Zach was listening to our conversation—I knew it—though he didn't appear to be paying attention.

"Just a snippet here and there," I said. "It was enough to make me want to ask the question."

Steve looked uncomfortable. "We had some mutual friends. I might have met her at a party once, but I can't be sure."

"But you never dated her."

"No, nothing like that." Steve looked at Zach, who had remained silent during the conversation. "What's this about, Chief?"

"We're trying to cross as many names off the list as we can," he said. "You know the routine."

"Sure, I just never thought I'd make it onto one of your lists."

"Neither did most of the people who've ended up there."

"What's taking that elevator so long?" Steve asked.

"I forgot to push the button," Zach said, as he finally did so.

"If that's it, I've got work I can be doing downstairs, unless you want me to hang around here and guard the door."

"No, I don't think that's necessary. I'll let you know when I need you again."

"Then I'll take the stairs. I need a little exercise anyway."

After he vanished down the stairway, I said, "You didn't forget to push the button at all, did you?"

"I wanted to hear what he had to say."

"Then why didn't you ask him yourself?" I asked as I pushed the button again. The elevator was as slow as cold molasses.

"I was about to, when you stepped in and did it for me."

"I'm sorry. I didn't mean to butt in."

Zach smiled at me. "On the contrary, it was better coming from you anyway. If I'd have thought about it, I would have asked you to talk to him before."

"What do you think about his answers?" I asked as the elevator finally arrived.

As we stepped in, Zach said, "I'm not sure. Is he hiding something? Did he have a relationship with Cindy Glass? He didn't make it sound like five thousand dollars was a lot to lose, but I have a hard time believing it, don't you?"

"Then we're no further along than we were before."

"That's not true," Zach said as the elevator opened and we stepped out onto the ground floor. "The more information we have, the better chance there is of solving the case."

It was overcast when we went outside. "Should we take the car? It looks like it might rain."

"It's just a block. Let's walk it."

"That's fine with me."

As we walked toward Grady's office, I asked my husband, "Should we call first?"

"No, I don't want to give him the chance to get away before we get there. It will be best if we can catch him off guard."

"I never dreamed this case would take this direction when Davis called you, did you?"

"No, but I can't help wondering what Grady was doing the first day we got here."

"You mean when he disappeared?"

"Exactly. He couldn't have been jogging the entire time, not if he just took it up. I keep trying to put each of my suspects in the killer's shoes. It would have been easy for Grady to take that photograph of you in his truck, and then stash the camera somewhere safe until he could get back to it."

"Davis could have taken it, too. Or Steve, for that matter."

"If we're naming suspects, I'd like to add Lorna's name to the list."

I was surprised by that addition. "Honestly, do you think she could have had anything to do with these murders?"

"Why, because she's a woman?"

"No, I fully realize that women can kill just as easily as men can. I just don't see her motivation."

"What if we're looking at it all wrong?" Zach asked. "What if these murders are part of a bigger puzzle?"

"What do you mean?"

"It might explain the clues on the backs of the notes and photographs, if they are indeed important, and not just a way to throw us off the killer's scent. What if the two murders are connected, but not in a way that we've been considering so far?"

"You've got my attention," I said. "But I'm not sure where you're going."

"Let's say Lorna is our killer. She could have killed Cindy and Hank as a part of a frame-up to make Grady look bad."

"Would she commit multiple murders just to get back at an old boyfriend? She seems so happy now."

"Did you know that a lot of people who are about to commit suicide act more serenely than they ever have in their lives? Once they make the decision to do it, a kind of peace comes over them."

"Do you really think she's going to kill herself?"

"No, I don't mean that. All I'm saying is that once she came up with a plan to ruin Grady, she could very easily have become more content with her life. She keeps pushing these breakfasts on you, and the two of you have never really been all that close before."

"I thought she wanted to make amends for the past."

"It's possible, but she could also be trying to get information about the investigation out of you."

I thought about that for a few seconds. "She *has* asked about it every time we meet."

"When are you getting together again?"

"We were supposed to have breakfast tomorrow," I admitted. "But I'm going to have to cancel on her. I'm eating with Sherry instead."

"Do me a favor. Put Sherry off and meet with Lorna. Try to find out if she knew Cindy Glass, since we already know she danced with Hank the night he was murdered."

"I don't know," I said. "I'm not crazy about doing that."

"That's fine. I'll ask her myself."

I shook my head. "No, she'll never tell you anything she doesn't want you to hear. I'll do it."

"You could always ask Sherry for a rain check."

"I'm going to do better than that. I'm going to see if she'll have lunch instead. It's going to be your treat, by the way."

"Fine, I'm more than happy to pay for it."

As we got closer to city hall, I pulled out my telephone.

"Who are you calling, Savannah?"

"I have to be sure Sherry's okay with the change of plans before I agree to do this."

I called my friend, and after a minute of conversation, I hung up. "She's fine with it. But we're going someplace nice."

"You should."

"Zach, it's no fun teasing you if you're just going to roll over like that."

"So, my plan worked," he said with a smile.

"Don't be smug. It doesn't suit you."

"Sorry," he said, though the grin on his face showed that he wasn't sorry at all.

WHAT IS IT? I DON'T HAVE TIME FOR A LOT OF FOOL-ish questions right now," Grady said as we were shown into his office. I was more than a little surprised that he'd even agreed to see us at all after our last conversation.

"This won't take long, and we're in Charlotte because of you, remember? Are you absolutely positive you didn't know Cindy Glass until the night of the ball?"

"That's what I told you, wasn't it? She was a last second fix up."

"Who made the match?"

Grady leaned forward in his chair. "What does it matter?"

"I won't know that until you answer the question."

"An assistant here got us together. Like I said, it was all last minute. Is there anything else? I'm busy."

Zach wasn't finished, not by a long shot, but I could tell by the expression on his face that he knew it was time to move on. "Were you a part of a land development deal with Hank Tristan?"

"You wouldn't be asking me the question if you didn't already know the answer. Yes, we made a few deals together."

"One in particular lost a great deal of money, didn't it?"

Grady scowled. "Trust me, he made more for me than I ever lost. The man had a real knack for turning a profit."

"But he didn't always make money, did he?"

"Remember, even the best baseball player on the field strikes out more often than he hits the ball when he's standing at the plate."

"Spare me the sports analogies," Zach said.

"Okay, I was trying to be nice fitting you into my schedule, but if you'll excuse me, I've got a city to run."

Before I knew what was happening, we were being expertly shuffled out of the room by his secretary.

"What just happened there?" I asked my husband.

"We hit a nerve. There's more to that story than Grady's telling us."

As we walked back toward the police station, it started to sprinkle. "Maybe I should have brought my umbrella."

"Come on, we don't have that far to go."

As we hurried on our way, I asked Zach, "So, tell me again why Grady holding out on us is a good thing."

"It's simple. The more we can shake things up, the better off we'll be."

"You do realize that most likely we're aggravating the killer, too."

"Hey, it won't work if we're not willing to take any chances. You're not getting cold feet, are you?"

"No way. I want to see the killer caught now more than ever."

"So be happy with our progress."

As we rushed up the steps to the station, I said, "If irritating the people we know is our goal, we're doing remarkable work. We've agitated Grady, who happens to be the mayor, and Davis, the new chief of police. Throw in Steve Sanders, and we're losing friends fast."

"That just leaves Lorna."

"There's time to pick a fight with her tomorrow, isn't there?"

"I'd really rather you did it now," Zach said.

I looked at him to see if he was serious, and there was no trace of a smile on his face. "Fine. I'll call her. Is there anything in particular you want me to say, or should I just start hurling insults at her?"

"It won't do any good if it's not focused. I want you to work into the conversation that I'm thinking about her ties to both victims."

"How does she know Cindy?" I asked as we walked back into police headquarters.

"As far as we know, she doesn't, but that doesn't mean you can't imply differently. What do you say? Are you up for it?"

"I'm here to serve," I said as we got on the elevator and went upstairs. I wanted a little privacy when I called Lorna, so I was at least going to wait until we were behind locked doors. I was kind of surprised when we got up there that

Steve wasn't outside the door. I figured he'd be there, despite my husband's earlier orders.

"Where'd your guard go?"

"Yeah, I thought he'd sneak back up here, too. He's probably off licking his wounds. You were kind of rough on him."

As Zach unlocked the door, I asked, "Does that mean that you don't approve?"

"Are you kidding? It was all I could do not to start applauding when you went after him. Do me a favor; don't get mad at me."

"As long as you behave yourself, I won't have to."

"Come on. What are the chances of that happening?"

"Too slim to count for anyone but a mathematician," I said.

I got out my phone as Zach locked the door behind us.

Don't pick up. Don't pick up.

She picked up.

"Hey, Lorna. It's Savannah."

"Hey yourself. I was just thinking about you. You're not canceling on me tomorrow, are you?"

"Not a chance. I'm looking forward to it. I have a quick question, though."

"Fire away."

"We know you were friends with Hank Tristan, but when exactly did you meet Cindy Glass?"

"Who?"

"The other murder victim."

There was dead silence on the other end of the phone. "What are you talking about? Who said I knew her?"

"Zach doesn't like me to reveal his sources," I said, and

my husband gave me a thumbs-up signal. I couldn't let that go without a comment. I told Lorna, "You know how men can be like little children sometimes."

"You don't have to tell me. Does he really suspect me?"

"Well he wants to cover all of his bases. I'm looking at your name on the board at the task force headquarters right now," I said, a full and blatant lie.

"I didn't realize anyone knew," she said softly. I wasn't even sure she knew that she'd said it aloud.

"Charlotte may look like a big city to an outsider, but it's really not all *that* big. People talk."

"It was nothing. We met at a seminar two years ago. I barely remembered her until I saw her picture in the paper. You've got to convince Zach that I didn't really know her at all."

"I'll try, but once he makes up his mind about something, it's tough to get him to back down. He's sure there's a connection here somewhere."

"You have to at least try, Savannah. Promise me."

If her tone of voice was any indication, she was more worried about Zach's theories than she wanted me to know. "I'll do my best."

"We'll talk about it tomorrow, okay?"

"Fine. I'm looking forward to it."

"Me, too. And Savannah?"

"Yes?"

"I didn't kill either one of them. I'm not a murderer."

"I'll tell him that, too," I said, and then I hung up.

"Wow, that worked better than I'd hoped."

"What did she say?" Zach asked me.

"Lorna met Cindy at a seminar two years ago, so they have a history together. How did you suspect that?"

"I didn't, but sometimes it's fun to guess, isn't it?"

I looked around the room, and then I asked, "What do we do now?"

"I don't know about you, but there's something that's been bugging me, and I'm going to dig through the files until I find it."

"Can I help?"

He shook his head. "No, this is a solo job. You can work on the clue segments, if you really want to help."

"You know I do."

A N HOUR LATER, NEITHER ONE OF US HAD MADE AN ounce worth of progress. The numbers and letters still meant nothing to me, and the more I stared at them and moved the sequences around, the more confused I got.

Zach looked over at me, and then shrugged. "Whatever it was I just had, I lost it."

"At least you had it to begin with. I keep staring at these sequences like they're Martian cookbook ingredients."

He walked over and touched my shoulder. "I know I gave you the worst possible job in all of this. The more we get into it, the more I think the codes were made up just to frustrate us."

"Then I'd say it was a roaring success. How about you?"

"I'm stumped, and I'm not afraid who knows it," he said.

"Is there any reason we can't move our think tank back to the hotel? I know you've got copies of just about everything here. Could you pack up a few boxes and take them with us? That way you'd have access to the information without having to live here around the clock."

"I suppose I could," he said reluctantly. "But what if there's something here I miss?"

"Would it be the first time that happened to you? In fact, it might help shake up your thought processes a bit."

"How do you get that?"

"Sometimes with my puzzles, what's not there is more significant than what is."

"Would you care to clarify that for me?"

"I wish I could explain. Come on. Let's do it."

Zach took an empty box, and I started collecting my random notes as he collected copies of his documents. By the time he was finished, I'd been standing impatiently by the door for a good ten minutes.

"I'm coming," he said. "Just give me one more minute."

"Take all the time you need," I said. "I'll just take a little nap while I'm waiting."

I pretended to snore, and then I heard my husband laugh. "You're good for me, Savannah; I've told you that lately, haven't I?"

"Sure, but a girl can never get tired of hearing it. Or a woman, either."

"Then I'll try to say it more often," he said. He looked around the room again, and then nodded. "That should do it."

"Are you sure? I don't want to have to come back here tonight."

"Maybe you're right. Give me one more minute."

Me and my big mouth. I should have known better than to tease him.

He stuffed a few more copies into his box, and then he smiled at me. "You were right. I'm finished."

I was about to ask him if he was sure about that, but I knew better. "Then let's get out of here."

We walked out the door, and as we were locking it behind us, Davis came out of the elevator with a heavy frown on his face.

"What happened?" Zach asked.

"We got another note, and this one's a direct threat toward both of you."

Chapter 18

•••

ZACH AND SAVANNAH STONE. UNLESS YOU LEAVE CHAR-*lotte by midnight tomorrow, I will take my next vic-tim. Your blundering has cost me my patience, and I'm weary of your meddling ways. Remember, if you fail to act, the next murder will be blood you've spilled your-selves.*

Zach studied it after he'd read it aloud, and then he flipped it over. Instead of a number and letter sequence, there was some kind of odd-looking grid on the paper, barely discernable.

"Can I have that a second?" I asked.

The note was in a plastic evidence bag, and Zach handed it to me.

There was definitely something there. "I need to get to the copier."

"This is no time to make copies," Davis said. "This is serious."

"Really, Davis? Is it? Because I wasn't sure, what with the murder threat and all."

"Easy, Savannah," Zach said as he unlocked the door again.

I ignored everyone, turned the copier back on, and then turned the exposure to its darkest setting.

What had been faint before was now clearly outlined on the copy of the original. In this case, the duplicate was better than the source.

But it still didn't make any sense. There were oddly shaped ovoids and faint numbers placed randomly on the page.

"What does it mean?" Zach asked as he looked over my shoulder.

"I have no idea. But I will. If the killer thinks he's going to run us off this way, he doesn't know either one of us very well."

"You're staying?" Davis sounded incredulous as he asked the question.

"Of course we are," I snapped. And then I thought to look over at my husband. "Aren't we?" I asked softly.

"I'm willing to hang around as long as you are," he said.

"Then that's settled. Are you ready to go back to the hotel now?"

"You're not going to work on the case here at head-quarters?" Davis asked. I saw his gaze take in the foam insulation boards filled with copies, notes, and drawings that Zach had been putting together.

"No. I need some fresh air. Let's go." There was no

room for misunderstanding in Zach's tone of voice. It didn't matter that his former subordinate was now his boss. This was a command, and it was going to be obeyed without question, or there would be consequences.

Davis left the room first, and I was on his heels as Zach stepped out of the room and locked the door behind us. After he did that, he took the key and put it back into his pocket.

"You know where to reach me if you need me," he said to Davis.

"Yes, of course. I'll be in touch if anything else comes in tonight."

"Thanks, but it won't," I said, not realizing that I'd just vocalized my thoughts.

"Why do you say that?" Davis was looking at me oddly, but Zach just smiled.

I'd started this, so I had to explain my reasoning. "There's no need to. We've been warned, and until midnight tomorrow, the killer is going to wait and see before he does anything else."

"You're putting a great deal of faith in a theory," Davis said.

Zach answered for me. "She's right, and you know it."

We got on the elevator and traveled down to the ground floor. Davis was surprisingly quiet all of a sudden, and I thought I knew why. Zach had backed me to the fullest, instead of taking Davis's side. It had to sting, but what did he expect? He and Zach might have been friends and co-workers at one time, but I was his wife.

It helped that I was right, too.

We left Davis on the ground floor and made our way to

our car. Even though we would still be working in our suite, it was a much more conducive atmosphere for critical analysis. We didn't have to worry about anyone trying to get into our room. It was our sanctuary, and the way things were going, we were going to need it. I wasn't sure how long we were going to be able to ignore the killer, but I had the feeling that by tomorrow night, I might be packing my bags if we weren't able to name the murderer.

Blood on my hands was something I just wasn't willing to risk, no matter how brave I'd sounded talking to Davis.

"**I** CAN'T BELIEVE HOW LONG THIS DAY HAS BEEN," I SAID AS we walked into our suite.

"It's going to get longer. That note has put us under the gun. It's long past personal."

I stared hard at my husband. "Zach, what are we going to do if we can't figure this out in time? I can't stand the thought of someone dying because of us."

"He's counting on that, you know. We must have struck a nerve over the last few days."

"I don't doubt it, but who's guilty?"

"I have a few ideas." He tapped the box in front of him. "It's in here. I just know it."

"I have faith in you."

"I'm thankful for that, believe me. Are you having any luck with the latest note? I can't imagine what that clue was supposed to mean. I'm guessing he's just trying to muddy our thinking."

"I have to treat it seriously, though. If there's something there that could help us, I have to keep searching for it." I studied the latest copy, and then added, "Even if the clue is inadvertent."

"What do you mean?"

I sighed. "I don't really know how to explain it. Do you know how you can tell when someone's lying to you?"

"Any number of ways, actually. The suspect's eyes shift downward, he covers part of his mouth with his hand, or maybe his inflection changes."

"But sometimes he does none of those things, and you still know."

Zach nodded. "Okay, I agree that there are parts of my mind working on levels I can't easily access."

I smiled at him. "Kind of like women's intuition?"

"More like a seasoned cop's gut feeling."

"Same thing," I said.

"Maybe. What's that got to do with the codes we've been receiving?"

"Numbers can lie, too."

That got his attention. "How can that be true? A four is always a four. It can't tell you it's a three."

"There are some mathematicians who believe that the entire world of statistics is one big lie. In fact, I had a stat professor in college who had a plaque above his door so everyone would see it when they left the classroom. It said, 'Figures lie, and liars figure.' He taught me that you can manipulate data to suit your purposes."

"Okay, I can see that," my husband said. "But that four is still a four."

"Sure, but what if it's disguising itself as one plus three?"

He shook his head. "It's still a four."

"But isn't one way of lying telling only part of the

truth? Numbers are perfect for that kind of sin of omission." I tapped the latest copy. "There could be something in here disguised as a lie, but it's really the truth."

"If that's the case, you're going to have to find it, not me. I'm lost as usual when it comes to your number discussion."

"That's okay," I said as I touched his hair lightly. "You're good at other things."

"I just wish one of them was solving this case."

"Forget about the big picture and focus on the details," I said. "Sometimes tackling a problem from a different direction is enough to show you the way. At least that's how it works with my more complex puzzles sometimes."

"I don't see how it can hurt," he said.

Zach pulled the coffee table over to the bank of windows, and he started laying out notes on it. There was barely room for me.

"Sorry. Did you need some space, too?"

"That's okay. I've got the floor, if I need to spread out," I said.

"I can give up a little room."

"No, honestly, I'm just dandy right here."

I stood and decided that the small end table would give me enough space for my needs. As I started to put the lamp and the telephone on the floor, I saw that the message light was blinking.

I picked it up and dialed zero. Zach didn't even look up.

"Hello, I have a message."

"I'll connect you, Ms. Stone," the operator said.

I was expecting a computerized voice mail system, so I was surprised when Barton Lane picked up.

"Good evening, Savannah. Thank you for returning my telephone call."

"Sorry it wasn't sooner, but we just got back in."

"That's fine. There isn't a time constraint on our conversations."

It was odd in one way to have a multi-millionaire at my beck and call, but I didn't have time to enjoy it. I had bigger things to deal with at the moment.

"What can I do for you?"

"I wanted to thank you again for helping me with Cindy's things."

"No more thanks are necessary." At that moment, something was clicking in my brain, something I'd seen in that puzzle.

"Oh, my word; I just figured it out. I have to go," I said, and before he even had a chance to say good-bye.

"Who was that?" Zach asked.

"Barton Lane," I explained as I started looking through the copies Zach had made up for me.

"You realize that you just hung up on a millionaire," he said.

"Zachary, would you please shut up for a second?"

I found the sheet I wanted, and looked at the code on it.

Only I'd remembered it wrong.

I didn't have anything after all.

I let the copy slip out of my hands, and I stared numbly out the window.

Behind me, I heard my husband say softly, "I'm sorry if I made you lose your train of thought, Savannah."

"It's okay. I was wrong."

"Don't let me off the hook that easily," Zach said. "I know better than to interrupt you when you're thinking."

"I just don't get it," I said. "I thought I had something there."

The phone started to ring, so I asked Zach, "Would you get that?"

He did as I requested, but I zoned him out after that. I kept staring at the codes, trying to make some kind of sense out of them.

I finally gave up, though. I knew I couldn't force the solution, just as I couldn't force one of my puzzles.

"Who was that?" I asked as I finally met my husband's gaze.

"Barton Lane. He wanted to make sure you were all right."

"What did you tell him?" I felt bad about hanging up on the man, but when a thought comes unbidden, it's best to grab it with both hands.

"I didn't have to say anything. He's coming up, so make yourself presentable."

Oh, no. Now I'd angered our host. Was he going to evict us, even when we were on a tight deadline to solve his assistant's murder?

"I'm sorry. I shouldn't have been so rude to him," I said. "Was he really upset?"

"I'd be lying if I said he wasn't," Zach said.

"If we get booted out tonight, we could always go to the Motel 6."

"Or we could share Davis's couch. It's not too bad."

"I get the pillow," I said.

"I'll toss you for it."

There was a knock at the door, and I noticed that though Zach was more than a little distracted, he still asked, "Who is it?"

There was a moment's hesitation, and then we both heard a voice say, "It's Barton Lane."

Zach looked at me for confirmation, and I nodded. It sounded like Barton, though I didn't know his voice that well. That's when it hit me. Regardless of how insane it must be, his voice was quite a bit like someone else I knew, someone I cared about a great deal.

Zach must have noticed something in my expression, because he didn't open the door. "Are you all right, Savannah?"

"I think I'm losing my mind," I admitted.

"What is it?" There was real concern in his voice, and I loved him even more for it.

"I'm about to do something stupid, and there's a one percent chance I'm right, and a ninety-nine percent chance I'm about to make a complete fool out of myself."

"What does your gut tell you?"

I thought about it a split second. "That I'm right."

"Then go for it, and let the consequences fall where they may."

"Excuse me, but may I come in?" Barton called out.

That sealed it for me. How had I not heard it before? Could it be that over the telephone, and in person, his voice was somehow changed, but through a closed door, the nuance of it came out? It didn't matter anymore.

"Sorry, of course you can. Come on in," I said as I opened the door.

"Thank you."

After he was in the suite, and the door was closed behind him, I said, "I've got something of yours I need to return."

"You found the necklace after all?" he asked, his voice full of hope.

"No, that still hasn't turned up."

"Then what is it?"

"Ten thousand dollars. My mother didn't spend it, and I don't think it's right that I do, Uncle Jeffrey."

He frowned for a few moments, and then he said softly, "Pardon me? I have no idea what you're talking about."

I wasn't about to let him get away with it, though. "I just spent a day with Uncle Thomas, and while there isn't much family resemblance between the two of you, I can hear his voice when you speak. I'm willing to bet that Barton is my uncle's middle name. Should I call Uncle Thomas and find out?"

Barton Lane slumped down, and I knew I had him. "That won't be necessary. It's true. I'm your uncle."

I didn't know what he was expecting, perhaps a tongue-lashing and a scolding, but he was clearly surprised when I wrapped him in my arms. "Why did you stay away so long?"

"I had no choice," he said. He finally managed to pull away from me, and I could see that his face was flushed. "You understand, don't you?"

"I don't have a clue what's going on," I answered honestly.

"No one told you? There weren't horrible tales of J.B., the thief, when you were growing up?"

"What are you talking about?"

"That ten thousand dollars I sent your mother was atonement for something I did many years ago. I left when

I was eighteen, but I didn't go empty-handed. Your grand-father didn't believe in banks, and he didn't believe in me when I asked him for a loan so I could make my way into the world. He refused me, so I took it anyway." Barton's face seemed to melt as he told his story, and I could swear I saw the man shrink before my eyes.

"I was so ashamed of myself. I tried to pay him back five years later, but he tore up the check and returned it to me. He said as far as he and the rest of the family were concerned, I had died the day I left them. It took forever for me to get the courage to write your mother, and when I never heard back from her, I assumed that no one had forgiven me."

"So you sought me out?" I asked, incredulous about the news.

"Quite the opposite. I've stayed away from you, per your mother's wishes. When I discovered you and your husband were coming to town to investigate my assistant's murder, I couldn't help myself. I offered you my finest suite in the hopes I could get to know you without the stigma of what I'd done to taint your impression of me."

"Like I said before, I never knew you took any money from my grandparents."

"Are you honestly saying that neither Thomas nor your mother told you?"

"No. I've got a feeling if you tried again with Uncle Thomas, you just might be surprised. He's softened quite a bit over the years." I looked at Zach, who nodded his head. In some ways, he knew my uncle better than I did, and if there was a chance for forgiveness, he would most likely be the one to know it.

"I hope with all my heart that it's true, but being here with you right now is enough for me."

"Whatever sin you committed was never against me, so I'd have a hard time holding a grudge for it, wouldn't I? We can try to get acquainted, but there's something you have to do first, or I'm not interested in pursuing this."

"I can pay you any amount you name." He reached into his jacket and pulled out an envelope. "In fact, I've calculated the amount I took, compounded the interest, and I've written you a check for the full amount. I did it just before I came upstairs."

"It's about money, but that's not what I want."

The envelope dipped slightly in his hand. "Then name your price, and I'll gladly pay it."

I reached into my purse and got the receipt Garrett had given me when I'd deposited the money from my mother in the safe.

"You can take this back. After all, it's yours."

He looked at the receipt, and then his expression changed into pain. "Then you don't forgive me?"

"You don't understand. It's not my money. Even if it belonged to my grandparents, that doesn't make it mine. Give it to Uncle Thomas, if you have to, but I don't need it. We're doing just fine."

Zach nodded his approval, and I felt even prouder that I'd chosen him.

"I don't know what to say," he said.

"Don't worry, I'm sure you'll think of something."

Barton's face brightened, and I knew I'd have a difficult time ever calling him Jeffrey, or even J.B. "May I keep calling you Barton?"

"Savannah, you may call me whatever you wish," he said with a smile. "Just as long as you call me."

"That's a promise," I said.

Zach coughed, and then said, "You two have a lot to talk about, and none of it concerns me. If you'll excuse me, I'll go into the bedroom so I can get back to work."

I remembered the codes I was supposed to be working on, too. "Barton, would it be all right if we postponed this reunion for a few days? We're really pushed for time here."

"Of course you are," he said. "We can get acquainted anytime."

He moved toward me, and after a moment's hesitation, Barton hugged me.

"Good night," he said after quickly breaking it. "And thank you for giving me my life back."

"It looks like you're doing okay without us," I said.

"That's where you're wrong. Without my family around me, all of this means nothing."

After he was gone, Zach looked at me and whistled. "Wow, and people think I'm the detective in the family."

"You would have figured it out, too, if you'd just spent the day with Uncle Thomas."

"You're giving me way too much credit again. Savannah, remind me never to get into a detecting contest with you. I've got a bad feeling that I'd come in second place if I did."

"Let's not worry about that right now. We have work to do."

"We sure do, but I don't know how you're going to be able to focus on it. After all, you just found out you're rich."

"I'm not rich, my uncle is," I said, the taste of the words feeling funny in my mouth.

"True."

"And if I were, you would be, too."

"Not me. I just married money."

"And here I thought it was for love."

He kissed me, and then Zach said, "Love's the cake, the rest is just icing, no matter how much of it there is."

"Let's get to work. You're making me hungry, talking about cake."

"We could always order room service," Zach suggested.

"That sounds like a great idea."

I picked up the phone, ordered for both of us, and then found my husband staring at me. "Don't you think you should have asked me what I wanted before you called?"

"I'm sorry," I said as I picked the phone back up. "What did you want?"

"Steak, garlic mashed potatoes, and creamed spinach."

"But that's what I just ordered," I said.

"I know, but it feels good when you ask."

We both laughed, happy to have something to break the tension we were both feeling.

As we waited for the food to arrive, I took the copies and laid them out in the sequence they'd arrived in so I could study them better as a whole, and not just parts.

I wasn't sure, but there was something there.

I just wasn't seeing it yet.

"I GIVE UP," I SAID AS I STARED AT THE COPIES FOR THE HUNdredth time after we'd had our dinner. Zach didn't even hear me he was so intent studying the timeline he'd created. It was a work of art, the size of a regular sheet of paper, but with every suspect's whereabouts drawn in a different colored pen, looping in and out, making contact, and then splitting off again.

"What was that?"

"Nothing," I said. I had a puzzle to do for tomorrow, but I was tempted to have Derrick run one of my backups again, no matter how much grief he gave me about it. This was too important.

Then again, maybe the distraction of creating a more complex puzzle was exactly what I needed.

I started reviewing the types of puzzles I liked to create on my notepad, but before I could make up my mind, my telephone started ringing.

Zach didn't even look up as I answered.

It was Lorna.

"We're still on for tomorrow, aren't we?" she asked.

"Yes, unless you want to cancel."

"I wouldn't miss it for the world," she said, and then she hung up.

"Who was that?" Zach asked. So, it had caught his attention.

"It was Lorna. She wanted to be sure I was still meeting her in the morning."

"She could have been calling for another reason," Zach said.

"What's that?"

"To see where we were."

"Why should she want to know that?"

"She wouldn't, unless she's the killer."

"Come on, Zach. You can't read too much into everything that happens to us."

He shrugged. "I'm not saying it's true. I'm just saying it's a possibility."

"Fine; whatever you say. Frankly, I'm too tired to argue."

I walked back to retrieve my pad when I glanced down at the copies on the floor. I glanced from my grid to the copies and back again, and then I looked at the last clue we'd gotten.

Could it honestly be that easy, or was I letting my imagination get the better of me?

There was only one way to find out.

I studied the letters in the sequence they'd been received, and wrote the combinations below the square on the horizontal axis. And then I remembered the 4O I'd so casually dismissed. What if it wasn't a zero, but a letter O instead? That would make it 4-O.

I added it to the others, and wrote A3, E5, E2, A4, E1, and 4O.

So far, we'd received As, Es, and an O on the last one before the oblong circles.

The first part of every sequence was a vowel.

Five columns wide had to mean A, E, I, O, and U. I knew Y was sometimes a vowel, but there wasn't room on my grid, and if I needed it later, it wouldn't be too hard to add.

What about the y-axis going up the rows? We had a 1, 2, 3, 4, and 5. Each row had its own number.

I wrote it in quickly, and then called Zach.

"Come here. You need to see this."

"What is it, Savannah? I'm onto something here."

"If it weren't important, I wouldn't ask you to look," I said.

He came over to me, and I handed him my pad.

He stared at the grid. "There are a lot of spaces we still don't know about though. There's no way we could be expected to solve this with the clues we've gotten so far."

"That's why the killer sent us this last one," I said. "He ran out of time, so this has to be the key."

Zach took it from me, studied it, and then said, "But the question is, what lock does this key fit into?"

"I haven't gotten that far yet," I admitted. "Do you think I've lost my mind?"

"Yes, but for completely different reasons. This could actually be it. Good work."

"I'm not there yet."

"You'll get it," he said.

I laid the original clues out again, this time being careful to put them in the proper order. As I did, I stared at each note.

3A, 5E, 2E, 4A, 1E, O4.

After that, I decided to add the order they arrived in, and got something like this: 3A (1), 5E (2), 2E (3), 4A (4), 1E (5), 4O (6 or 1).

Could the sequence of the notes represent the numbers that belonged in the corresponding squares?

I laid out my grid, and started filling in numbers. When I finished, it looked rather stark.

If I only knew what it meant. As a puzzle, it was nearly empty, and if it was one of mine, there was too much information that was still missing.

I just hoped I didn't run out of time before I unlocked the key.

Chapter 19

■ ■ ■

"**H**AVE YOU HAD ANY MORE BREAKTHROUGHS?" ZACH asked as he walked into the bedroom where I'd been working.

"No, I'm afraid I burned out my thought process. How about you?"

He grinned at me in a special way, something I'd seen before.

"You're on to something, aren't you?"

"Maybe."

"Come on, don't hold out on me."

"I need to sleep on it, and then I have to check a few things out tomorrow." I knew my husband's methods. He'd talk when he was ready, and only when he was ready. Otherwise, his internal thought process could short-circuit if he spoke his theories aloud. I understood it completely, and had learned to respect my husband when he was reticent about a case.

"Good enough." I started gathering my copies and notes.

"You don't have to do that on my account. I could always crash in the other bedroom."

"I don't spend enough time with you as it is. Besides, I'm just spinning my wheels right now."

"Don't worry. You always do better in the mornings."

"We can only hope."

After we were in bed, I snuggled up close to my husband. "I'm glad you're with me."

"Tonight, or all of the time?"

I punched him lightly. "All of the time, and you know it. Can you believe Barton Lane is really my uncle?"

"It's hard to grasp, isn't it? How do you think Tom's going to take it?"

"One thing's for sure. He's either going to be thrilled, or he won't talk to his brother at all. There's nothing wishy-washy about my uncle."

"Which one?" Zach asked, and even though it was dark, I could hear the smile in his voice.

"That's got a nice ring to it."

"What are you going to do about it?" Zach asked softly.

"What do you mean?"

"He stole from your family, Savannah. I'm sure it was probably everything your grandparents had. Are you going to give him a free ride for doing that?"

"He tried to make amends," I said.

"Too late to do your grandparents any good, though."

"Zach, do you think I should turn my back on him because of something he did before I was even born?" While I prided myself on being my own woman, that didn't mean that I didn't take my husband's advice seriously. He was a smart man, and he loved me. I respected him enough to listen to what he had to say, though I didn't feel bound to follow it. It was a marriage, an equal partnership, at least as far as we were concerned.

"Hang on. I'm not saying that. I'm just not sure you should make it too easy on him."

"How many hoops should he jump through first? Would seven be too many? Are three not enough? What's the magic number?"

"Nope, I'm not going to do it," he said.

"Do what?"

"Let you work out your frustration on me. I know you're as torn as I am about the whole thing. Let's table it for now, shall we?"

I realized that he was right. I'd been projecting my ambivalence onto him, and that wasn't fair for either one of us. "How'd you get so smart?"

"It helps marrying the right person," he said as he hugged me. "You've been training me to be a better man since the day we met. Who knows? Someday you just might succeed."

"I think we've both done pretty well."

"You bet."

Soon, I heard my husband snoring softly, but my mind was in too much of a whirlwind to just drift off like that. Zach could turn his thoughts off at night like they were on a switch, but I wasn't that lucky. How would Uncle Thomas react to his brother? Would they force me to take sides if the two of them clashed? Should I have made it a point to give that money—cash that we could have used—back to a man who was worth millions?

There were just too many questions, and not nearly enough answers.

I didn't think I'd ever get to sleep, but I must have at some point, because I woke up the next morning groggy from my nightmares. Fortunately I rarely remembered them for long, but in this one, I was being chased by a long line of letters and numbers. They'd formed a perfect line and were holding hands as they chased me through one of my own puzzles.

The image had been enough to jolt me awake.

Zach was still sleeping, so I slipped out of bed and decided to take a shower. The multiple jets helped a little in bringing me fully awake, but I could feel the lack of real sleep, and I knew I'd pay for it through the day. When I'd been in my late teens and early twenties, I'd been able to pull all-nighters writing papers or studying for exams, but the older I got, the more I felt missed minutes of slumber, let alone the hours I'd lost last night.

I wasn't a coffee drinker by nature, but I loved sweet tea. After my shower, I placed an order just for me; a pitcher of sweet iced tea, and a stack of cinnamon sticks.

I tried to be quiet as I got dressed, but I heard Zach's voice from under the covers. "You had a rough night, didn't you?"

"Sorry if I woke you," I said.

"Which time; now, or when you shouted out the sequences were after you?"

"Oh, no. Did I actually say that out loud?"

"You did. Care to share your nightmare with me?"

I shook my head. "Not before I've had something to eat."

"Savannah, you know it's just superstition, don't you? Your bad dreams really won't come true if you tell them to someone else before you've had breakfast."

"I know it's irrational, but I won't do it, so stop asking."

There was a knock at the door, and Zach popped out of the bed like he was on springs.

"Easy, tiger. I ordered some sweet tea to perk me up, and some cinnamon sticks just because I could."

"Not breakfast for me? I'm starving."

I laughed and threw a pillow at him as I walked to the door. "I'll order you something as soon as I answer that."

"Yes, but will you share with me until mine gets here?"

"We'll see," I said.

"**W**HO IS IT?" I ASKED AS I WALKED TO THE DOOR. "Sweet tea and cinnamon sticks," the voice said.

I was surprised when I opened the door to find Garrett standing there. "Wow, I didn't realize the manager of the hotel delivered room service."

He smiled at me. "Not normally, no. But I've been told you are to receive VIP treatment during the rest of your stay."

"Funny, I thought I already was."

As he pushed the tray inside, he said, "No, ma'am. You got Important Person treatment before. The Very was added sometime last night."

"Trust me, there's no need to go all out. I'm sure you have other duties to perform around here."

"Until you check out, that's not the case. If there's anything you'd like, all you need to do is ask."

"Well, for starters, could we have a repeat of yesterday's breakfast order? My husband's a little peckish this morning."

Garrett smiled then retrieved a radio from his pocket. After a whispered conversation, he said, "It's taken care of."

"I need to get one of those," I said with a grin.

"That's not a bad idea," the manager said.

Zach came out wearing a bathrobe. "I smell something delicious." He looked surprised to see that Garrett was still there.

"If you'll excuse me," he said.

"Was that really the hotel manager just delivering your breakfast to you?"

"I wouldn't call it breakfast. It's more like a snack."

"You know what I mean."

"I'm guessing Barton had a chat with him last night. It appears that our level of service just went up a notch."

"Where do you go from platinum?"

"That's what I wanted to know. You have to give Barton credit for one thing. He doesn't do anything in half-measures."

Zach reached for a cinnamon stick, and I decided not to smack his hand away. "What about me?"

"I'm sure you'll be taken care of, too."

"Then let's order my breakfast."

"I took the liberty of getting a repeat of yesterday for you. You don't have any problem with that, do you?"

"Not unless you expect me to share," he said with a smile. "I've got time to shower."

"I wouldn't count on it. I'm guessing this won't take long."

"I'll be quick," he said.

"In that shower? I'll believe it when I see it."

He made it out in time, beating his breakfast by a full thirty seconds. After Garrett brought the food in, he handed me a small radio. "For you."

"I was just teasing."

"This will eliminate the need for you to go through the switchboard. It's set to my frequency. If you need anything, you have only to ask for it, and it will happen."

"Wow, so it's a magic radio."

Zach was ignoring us, diving into his meal.

"You might say that," Garrett said with a smile.

After Garrett was gone, I helped myself to a glass of tea, and grabbed a stick from Zach's plate.

"Hey, you've got your own."

"But they aren't as hot as yours are," I said.

Zach appeared to think about that, and then he nodded his approval. "Point taken. Are you ready for your breakfast meeting?"

"As ready as I'll ever be. Do you really think Lorna's a murderer?"

"I'm not saying just yet. Push her, and do it hard. I want to see what happens."

"What if she snaps?"

"Would you feel better knowing that I've already covered that? I've got a plainclothes detective staking out the restaurant. You'll be protected the entire time."

"Don't I rate getting you?"

"She knows me, Savannah. I'm afraid Lorna won't open up if she sees me there."

"You've thought of everything, haven't you?"

"I hope so. It's not too late to back out, you know."

I glanced at the clock and realized that Lorna was already on her way. "No, I said I'd do this, and I will."

"That's my girl."

I kissed him, and then I walked out the door.

"Good luck," he called out.

"Thanks."

The trip down the elevator was much too fast for my taste this time. I was going to have a rather public conversation with one of our murder suspects, and I wasn't looking forward to it at all.

"**THERE YOU ARE**," LORNA SAID AS I WALKED INTO THE restaurant. "I was beginning to think that you weren't going to show again."

"I said I'd be here," I said.

"I'm glad."

As I joined her, I scanned the room full of diners, wondering who the plainclothes detective was that Zach had promised me. No one stood out, so I supposed that was a good thing, at least for him, but I could have used the sight of a uniformed officer at the moment.

After we ordered, I said, "You were going to bring me a present today, weren't you?"

Lorna looked surprised. "Can you believe it? I left it on the counter at home."

Was she lying, or had it just been an excuse to pick my brain about Zach's investigation again? If it was, it was going to bite her this time.

"You've got to tell me what it is," I said. "I'm just dying to know."

"It's a frame of your first puzzle that ever ran," she said. "I called the *Lenoir Dispatch* and they dug a copy out of their archives for me. I hope you like it."

The first paper my syndicate had sold a puzzle to was indeed a small, independent paper in the city of Lenoir. I'd been as proud of that puzzle as I could be, but I'd forgotten to save one for myself.

"That's really thoughtful," I said. "Thank you."

"It would have been even better if I'd brought it with me," she said. "I'll have it messengered over to you today."

"I'd appreciate that," I said. "What made you think of doing it?"

"You broke up my relationship with Grady. I owed you something out of gratitude. It was the wake-up call I needed to save me from my bad choices. Grady was exactly the wrong man for me at the wrong time, and I don't know what would have happened if we'd stayed together."

"I told you, I didn't say a word to him about you."

"I didn't know that when I had the newspaper framed, though. For whatever reason, splitting with Grady was what saved me."

Our food arrived, and as we began to eat, I realized that I'd stalled long enough. I had to pressure her, and do it fast, before she walked out.

I finished a bite of my omelet, and then I asked, "Aren't you going to ask me about Zach's investigation?"

"You made it pretty clear the last time that you weren't comfortable discussing it with me," she said.

"Funny, but I never thought you'd give up that easily."

She waved her fork in the air. "I thought about what you said, and you were right. It really never was any of my business."

"You might be surprised."

"Why is that?"

"Zach still has you on his list of suspects." I said it as flatly as I could, but Lorna looked at me as though I'd just lost my mind.

"Come on, that's not amusing at all."

"It wasn't meant to be," I said. "You had a reason to want Cindy and Hank both dead. Zach can't ignore that just because we're friends."

"I told you before. I didn't kill anyone," she said loudly enough to attract attention to us. Was one of the folks watching us the cop sent there to protect me? I certainly hoped so.

"You don't really have an alibi for Hank's murder though, do you?"

"I have one for Cindy's," she said.

"Really? What is it?"

She ignored the question. "If I'm really a suspect, why hasn't anyone pressed me about an alibi? The two murders are tied together, if the *Observer* has it right. I couldn't have killed Hank, because I didn't kill Cindy."

"It's easy enough to say, but can you prove it?"

Lorna threw her napkin down on her plate, though her meal was less than half eaten. "I don't have to sit here and listen to this. To think I tried to do you a favor."

"Do yourself one," I said. "Tell me your alibi, or tell the police."

"You wouldn't sic your husband on me, would you?"

"Try me," I said, trying my best to press her into saying something she didn't want to tell me.

"I was with Davis Rawles all night, okay?"

That was shocking to hear. I'd known about Lorna and Grady, but I'd never suspected Davis. "Excuse me if I don't believe you," I said.

"Believe what you want to."

"He's a married man, Lorna."

"Don't you think I know that? I'm not proud of myself, and neither is he. Maybe I haven't changed as much as I thought I had. We were both drinking, and a little harmless flirting went way too far."

"So, that's why you didn't tell the police your alibi."

"You want to know the truth? They never asked. I figured it was because Davis cleared me, and none of his cops wanted to step on their boss's toes."

"Zach's going to talk to him to confirm your story; you know that, don't you?"

"What do I care? Let him." She stood, and loomed over me for a second. Where was my protection? Was she getting ready to strike, even in a crowded dining room? "Savannah, you and I are through. I thought we could really be friends this time but I was wrong."

"Is that it?" I asked, the relief washing over me.

"What more did you expect, a dramatic drumroll? Good-bye, Savannah."

"Bye-bye," I said almost merrily.

I WENT BACK UPSTAIRS TO OUR SUITE. I SUSPECTED ZACH would already be gone, but he was still there, waiting for me.

"I thought you'd be at the station by now," I said as my husband hugged me tightly.

"I wouldn't have been able to concentrate. I should have gone downstairs with you."

"I was protected all the time, remember?"

Zach paused and grinned. "Did you spot her?"

"Who are you talking about?"

"The detective I sent."

All that time, I'd been imagining a big, burly cop, when a woman had been guarding me instead. "No, I didn't."

"Then she was doing her job well. What did Lorna say?"

"She claims she was with Davis the night of the murder."

My husband whistled softly. "That explains why neither one of them volunteered the information. I wonder what Davis's wife will think when she finds out?"

"Are you going to tell her?" I was surprised by the comment, since my husband was normally the model of discretion.

"Not me, but it's a small force, and husbands talk to wives. She'll find out soon enough."

"You're going to confirm it with Davis, aren't you?"

"I have to," Zach said, "though I'm not looking forward to it. Way to go, Savannah. If this checks out, you've just eliminated two suspects with one confession."

"It wasn't exactly freely given," I admitted. "I threatened her with you."

"However you did it, good work."

"What are you going to do?"

"Do you mean after I talk to Davis? If it checks out, I'm going to focus on Grady. I was pretty sure he was the killer before, but now I'm almost positive. I just can't believe one of my closest friends is capable of murder."

"Are you going to arrest him?"

"That's the problem. I don't have enough real evidence yet. But trust me, I'll get it."

"Don't do anything stupid, Zach," I said. "You know the temper Grady has. He could do anything."

"Trust me, I'll be careful. What are you going to do in the meantime?"

"Does that mean I can't come along with you when you corner Grady?"

He laughed. "Not a chance in the world, and you know it."

I glanced at the clock. "I don't feel like waiting around for lunch with Sherry. I'm going to call her and see if I can come by early. I didn't even have a chance to eat my breakfast."

"Have a good time, and send her my love."

"I will. Zach, I meant what I said. Be careful."

"Always," he replied as he headed for the door.

I just wished that were true.

I SPENT AN HOUR AT SHERRY'S BUT IT WAS CLEAR TO BOTH of us that I was worried about my husband, and we broke it off early, with the promise that we'd get together after all of this was over.

As I drove back to the hotel, I knew that Zach was closing in on the killer, but I believed in my heart that Grady had to have slipped up making that puzzle for us to decipher. If I could find a signature clue there, it would make my husband's case that much stronger.

I might not be able to help in most ways, but I could at least do that.

When I got back to our suite at the hotel, I tried to look at the clues we'd been given with fresh eyes. No matter how much I tried, though, I kept coming back to the last note's odd appearance. It was so different from the others that I couldn't get my mind off it. Had I missed something there before? It was so strange.

And then I realized what was so troubling to me about it.

There wasn't a single letter or number on it.

Or was there?

Chapter 20

■■■

I STARTED LOOKING CLOSER AT THE OBLONG CIRCLES AGAIN, and then I suddenly realized that there might have been a clue there all along, but we'd all just missed it.

When the sheet was examined closely, it was clear that the lines were broken in many places. At first, I'd just assumed that it was from the way it was copied, but as I stared harder at it, I began to see that there was more than just a series of oblong circles.

Zach had a magnifying glass on his key chain, and I prayed that he'd left it behind, since he wasn't driving our car. For my husband's fortieth birthday, I'd gotten him a magnifying glass, though miniaturized, like Sherlock Holmes might have used. It hung from his key chain, and even sported its own little case.

Thankfully, it was still on the dresser. I took the shade off one of the lamps and held the copy up to the bulb.

Without the magnifying glass, I could really see the breaks with my naked eye, but when I saw it under magnification, my heart started pounding.

Those weren't just lines.

They were a series of numbers, all in the same sequence of number-letter combinations that we'd been getting from the start. In a way, it was exactly like my nightmare.

I had a key to the puzzle now.

It was time to get to work.

AFTER I FINISHED RECORDING THE NUMBERS AND LETters, I stared at the list on my pad. I was happy to see that the sequences we'd already received were included in this list, telling me that my hunch was on the money. I quickly filled in the grid with the new additions, but there were spaces still left open, and several sequences that didn't seem to fit into the grid.

Along with a series of numbers, there was something that appeared to be a set of other numbers that didn't fit: C13, B12, D11.

But what did they mean? If they were a part of my grid, they wouldn't match the vowel axis I'd penciled in.

They had to mean something, though.

I started to pick up the phone, and then I remembered the radio in my pocket.

"Hello?" I asked tentatively as I pushed the button. "Is anyone there?"

"Hello, Savannah. How may I be of service to you?"

I still couldn't get over the fact that I had the hotel's manager at my beck and call.

"Could you send someone up here with an almanac, a

road atlas for the area, and a fact booklet on the city of Charlotte?"

"Of course."

He signed off, and I wondered how long I would have to wait.

Four minutes later, there was a knock at my door.

"Yes?"

Garrett said, "I have the information you requested."

As I opened the door, I said, "Wow, that was fast."

"I was about to apologize for the delay. I had to retrieve a new copy of *Charlotte's Got A Lot*."

He handed me the stack of requested items. "Will there be anything else?"

"No, not that I can think of."

"If you require anything, don't hesitate to ask."

"Thanks, Garrett."

After he was gone, I started leafing through the reference materials, trying to come up with some explanation for the different set of numbers I'd found. The almanac had a great deal of information, but there wasn't anything that struck a chord with me. I browsed through the map, but again, no bells. I got excited at first, but when D11 turned out to be Raleigh, I knew I was on the wrong track. These crimes were limited to the Charlotte area.

Then I picked up the Charlotte guide. As I leafed through it, searching for any number/letter combinations that might make sense, I kept drawing a blank. The magazine had a lot of useful information, but there was nothing that matched the new sequences.

I tossed the magazine aside, and it landed on the open road atlas. I picked it up again, and saw that the coordinates still didn't match anything else.

And then I flipped the page.

On the next section, there was a grouping of smaller maps of several North Carolina cities, including Charlotte.

D11 had part of Sharon Road within its boundaries, the scene of one of the homicides.

My hands were shaking as I circled the other two locations.

One was the other crime scene.

I wasn't sure what the significance of the last sequence was, but I had something to work with now.

I took out my puzzle grid. For the moment, I forgot about my vowel lines, and wrote the start of the alphabet below them, A, B, C, D, and E.

But I didn't immediately go up the vertical axis. I started fiddling with the puzzle, and discovered that if I used the first digit for the vertical axis, I could use the second to fill in the number for that open block.

It worked like a charm, but I had one number left, one that didn't match anything else.

19 squared.

I kept staring at it, wondering how it could fit into the puzzle to make things perfect.

And then I started counting, and realized that 19 squared could also be written as S X S.

Savannah Stone.

Was this a warning directed straight at me?

As I stared at it, I realized something else.

There was another player in this who shared my double S initials.

It might not be telling me the next victim at all.

The killer could have been signing his work, thinking

that he was too clever for anyone ever to figure out what he'd been up to.

Steve Sanders.

I was reaching for the phone to call Zach when I glanced at the map again.

In a flash of insight, I realized the significance of the last set I hadn't been able to place before. I stared at the map, and then I realized the importance of that sequence.

The last letter-number combination represented the grid that my hotel was in.

As I dialed my husband's number, there was a knock at the door.

"Who is it?" I asked as I waited for my husband to answer.

"Housekeeping," a muffled voice said from the other side of the door.

Without even thinking to check twice, I opened the door as my husband's phone went to voice mail.

Steve Sanders was standing there instead of a maid, and he had a wicked-looking knife in his hand.

I'd been right figuring out the killer's identity, but it wasn't going to do me the least bit of good.

A S HE FORCED HIS WAY IN, STEVE REACHED OUT A HAND for my cell phone. "I'll take that, if you don't mind."

He grabbed my phone out of my hands, threw it to the floor, and then smashed it with his heel. "We don't want to be interrupted, now do we?"

"You were a little too cute with that last clue. I knew it was you."

He looked surprised. "Come on, you're not that clever, Savannah."

"S squared, naming the victim and the killer, and the last coordinates from the map are of the hotel."

Steve nodded. "Bravo. I didn't give you enough credit, I can see that now. Not that it's going to do you any good."

"You honestly don't think you're going to get away with this, do you? My husband will never rest until he brings you down."

Steve laughed. "That's where you're wrong. Zach is going after Grady, so I had to strike while I could, before the mayor was in custody, or something worse happened to him."

"Why me, though? I thought we were friends."

He looked sincerely regretful. "You're collateral damage, Savannah. I have to blind your husband with rage, and killing you will do just the trick. I'm hoping he kills Grady for me."

"Your plan was to bring the mayor down? Why?"

"He endorsed Davis, not me." Steve's voice was growing agitated, and that was a good thing. I had to distract him somehow until help arrived. The only problem was, how would anyone know that I was in trouble, until it was too late? My cell phone was in a thousand pieces, and the house phone was too far away.

But I still had a radio.

If I could get Steve to brag about his brilliance, I might be able to summon help on it.

"It was clever casting suspicion on Grady, I'll give you that. But what reason would he have to want me dead?"

"You were about to expose him," Steve said. "In the scenario I'll suggest as motive, it will appear that you held on to some evidence you found at his house the day you and your husband were there." Steve reached into his pocket, and for just a second, he took his eyes off me.

I casually put my hand in my pocket, hoping he wouldn't notice.

He must have seen something in my eyes, because Steve lashed out and struck me with his clenched fist, exhibiting a swiftness that startled me, driving the air out of my lungs. As I fell to the carpet, I struggled to catch my breath and signal Garrett.

At least he hadn't used the blade in his other hand.

Not yet, anyway.

I didn't know if I made it or not. Steve reached into my pocket and pulled out the radio before I could try again.

He was angry, until he looked at it a little closer. "I don't know what you thought you were doing, but you turned it off. Thanks for saving me the trouble."

He smashed it as well, taking glee seeing it strike the wall and shatter.

"No one's going to save you," he said as he stood over me.

The knife shifted in his hand, and I realized I was about to die. I had to do something to stall him. My breath was starting to come back, but when I spoke, my voice was still muffled. "How are you going to frame Grady? You might as well tell me. No one else is ever going to know."

It was clear that Steve felt he had all of the power, and he seemed to draw strength from it. "I was about to show you, so I don't see what it could hurt now. It's not like you're going to be able to tell anyone."

He pulled something out of his pocket, and I knew what it was in an instant. It was Cindy Glass's cow necklace, the one Barton had been so desperate to find.

"That won't do any good."

"It's just one more piece of the puzzle, Savannah. I've got other little trinkets, and Grady's watch is one of them."

Grady had mentioned that it was missing when all of this started, but none of us had suspected at the time that it was going to be used to frame him for murder.

"That's pretty clever," I said. "You killed Cindy to put suspicion on Grady, and then after the public fight between Grady and Hank, you had a perfect opening. But I don't understand something."

The knife hesitated, and I started breathing again.

"What's that? Quit stalling. You're not making this any easier on yourself."

"Why not get rid of Davis, so you can take his job?"

"My job, you mean," he said viciously, and the knife shot out and caught my shoulder. It wasn't a deep cut, but it still crippled me. I felt a searing stab of pain, what I was afraid was going to be the first of many.

"Your job," I corrected, holding my free hand to the wound. I had never experienced that level of pain before.

"It wasn't Davis's fault. He's a good cop, but he shouldn't be chief. I never blamed him for going after the job. Grady is the one who ruined it for me, so he's going to pay."

"Were you the one who followed me to Hickory?" I asked, stalling for time.

"You caught that? I've got to say, I underestimated you, Savannah. Following you was rash of me, but you got my curiosity going. I nearly ran you off the road when I had the chance, but it didn't match my puzzle."

"That's the last question, isn't it? Why did you choose a puzzle to taunt the police with?"

Steve laughed. "I knew Davis would be in over his head, and that they'd bring your husband in. Zach has to pay for recommending Davis and not me. If neither of them could figure out what I'd done, they both could be discredited, and I might be chief after all. Wouldn't that be something?"

"But you thought you were too smart for me." I had a desperate idea, but there wasn't any choice. If I did nothing, I knew that I was about to die.

I took a deep breath, and then said, "There's a flaw in your puzzle; you know that, don't you?"

"What are you talking about? The S squared? It works out, if you're clever enough to see it. 19 times 19 equals 361. 3 plus 6 plus 1 equals 10, and 1 plus 0 equals 1. The last block is filled in with a one."

"The math doesn't work out," I said. It wasn't true; I could see the answer clearly in my mind, and I realized that while Steve was a killer, he wasn't stupid.

"You're wrong," he said.

"Check it. My notepad is over there."

I pointed to the window, and he moved toward it, forgetting all about me for the moment.

It was the chance I needed.

I drove myself upward, ignoring the screaming pain in my shoulder. I never thought for a split second to try to disarm him. He was a cop, trained in self-defense, and besides that, he had a knife.

Fight or flight quickly came down to flight.

I hit the door running, threw it open, and ran as fast as I could. Behind me, I could hear him scream in some kind of demented anger, and I knew that if he caught me, the cat-and-mouse game he'd been playing with me was going to be over.

The elevator was out of the question, so I raced for the stairway. If I tried to go downstairs, he'd have the advantage, being able to jump on me from above.

There was nowhere to go but up.

I raced up the stairs, and as I cleared the next landing, I felt something knick the back of my jeans. He'd taken a chance and lunged out at me, and only the luck of timing had saved me from having my calf split wide open.

I lost a good pair of jeans, but I could cope with that if I lived though this.

The next floor was Barton's, but I knew his door would be locked. That left the roof. He'd shown me his garden up there, and I prayed the door was unlocked, as he'd promised it would be.

If it was dead-bolted, I was a goner.

It swung open, but I knew I wasn't in the clear yet. I made it out onto the roof, and I put my weight against the door to keep Steve from following me. I thought I had him for a second, but the door locked with a key on both sides, and I wasn't strong enough to hold it, especially with my weakened shoulder. Blood had run down my arm in my efforts to escape, and when it hit my hand, it made everything I touched too slippery to grasp well.

I looked around at Barton's sparse garden, searching for some way to defend myself.

The only thing I could find was a handheld garden

weeder with three tines protruding from it. It was metal, and it was sharp, but it was also less than nine inches long. If I was going to use it, I was going to have to get within a foot of a serial killer.

As weapons went, it wasn't much, but it was all I had.

Steve came through the door like a prowling cat, the knife held out as if it were seeking my heart.

"You're going to pay for that," he snarled. When he saw the meager weapon in my hand, Steve actually laughed. "Do you think that's going to do you any good?"

"I might not kill you, but if I can mark you with this, Zach will know you had something to do with my murder."

"It still won't save you," he said.

"No, but you won't get away, either. If I'm going to die, I'm going down fighting."

He paused for a second, and then shrugged. "I'll take my chances."

I prepared myself for his attack when I saw the door open behind him.

I'd been hoping for Zach, or even Garrett.

It was my uncle Barton instead.

"Go back," I shouted.

It was enough to make Steve pause.

"I won't," Barton said. "I can't."

Steve pivoted around. "Get over here, or she dies."

"If you come, he'll just kill us both." I hoped I was getting through to him, but my heart sank as my uncle walked toward us.

He was two steps away when someone came out of the door behind him, holding a gun on Steve. "Drop it or die."

I saw Steve look at the gun, and then judge the distance to the edge of the roof. It was clear he had no interest in paying for his crimes.

He started for the edge, but before he could get there, I drove the weeder into his thigh as he raced past me. We both screamed in pain, him for his leg, me for my shoulder, and we collapsed on the rooftop together.

Barton rushed to me, and before Steve could recover, my uncle pulled me to safety away from the killer, and the edge of the roof.

Chapter 21

· · ·

"**T**HANK GOD YOU'RE OKAY," MY HUSBAND SAID AS HE rushed toward me. I was sitting in an examining room in the ER, having just gotten eight stitches for my shoulder wound. Barton hovered just out of sight. He had stayed with me the entire time, even riding in the ambulance with me.

Zach said, "I can't believe I was wrong about Grady."

"Steve had us all fooled until the last second," I said, reliving the fear and pain of my experience. "Is he going to be okay?"

Zach smiled, but I could see tears tracking down his cheeks as he did. "He's going to be limping for a while. You probably just should have let him jump."

"I know it would have saved the taxpayers the cost

of a trial, but I couldn't let him get off that easily. Could you?"

"Ordinarily I'd say no, but in this case, I might have been willing to make an exception." Zach turned and patted Barton on the shoulder.

"I hear you saved her life."

"Not by any stretch of the imagination could you say that," Barton said. "I was coming up to my garden for lunch when I saw blood on the doorknob. I hit my panic button, and my security chief came up and intervened."

"Don't let him get away with that," I told Zach. "Barton had every chance to turn around and run, but he walked toward Steve while he was holding a knife to try to save me. That delayed him long enough for reinforcements to get there. He's a hero."

"I just did what any uncle would do for his niece."

"Maybe, but I doubt it."

Zach asked me, "Do you have to stay here overnight?"

"No, they're going to clear me. I lost a little blood, but they gave me a tetanus shot and stitched me up, so I'm going to be a little sore."

"Don't worry; I'll take good care of you."

The door opened, and I was surprised to see my uncle Thomas come in.

"How did you get here so fast?" I asked as he hugged me.

"I had to come to Charlotte on an errand, and Zach called me. Are you okay?"

"I'm a little worse for the wear right now, but I'll be fine."

"Good."

He turned to Barton, and I saw a look of panic in my prodigal uncle's eyes. Thomas held out his hand, and Barton quickly took it. "Thank you, J.B."

"You're welcome."

Thomas didn't let go of his grip, though. "You evened the scales today as far as I'm concerned."

"I keep telling everyone that I didn't do anything."

Uncle Thomas grinned at him. "So, does that mean you don't want to get to know your little brother again?"

"I never said that," Barton said, his voice trembling.

Thomas hugged him, wrapping Barton up in his arms. "Welcome home, J.B."

THE BROTHERS LEFT TOGETHER, AFTER BEING SURE THAT I was being taken care of by my husband and the entire hospital staff.

Zach sat down in a chair beside the bed I was sitting on. "Who would have believed it?"

"What, that Steve was a killer?"

"That, too, but I'm talking about your uncles. It's hard to imagine that a couple of murders would bring them back together again."

"I'm just happy it turned out all right. How's Grady?"

"He was pretty upset with me when I called him a killer, but the second he heard about Steve, he got over it. He's outside right now, but I told him he had to wait before he could see you."

"Are you telling me that you're keeping the mayor of Charlotte stewing out there so we can chat?"

"That sounds about right," he said.

"That's just one of the reasons I love you."

"If you can think of any more, be sure to let me know."

I grinned at him. "Wait until my shoulder stops killing me, and I'll show you. Where are we going after this?"

"If you don't want to go back to the hotel, I completely understand." He glanced at his watch. "We can be back home in less than three hours, and that includes checking out of here and packing our bags."

"As much as I'd love to be back working in my garden, I think we should hang around a few more days before we take off."

"What's the matter? Are you afraid to give up room service?"

"That's part of it," I said with a laugh. "But what I'd really like to do is get to know my uncle a little better."

"He's offered us that suite on a permanent basis, if we want it."

"Tell him I said thanks, but no thanks."

Zach nodded. "Too many bad memories there, I understand completely. When I told him that, he offered us another suite on that floor, and he said he'd have it decorated however we wanted. It would be rude to say no to him. After all, we don't want to hurt his feelings, do we?"

I laughed, despite the pain. "We'll talk about it. For now, I just want to enjoy being with you."

"I can handle that," Zach said. He took my good hand in his, and squeezed it gently. "We seem to have a knack for getting ourselves into jams, don't we?"

"As long as we come out all right on the other side, I'm fine with it."

Zach glanced at his watch, and then looked away. "Am I keeping you from something?"

"No. I just realized that you have another puzzle due in a few hours. Want me to call Derrick?"

"No, I'll take care of that myself."

"You're not actually going to try to create a puzzle after all you've been through today, are you?"

"I don't want to, but I need to."

Zach nodded in understanding. "You have to wash the bad taste of Steve's puzzle out of your mind, don't you?"

"That's it exactly."

"I'll go find you a pencil and some paper."

As he went out on his search, I marveled at what had happened in the past few days. If it weren't for my puzzles, Steve might never have been caught. He'd picked the wrong gal to mess with, though.

Puzzles were in my blood.

I started playing with ideas in my mind, and realized that today's puzzle was going to have to be another simplified version, given all that had happened. Derrick wasn't going to be happy about it, but then again, he rarely was, anyway.

It would be enough to get a new, fresh look at the puzzles I loved so much.

And that, along with my newly expanded family, was all I really needed.